HELEN DUNMORE

With Your Crooked Heart

PENGUIN BOOKS

PENGUIN BOOKS

Published by the Penguin Group
Penguin Books Ltd, 27 Wrights Lane, London w 8 5 tz, England
Penguin Putnam Inc., 375 Hudson Street, New York, New York 10014, USA
Penguin Books Australia Ltd, Ringwood, Victoria, Australia
Penguin Books Canada Ltd, 10 Alcorn Avenue, Toronto, Ontario, Canada m 4 v 3 b 2
Penguin Books (NZ) Ltd, Private Bag 102902, NSMC, Auckland, New Zealand

Penguin Books Ltd, Registered Offices: Harmondsworth, Middlesex, England

First published by Viking 1999
Published in Penguin Books 2000
1 3 5 7 9 10 8 6 4 2

Set in Monotype Garamond
Printed in England by Clays Ltd, St Ives plc

12334022

*'You shall love your crooked neighbour
With your crooked heart.'*

('As I Walked Out One Evening', W. H. Auden)

One

Every day for a month now the sun has shone, and every morning you've brought the same things out into the garden.

A faded cotton quilt. A pillow for the back of your neck. A tall jug of water and a glass.

But today you leave the quilt behind and walk out naked through the French windows, pillow under one arm and jug and glass in the other hand. You kneel on the yellow stone, place the jug and glass where you can reach them, and the pillow where it will support the back of your neck.

You lie down on the warm stone, and wriggle your body until it fits. Then you relax, and the terrace bears you up as if you are floating out to sea. Sun has been pouring on to it since seven o'clock, and every grain of stone is packed with heat. Sun pours now on to the glistening mound of your belly, on to your parted thighs, your arms, your fingers, your face. No part of you resists, no part does not shine. The moist lips of your vulva are caught in a shining tangle of hair.

Inside you the baby thuds deep, touching your bladder. You look down through your eyelashes, and the stroke of a baby limb sweeps across you, under your skin. You look up, where a jet on its way to Heathrow unzips the sky. You wonder for a moment about the people in it, where they're going, where they are coming from, what they feel, what they want. You think of them with their hands on the arm-rests, tense for landing. But you're not really curious, just glad that you're down here on solid earth.

The days slip by, marked only by getting up to fetch another jug of water, or making a plateful of sandwiches, or trying to do the crossword until the black-and-white squares fizz and you collapse back on the pillow. You're not good at puzzles anyway; never have been. No good at crosswords, no good at riddles or charades or remembering jokes, though you always think you will remember them, while you're still laughing at them.

Here you are. No cloud in your sky, and there'll be none all day. There's a small, burning blue square above the high walls. You don't need the newspaper to tell you how hot it's been, though you quite like the headlines and the pictures of girls on their lunch-breaks, flat out on the grass in their bras and knickers. It's another world, one which you never want to go back to.

The birds don't really sing in the middle of the day. They drowse away the heat in the jungle of buddleia and bamboo, and sometimes you hear a bubble of song rising in their throats, but it never bursts. You turn your head into the crook of your arm and your world grows smaller still. You smell your skin and watch your flesh tanning until it matches the burnt brown of the grass you don't look after properly. Inside the sycamore by the wall, there's a wood-pigeon. Prr-*ccoo*, it goes, prrr-*cooo*. You love its hot and sleepy stammer more than anything else in the garden. That's why you won't let Paul prune the sycamore, even though he says it's nothing but an overgrown weed and you ought to cut it down. You could put in something worth having. A white lilac, or a tree of heaven.

There's a smell of cat-piss, and buddleia. A honeyed smell which draws the butterflies. The garden simmers with heat and wasps, cat-piss and cabbage whites. In the little fountain, water wobbles then spurts up.

One day you'll chop everything back, or Paul will. But you're at home in London gardens like this one, overgrown, rank and fat with weeds. It reminds you of when you were a child, when you were four or five, tagging after the bigger kids, in and out

2

of fireweed and rotten fencing. You like buddleia and bramble, and jam-jar traps for wasps, and flying ants, and the Russian vine that's climbed like a wave over the back wall, and swamped it. There's honeysuckle in your garden, and a stand of bamboo. You pull out the new shoots of bamboo from their shafts, and nibble the cold, moist tips.

You can lie naked in your garden and no one can see you. That's what money does. You have your privacy, bang in the heart of London. You can sprawl out on the stone. You're pregnant: what business is it of anyone else's? There's the fountain that was dry when you came, but you slashed back the thorns and bought a pump and now the water flows. You could listen all day long to the water bubbling up, a soft plucking sound as it rises, then the splash of drops into the bowl.

It's early August. Your legs are stalks while your breasts are heavy with green and blue veins. Your nipples are wide and brown, ready to give milk. You feel the child thudding inside you, and you feel the sun.

Paul put carp in the pond under the fountain. The water is deep, and the carp are blotched white. They swim in the murk and silt, and rise to nuzzle the top of the water when they want food. Then something steers them down. You are sure that they're blind, and that they're white because they were already old when Paul bought them. But neither of you knows anything about fish. You'd like to touch them, but you're afraid you'll hurt them. The white patches look like velvet, but they might be fungus.

You don't want anything. You don't even want the baby to be born. Time doesn't move any more, it drips like syrup. You've got a garden with high walls and a locked door, in the heart of London. You don't have to go out in the traffic if you don't want to. If you want shopping, you can telephone and get it delivered. You are happy here.

You sit up and pour water into your glass. It's clear and

warm and you drink the long glass thirstily, swallowing it into yourself. You want more.

You want to be touched. In your condition, Paul tiptoes around you. How can you know that it's out of consideration? Is he put off by the sight of you? It's true, you don't look like yourself. You're blazing with veins on your belly and breasts. You don't look anything like the neat pictures in pregnancy books. You look like one of those seed-pods that explode when you touch them. No one in his right mind would go near you.

The cat knows you. She's a scruffy orange cat with black paws, thin as a whip except when she's bulging with kittens. She slips out now, from the nest where she's put her latest litter, at the base of the bamboo. You can't see the nest from here, but you have tracked her once, and watched where she's hidden the kittens in a heap of dry leaves. She streaks across the garden, showing herself to you boldly, because you're always here and she can predict you. You never feed her, or try to touch her.

It's the pond that interests her, and the carp. She has had one of them already. You saw her wait and wait, flexed, the tip of her tail moving. From time to time she dabbed her paw above the water like a hypnotist swinging a gold watch. She waited until her shadow had become part of things for the fish in their deep world, and they lazed up and showed themselves at the water surface. She shot her steel claw through the water and got one. It was small. She couldn't reach the monsters with their ripe white flesh, but she plucked out this little burning orange fish and bit its head off. Her head closed around the carp and stripped it of flesh. She let you see her fast, convulsive eating, and when she'd finished she licked off her paws, dipping her head and rasping them with her tongue until she was perfect outside as well as in.

The sun is blinding. When you stand up, you stagger a bit, and the garden goes dark. There is sweat in a slick all over you.

You stoop and grope for the jug of water and when you have it by the handle you lift it high and pour it over your hot and sweating body. It runs down you as if you are the slick stone under a fountain. You feel each runnel of the water like sherbet prickling in your mouth, then it caresses you. You pour slowly, so you'll miss nothing. The surface of your skin drinks in the water thirstily, and you think of the baby inside you, packed tight, its thighs and arms crossed as you saw them on the last scan. Not free-floating any more. Packed tight, waiting, gathering itself for the dive. You feel pity for it that it has to come out, and you will never be able to protect it again as you can now. Your food feeds it, your heart beats for it, your warmth curves around it. You are enough.

The cat is there, her paw in the water, waiting. You think what it's like to be lazing at the surface like one of those carp, plump and ripe and stupid. And then the claw, like steel ripping you through, scooping out the guts and white strings of your body's innards so quickly that they think they are still alive, and they wince in the daylight. You think what that slash of the claw would feel like as it emptied you. It would be like having your heart held up to you, in front of your face. The thing nobody sees, the naked heart, red and wincing, thinking it is still alive.

You move towards the cat and she shrinks back into the bushes. You crouch and go forward between the buddleias. Their pointed leaves blaze black shadows over you. You are printed and touched with every step you take. The light is thick and insect-ridden. A spiderweb clings to your shoulder and you pull it off with sticky fingers. You wade deeper into leaves and sour undergrowth. There is the cat, back humped, eyes on you. Her eyes are big in the gloom. She nets every inch of you.

You sink down. A branch brushes the back of your neck and you squat, your belly pointing towards the cat. You are hidden, both of you. Even the passing white thread of an aeroplane can't see you. The leaves quake into stillness, now that you are still. The cat watches, and you watch the cat. You know she has her litter near, her second of the year, and her kittens are already half-grown. They will be feral cats, like her, living on luck.

You don't want to touch them or look at them, but she doesn't know that. You stare, she stares. You squat and you run your hands over your tense, strained thighs. In two months you'll have to give birth, but not here. Somewhere where there are people watching you, watching out for you. But you don't want them, you don't want the bustle of their faces round you. Not even Paul's: no. You don't want him with you when the baby is born.

The cat hisses, warning you off. You have stopped her catching another fish, and now you are coming too close to her nest. You retreat, and the buddleia leaves slap softly against you, then let you go.

You're out in the sun. You have never been so happy. All month the sun has shone and the traffic has growled outside the walls. You smell the fumes through the leaves. You are secret, on the inside of the wall, while outside the tarmac melts into sticky puddles.

The cat darts through a tangle of sunburnt grass. There is no cloud. You've done wrong, but your sky is savagely clear. You know you'll pay, but you don't feel that knowledge as any more than a small darkness inside yourself, like a hand of cloud.

You hear the key in the door, on the other side of the house. You steady yourself on your stalks of legs, you run your palms down your burning sides. You face the French windows he'll come through.

It's Johnnie. You knew it was him. He puts the key in the door a different way from Paul. Not your husband, but your husband's brother. He comes out of the house, into the sun. You seem to see him shrug the indoor darkness off him, so it

6

falls like a spill of ink at his feet. And he stands opposite you, saying, 'Well? How's it going?'

And you say nothing. He reaches out his hand. You draw back, smiling.

'How's Paul?'

'All right.'

He looks at the veins growing through your skin like blue and green roses, your brown nipples, your belly. You don't disgust him.

'Fucking unbelievable,' he says.

'*You* ought to believe it,' you say.

'Yeah.'

He moves away to sit on the edge of the pond. He lifts a handful of water, cups it, lets it fall. You watch a fish rise to his fingers. Under the water Johnnie's finger tickles its heavy, velvety side.

'I could lift it out,' he says, 'just like that. It wants to be caught.'

'It wouldn't want to be, once it was,' you say.

He turns a sharp bright flash of his look on you. You want him. You want him to come over with his wet hands and open you and fuck you. You feel your legs tremble under the weight of what they're carrying. But you won't, no. Once was good, once was right, once was enough.

Two

Behind that summer day there lies a winter night. Louise stares through the sun-stripes of the garden and sees it.

It's cold, and she's hurrying. *I was hurrying, going down the street. I'd told Paul I was going to take a cab, but there weren't any about. It was nearly two o'clock, later than I thought. The party was still going on when I left. Paul was sober, but all the clients were sweating with drink. Opposite me Johnnie was doing card tricks no one could follow. Cards flickering like leaves in Johnnie's hands. I told Paul I was tired.*

She hears footsteps behind her, timed to her own. There's not enough light to see who's there, even if she turned round. But she won't turn round. She hurries on through mucky orange streetlight, over the mucky, glistening pavement greased with burger packs and drink cartons, where her feet tap. His steps have slowed so that he walks in her footprints. His shoes touch the marks hers make on the wet pavement. His echoes are swallowed up in hers.

Between the streetlights the darkness swoops and blots her out, then she's back in the light, head up, hair glistening through the net of rain that lies on it. The belt of her trench-coat is drawn tight. Her heels are high, and her calves are round and gleaming. She walks away from him all the time, trying not to run, trying to hold on to the aplomb of a slender woman in tight-belted trench-coat and high heels. But now she's going too fast. Her heels skitter on the wet pavement, her pale legs flicker like the legs of paper dolls. Someone is after her and she knows it.

The streets are empty, shops shuttered with metal. Concrete bollards litter her way, set in the paving against ram-raiders.

Go quick now. Don't look back. Don't let him know you know he's there. She holds herself straight and walks upright, out on the edge of the pavement, away from grabbing shadows. She won't scurry. She won't try to run in these heels. She won't trip and sprawl under his feet. And his footsteps are now so perfectly tuned to hers that for a moment she thinks he's gone. Her blood shoots through her veins like an electric current as she thinks, *He's gone, he isn't there any more.* And then behind her, very softly, he starts to whistle.

The rain, the ghost touch of rain made flesh from the murk of mist. She can't run in these heels. She slows, he slows. She sees a flash of headlights on the main road and she hurries towards it, to where the late-night people are still coming out of clubs and there are taxis cruising and people cruising. People who'll see her, who'll notice that she's there or suddenly not there. They'll see her disappear.

But it's two a.m. and there's no one on this side-street but him and her. And he does what she does, his rhythm drums her rhythm, she leads, he follows.

He touches her shoulder. His hand grips the wet, off-white shoulder of her trench-coat. She turns to face him with black stains for eyes and white face burning. Like a cut-out from paper, he sees her.

'You going my way?' he says.

Her lips part, but she doesn't speak. Her whole body trembles as she takes him in. The tip of her tongue emerges and rolls itself over her bottom lip. He can hear her trying to hold her breathing steady. Her breath comes from the top of her lungs, in quick pants.

'What do you think you're doing?' she asks. 'You fucking lunatic.'

'You knew it was me,' he says.

'You could have been anyone.'

'You knew it was me. You know you did.'

'Well,' says Louise, 'that's enough. It's time I got home.'

'I know a better place,' says Johnnie.

In the depth of the park, in the dry shadow of a holm oak, she kneels on the ground. It is scratchy with forgotten leaves. Away from the streets the night is thick as velvet, pawing at her eyes, but not quite dark. There'll be other people here. There always are. They know the gap in the railings where they were forced apart with a crowbar once, and never forced back together again. You speak softly here or not at all, because you don't know who might be listening. And on the benches there are the stiff, bombed-out shapes of men. They could be dead for all the listening they do. Prime targets, prey for anyone who wants to know how it feels to connect a steel-tipped boot with a sleeping face. They live here.

But in the shadow of the holm oak Louise kneels up, her skin prickling.

'What are you doing?' he asks sharply, reaching after her.

'Wait.'

She sheds her clothes. Trench-coat, black silk dress. She leans forward and unhooks her bra and her breasts swing free. She pulls down knickers, tights, and piles them out of the way. Can he see her? He can. There's no real dark in cities.

'You do it too,' she says.

'You want to get us arrested?'

'Go on.'

Johnnie hesitates, on the brink of the cold water where she is already far out.

'OK,' he says.

He takes off his clothes more slowly than her, folding each item with care.

'What do you want?' he says.

'Nothing.'

He does the strangest thing. He takes her face between his

hands and holds it still, peering. There's enough leakage of city light for them to see one another's staring eyes.

'What's this all about?' she asks.

'You tell me.'

'We can't lie down on this lot. There might have been dogs.'

He pulls her to him. Like a four-legged animal they stagger until they're standing and she's got her back to the tree trunk. The soles of her feet grip roots and earth. Suddenly there's a noise, not far off. Someone laughing. And again, the pulse of a laugh, too close, low in somebody's throat. Not a nice laugh. And the thin whine of a dog. Sometimes they have parties in the park here, the crusties. They set fire to a tramp once, a real tramp, one of the old-style ones who've been around since before Louise was born.

Johnnie puts his mouth to hers and whispers, 'Ssh.' But she doesn't need telling. Her body presses back into the bark as if she's one of these girls in stories, who turn into trees when there's nowhere else left for them to go. She feels the roughness of it against her buttocks and the pads of her shoulders. She wills herself to vanishing point, and her heart thumps, even though no one's chasing her any more.

A can clatters, but not so close now. Safer. But there's the dog. Dogs can sniff out people. For a dog, this park is floodlit by the smell of her naked, him naked. A dog doesn't need to see. It has a map of scent spread out for it. She sees the wet, probing snout of the dog, coming close and finding them where they think they are hidden. But Johnnie's hands are lifting her, parting her legs. Between the harshness of the tree and the rough, hurried fuck she disappears, goes off elsewhere. While she pants in his ear she is miles off, looking down on the black spread of the holm oak and the little point of fire the crusties have lit. Their thin-flanked dogs snap at her.

She feels him shudder with it, the effort of holding up her weight, and keeping her spread. And maybe some pleasure, she thinks, after so much effort, as his head snaps back. For once he's not watching, not looking out, not on top of anything. It's her looking out, not him, her making out the shadows of dogs and men, separating them from the larger shadow that is the enfolding night. Then silence, and the rain coming down harder now, hissing on the tough evergreen leaves as if it means to get in and drown them.

And then she says, 'I'd better get home. You going to come back with me? Paul'll wonder if you don't.'

This is the night Anna is conceived, in the tenth year of Paul and Louise's marriage. Louise is thirty-one. They've been childless so long.

'It must have been a shock,' people say to Louise. 'You can't have been expecting it after all that time.'

She smiles. But really she knew right away, right that second in the wet park. She knew it was what she was there for. She washed herself carefully when she got home, dreamily, wiping her thighs with a big, dripping sponge. She locked herself into the bathroom and stared at the body she'd taken for granted since she was thirteen, and knew that was it, she'd seen the last of it, it was gone. That was gone, and most of her life was gone with it. She heard Paul's keys chink on the bedside table. Already, she knew that the conception was spreading inside her like a bruise, like knowledge, changing everything it touched.

Three

There is a brass plate on the door, with his name and qualifications burnished. Louise can see herself in it much too clearly. The heaviness of her face, her pouched eyes. Below, the shape of her body dwindles, distorted by the slight curve of the plate. Or so she hopes. Her image looks at her angrily, as if it blames her for what it has become. *We used to like each other, you and me. Look at what you've done to us.*

Louise puts up her hand to her cheek, as if she's been slapped. The shadow Louise does the same, and looks back at her with wide, frightened eyes. Baby eyes in the face of a pig, she thinks savagely. *Here we are*, says her reflection. *What are you going to do about it?* Louise braces herself. She's not finished yet. She won't give in. Ten years ago, when she went to restaurants with Paul and Johnnie, the waiters pulled out her chair, settled her lingeringly, stroked her coat on to the hanger. And she sat with her head high and her back straight and sent a slow smile to the two men who sat with her. Before Anna was born. Now she goes alone, rarely, on days when she's looked out of the window and seen that the dark's come, and there's no food in the house. She's often muddled about the time. Sometimes she is sure she's booked a table, but she can't quite remember. They frown and tell her they are sorry, there isn't a table booked in her name. And the other people look up from their dinner for a moment, their faces like cats' faces, sleekly in place. Sometimes the big men who stand at the doors of bars put their arms out, firmly and finally, and say, 'Not you.'

Louise braces herself. She gives herself the same dry, maternal smile she gives to Johnnie when he needs reassurance. Already it is becoming clear to her that all this is a mistake, but she's going to go through with it. The surgeon was recommended to her. She has made the preliminary visits, had all the tests. She thinks of Anna, safe at school, and touches the discreet brass bell that makes no sound when it is pressed.

The man on the other side of the desk puts his hands together in a steeple, and looks at her. Mrs O'Driscoll. Louise O'Driscoll. She doesn't look Irish, but then she will have given her married name. She might be middle European – Romanian, or even Russian, with those high, broad cheekbones. The voice is London, and the address as well. He notes the postcode with annoyance. He could not afford to live there himself, not yet. He piques himself on being able to put a background to every face, but in her case, he suspects, it's mostly foreground.

'Liposuction isn't always the answer, Mrs O'Driscoll,' he says. He holds her eyes for the flash of a moment. Not too long, you've always got to be careful. He changes tack slightly, in case he's underestimated her. 'In some cases, it's not the most appropriate therapy.'

'But you're an expert,' she says. 'I've been recommended to you. That's why I've come.'

'Yes, and as you know, Mrs O'Driscoll, we follow a very careful procedure here, to make sure that each patient understands exactly what they are undertaking, and what they can expect. This type of surgery is a highly individual matter. I am speaking to you now on the basis of the extensive tests and interviews which you have already undergone.'

She blinks. Not nervously, but slowly, the way a cat blinks. He notices the tiny clot of mascara in the corner of her eyes. Her eyes are rimmed with kohl, and the mascara is too heavy.

'I know it doesn't always work,' she says. 'I know you can't give me any guarantees.'

'No,' he says. 'No, we can't. But that isn't exactly what I'm trying to say to you. You see, I cannot undertake this course of treatment unless I have reasonable confidence in the outcome. And in your case, I'm afraid . . .'

He pauses, looks at her again over the steeple of his fingers, then picks up a pen as if he's about to write her dismissal. He wonders briefly why so many women keep on wearing the make-up that suited them when they were eighteen. As if catching his thought, she flushes as people do at a remembered sexual humiliation. Then she recovers herself, pulls her shoulders back and stares at him. Three stone overweight, at least. There's fat on her upper arms, pads of fat on her shoulders, abdomen, thighs. He's a connoisseur of fat, and he knows that her kind is hard to shift. She's waiting for him to whisk it away in her sleep, and leave her with the lithe, smooth body she remembers she once had. And perhaps she did. But he's going to have to tell her that her fat is hers and she owns it, to keep or to lose. He's done it often enough, placing truth delicately between the tongs of medical terminology, speaking of anaesthetic risks or respiratory problems, of the desirability of a three-month detoxification process, prior to surgery.

But all that won't do for this one. She's too much of a risk. He assesses the puffiness of her face, the webbing of tiny burst blood vessels under the coat of foundation and powder. Her blood pressure is high, and she is slightly asthmatic. There are contra-indications to general anaesthesia.

'We are talking about a major procedure here,' he says. She stares at him. 'It's complex, and it's invasive. It's not right for everyone.' He remembers the skin on her naked body, when she slipped off the white cotton gown. She was webbed with stretchmarks.

'I know,' says Mrs O'Driscoll. 'I've watched your video.'

You don't know anything, he thinks. The video is about flowers, white masks with concerned eyes peering over them, gleaming nurses, changed lives, proud husbands. It has something to do with what he does, but not too much. He made the video on the advice of his P R consultants, but he's beginning to think it wasn't such a good idea. It undermines what he thinks of as the heart of his business, this one-to-one talk in the confessional of his consulting room. The decisions are made here, and he makes them.

'I do know,' she repeats.

You know nothing, he thinks to himself, keeping his eyes lowered. He knows. He knows the noise lungs make when air's pushed through them down a tube in the paralysed throat. He knows about fat beaten from solid to liquid until it can be sluiced away. He's heard every fart and wheeze that stunned flesh can make. He knows about faces scrubbed clear of charm and make-up, baggy under the hot lights of the operating theatre. He knows the yellowness of subcutaneous fat, and the bright blood that guards it. He's a surgeon at heart.

They want to yield to him. They're so tired of failure, and he can take it all away. Some of them want to know every detail of what happens, and he goes through it with them gently, outlining the risks without dwelling on them. They are set on what he can give them. He can make them back into what they believe they were. Through hurting them, he can take away the pain. He thinks about it a lot. People say doctors have no imagination, but sometimes he lies awake at night, beside his quietly breathing wife, and thinks of them all out there, waking or sleeping, shifting their bruised bodies under the sheets and thinking of what he has done for them. Those who trust him most heal the best.

He glances down at the file in front of him. Plenty of money here. She didn't even ask the cost of a course of treatment. His fees are competitive, his operation small, but sleek. His results are about what they ought to be, and his methods are entirely professional. These women require a service, and he provides it. He doesn't judge. Once you start going into ethics, what's so ethical about a woman left on her own at forty-five because her husband wants taut skin and a body that looks good beside his? No one tries to put a stop to *that*, he thinks, and the thought brings with it a familiar, warm wash of self-righteousness.

The air-conditioning hums, and he looks up at Mrs O'Driscoll again. No question of this one having to re-mortgage the house, or take out a bank loan. He knows them all: the inheritors, the actors, the wives of waning football stars, the high-flyers whose faces are falling. When he sees a sleek girl on the street, and gets the haughty stare of her sexual omnipotence, he has his revenge. He maps the way her wrinkles will divide her face into a thousand postcodes. He knows where thread veins will stitch blue knots under the milky skin of her thighs. He is a connoisseur of flesh which has yet to grow, the jowly shadows that will capture her pure profile.

His fingertips know everything there is to be known about female flesh. He can judge the elasticity of skin blindfold, and he knows more about these women who come to him than they know about themselves. In the consultations beforehand they shut their eyes and lift up their faces as if the sun is going to touch them. He comes close. When he puts gloved fingers on to flesh, he notes that their mouths open. The nurse sits at their heads, comforting them when the procedures are painful. He knows how they look inside, raw as battered meat, scarred. But the inside of the human body is beautiful to him, no matter how foul the damage done. What no one else sees, he sees. He scrapes and cleans and harvests, and laces up the keyholes in their skin. He loves the hot, casual alertness of the operating theatre, the smell of the antiseptic washing over stomachs, the first, iron smell of blood. He knows how they will heal, how their flesh will swell around his stitching, turn from ruddy purple to green, then brown.

Mrs O'Driscoll should think herself lucky, he says to himself with a coarseness which he never lets into his more public thoughts. Some surgeons would go ahead and do it. But not him, because he has a reputation to maintain. His patients are his best advertisement. They whisper his name, the whisper travels, and soon there's another patient in his waiting-room, counting dreams. It's not a miracle, he tells them. All I can do is help Nature out a little, when she's having a hard time. Nature intends you to be beautiful.

'So you won't help me,' says Mrs O'Driscoll.

She frowns, making her face still heavier. There's something about her that riles him, though he is far too well trained to show it.

'You are welcome to read the reports on which I've based my decision. I should warn you, you will find some clinics which will be willing to accept you. But here we follow the most scrupulous procedures. I advise you to think very carefully indeed before you go anywhere else.'

She's silenced, as he knew she would be. Her fingers move restlessly in her lap. The ring on her third finger sits deep in her flesh. An expensive ring. She's what – forty? She looks older. One child, born ten years ago after a decade of primary infertility. She's the type that ages early. One of those girls who are all glow and surface: no bones. Unhappiness makes short work of them. The body swells, demanding something. They eat too much, or they drink, and the skin coarsens, the hair dulls. Drink, in this case. It was perfectly obvious, even before the liver-function tests came back. There's a characteristic smell that comes off an alcoholic, though she's unlikely to be aware of it. She'll have taken care not to drink before coming to see him, but that makes no difference at all. The smell always reminds him of boiled sweets: pear-drops, perhaps. No, that's not quite it.

He leans forward, like a wine-taster rolling the finer points over his palate. 'I'm sorry not to have been able to be more helpful,' he says. Her eyes just keep on looking at him, unblinking now, as steady as his. She places both hands on the chair's arm-rests, and heaves herself up. He thinks she's going to turn round and go, but she doesn't. She takes a long look at the photograph of his wife and two blond boys, in its silver frame.

'Did you operate on her yourself?' she enquires.

'My wife hasn't –' he says, too quickly, too indignantly.

'Ah,' she says. 'It was just a thought.' Her plum-like eyes refuse to veil themselves. They stare at him out of the wreck of her face with steady sexual confidence. She's not even ashamed of herself, he thinks angrily. She acts as if she's still beautiful. He compares her to the cream of his clients. They are women who take care of themselves. They've suffered, but they haven't let themselves go. Beneath their polish, there is a timidity which he can always ease. They look out at him past their fat, or out of their fallen faces, and they plead with him to know them for what they are. *I'm trapped in here. Help me. Recognize me.* He would recognize them anywhere; not individually, of course, but by a certain look. It means something to him to be surrounded by women who trust him. They confide in him, let him see the weaknesses they show to nobody else, and accept his reassurances. They are doing their best, and so is he. But these unwinking, plum-coloured eyes – he doesn't like them. God knows what she is really after.

'Don't worry,' she says. 'It's too late anyway. It was a mistake to come.' She stoops to pick up her handbag, and when she straightens her face is flushed.

'Since we're not going to see each other again,' she continues, 'there *is* something I ought to tell you.'

'What?' he barks before he can stop himself. He should have had a chaperone in with this one, even though there's no examination today. Trouble from the moment she walked through the door.

'Your hair,' she says. 'You shouldn't wear it like that. It's not a good look for men who are getting thin on top. It looks as if you're trying to hide something. Much better to cut the whole lot short, don't you think?'

His hand flies up to the richly groomed wave of dark-brown hair that dips over his forehead. He snatches the hand back.

'No, that bit's fine,' she says. 'It's higher up, where you can't see it. That's where the problem is.'

And she walks to the door, opens it, nods her head at him as if they are old friends, then departs.

Four

You depart. You come down the white stone steps, and find that you are holding the handrail, and standing still. It's a beautiful day. Big clouds scud high above the houses, and a breeze blows fabric against flesh as people hurry down the street. You watch the outlines of them, the swell of thighs and breasts.

You are glad you said it. You know that he hated you and wanted to hurt you, and you feel your own rancour pinning you there on the steps, away from the flowing street. You'd have liked to watch him slump and die in front of you. But the breeze blows harder, becoming a warm wind, and suddenly you are out in it, walking southward. You don't care. No one is going to stick knives and tubes into your body, or hoover out the fat from under your skin. You must have been mad to go there. Imagine if it was Anna; imagine living to see your daughter so desperate she would let a man with a knife go at her in the hope of relief. There are plenty of things that we'd call crimes, you think, walking into the ripple of wind, if we hadn't made them seem normal.

You wanted the surgeon to wipe everything away, and let you go back to where you were. He couldn't do that. You wanted to be back to that winter's night nine months before Anna was born, at the table with Paul and Johnnie, both of them looking at you, you smiling, the light falling on to the white cloth and your faces. At the party, before the clients arrived, when everything was perfect. Flowers, knives, table-cloths, fresh, bright, unstained. Your black silk dress that fitted so perfectly over thighs and buttocks and breasts. Paul looking at you and thinking of how he would touch you later. You looking back, charged with Paul and with the thought of Johnnie which you held to yourself and never acted upon. There they both were, and you held them, you possessed them both and you loved them as you'd never loved them before and never would again. You could smell perfume rising, warm and dry, from between your breasts. You shifted position so that the silk moved over your skin and you almost shivered. You saw Johnnie's eyes change, as if he felt it too.

Your mother told you your breasts were beautiful. She touched your waist where it was narrowing between the swell of your breasts and your hips. She said your figure was perfect, and took you to be measured for hand-made bras, then for coffee and cakes afterwards, in celebration. She drank Turkish coffee, and at home she had little copper cups with long handles, and a copper coffee-maker. The coffee was dark and thick as syrup and it made your heart bump beneath your new breasts.

Your mother never went back to Romania, although she had uncles there, and there are second cousins you've never seen. Her parents were dead. You don't think of them as your grandparents; they belong to your mother, like treasure she had hidden and now could not find. Your mother had no sisters or brothers. She was sad that you, too, were going to be an only child, but you didn't care. You had a bedroom of your own, unlike any of your friends.

Your mother told you about coming to England. She came by train from Bucharest, across Hungary and Germany. The trains burned soft brown coal, and her skin and hair drank in the smoke. She smelled of train-dirt until she came to England and washed herself over and over with a slab of green soap which she did not yet know was for washing floors, not people. She took her first job in the Queen Alexandra Hotel near Regent's Park, and she lived in. She worked in the laundry, where she sorted and darned Irish linen table-cloths and napkins. People didn't mind a darn then, it was quite normal. In fact, darning was an art, in those years after the war, and your mother possessed it. At night she went to English classes, then back she came up the endless stairs, to a room which did not need curtains because it was so high.

Your mother's eyes were like black velvet curtains. They took in everything, and rarely gave it back. She married an Englishman she thought would prove as clean and strong as the linen, and he didn't fail her. They were old when they had you, your mother touching forty, your father two years older. The one thing he could not abide was organized religion, and on Sundays you walked, the three of you. You took the tube to Kew Gardens, or Hampstead Heath, or you walked through central London from park to park in the bloom of Sunday quiet long before the shopping laws changed.

Your mother told you that you were baptized. She had had it done somehow, quietly, so as not to impinge upon your father. When you had to fill in forms at school you had to write *Russian Orthodox*, which was hard work compared to *C. of E.* or *R.C.* Sometimes she took you to the Orthodox church. She answered in English when people spoke to her in Russian or in Romanian. You took it all in like breathing.

One day your mother told you it was Easter. You knew it wasn't, because you'd had your Easter eggs two weeks before. She reminded you that the Orthodox Easter came according to a different calendar, and even though she spoke to you in English, as always, it was clear which calendar was right, and that it was the true Easter which you were about to observe. *The Gregorian Calendar*, she told you, as if she was giving you sweets after promising herself not to.

You don't think that it was Easter Day itself. It was Passion Sunday, perhaps. Certainly it was a Sunday. You remember thin, bright sunshine, and the peaceful echoes of your feet on empty pavements.

Your mother held your hand. Her right sleeve brushed your face. You were seven or perhaps eight, and small for your age. You didn't know that you were about to start growing, and nor did your mother, who worried because you were the smallest in your class. Soon it was all going to be the past. *Do you remember when Louise wouldn't grow? How we used to worry about her?* She gave you Virol and Cod Liver Oil, and bought orange juice with a blue foil top from the milkman for your breakfast. No one else drank it, only you, because it was expensive. After she gave you the Virol you held it in your mouth for as long as you could without gagging, then spat it down the toilet. At school you refused to eat foods if they touched one another, or were connected in any way by gravy or custard. Your teacher stopped your mother in the street and said, 'I don't know why you waste your money on school dinners for Louise, Mrs Hapgood. She never eats them.' Your mother was angry, but with the teacher, not with you.

'It's not her business what happens to the dinners. They are paid for.'

The entrance to the church was black with old women. You doubted if there'd be space to squeeze through. But your mother saw no problem, and you went through in her wake, through waves of flesh. Your mother stopped, and put money into a box, then went into the little church.

The men stood on the right, the women on the left. You stood beside your mother, so close that you were touching, but her face looked out and away from you, towards the iconostasis. People were going forward, bowing to kiss the icons. You didn't know what was going on. You hadn't been to church often enough to make sense of it, or to predict what would come next.

'Why are all these people here?' you asked, as your mother made room for you. You had never seen the church so packed.

'They are here to remember the sufferings of Christ,' whispered your mother, and her little ironic smile twisted her lips. She began to join in the prayers everybody around you was murmuring, even though you didn't know or understand the words, and you hadn't known that she knew and understood them. Your mother crossed herself and you crossed yourself too, looking ahead as she did, at the iconostasis behind which lights moved and people moved, intent as builders. You didn't know what they were making in there. You wanted to see, but at the same time you were happy to be where you were, not seeing. You knew that later on the priest would emerge, and that he would move about in front of the people, wrapped up in his tasks.

The old woman on your other side was so shrunk and bent that you were nearly as tall as her, even though you were only eight – or perhaps seven – and small for your age. She was finding it hard to stand. She could have gone to sit at the side of the church, in one of the tall seats that faced into its body, but though another old woman gestured to her and indicated a place, she wouldn't go. She stayed beside you, her elbow touching your elbow, her body swaying as she listened to the cantor. Sometimes she groaned quietly, and she sang the responses in a queer rough voice, like a man's voice, as she crossed herself over and over again.

You saw her begin to struggle and you thought she was falling over, so you pulled your mother's arm. But your mother simply glanced at you, and frowned, and looked forward again, where the priest was moving behind the iconostasis. Slowly and clumsily, the old woman clambered to her knees. You watched every movement as she shuffled her body forward and down. The lumpiness of her, with her bum thrust up in its black worn coat. Stiffly and oldly, she sank until her face touched the ground. Her back went flat so you could have put your foot on it and stood on her. And then, on your left hand, your mother went down too, past your elbow, shrinking to her knees and then to her face on the floor. The cantor sang in his raw, rich voice that made your eyes sting. In front of the icons candle flames dipped, then sprang tall, and the black eyes of God's Holy Mother watched you. There was your mother, on the ground with the old women, and here were you left standing, the tallest thing of all, like a house in a knocked-down street. There wasn't space for you even to kneel. If you moved you couldn't walk, you'd be wading through flesh.

Your mother got up easily, in one springing movement, and was tall at your side again. The old women scrambled and heaved. You heard them groan to themselves beneath the sound of chanting: *Euch, euch*, as if their bones hurt. There was a smell, and you knew someone nearby had farted with the effort.

For a strange moment your mother folded her arms and stared straight ahead, through the gap in the iconostasis, as if she was arguing with someone there. The chanting rose round you, black and silver like the icons. Your head ached, you swayed against your mother's blue jacket, and the cloth rubbed your cheek. Your mother glanced at you, then she opened her handbag and took out a piece of paper and a little betting-shop pencil. She drew a line down the paper, dividing the left from the right. She began to write two columns of names, one on the right, the other on the left of the paper. She wrote as if she was writing a shopping list for the things she bought every week, rapidly, and without hesitation.

'What are you doing?' you whispered.

'I'm having prayers said for them.' She pointed at the names. Her father's name, her mother's name. More names, but people you didn't know. On the right side, your name, and your father's name. 'The names of the dead are on the left,' she told you. You put out your finger and touched the names. Now you knew they were the names of the dead, who needed prayers more than the living. Even your prayers, though you'd never

26

met them. Your mother asked you, as if you were grown-up like her, and not her own child, 'Do you want to put a name here?' You said yes. You wanted to put her name, your mother's, and your father's, side by side, but you didn't want to tell her in case she guessed you were afraid she might die. She gave the pencil to you, the little, plain, wood-coloured pencil your father must have brought home from the bookies'. 'You can write it yourself,' she said. You bent over and leaned the paper on your knee, and then you wrote both their names, on the right-hand side. *Daniela Maria Hapgood. Arthur George Hapgood.*

Your mother took back the paper without reading it. 'Wait here,' she said, and went forward with the paper and her purse, to the doorway in the iconostasis behind which the priest was at work. You saw her hand the paper to someone, and take money from her purse and give that too. People had closed in around you, taking away the space where your mother had been. You were afraid she would never be able to find you again, and you didn't dare call out to her. But she slipped through the mass of people easily, and smiled at you, and took up her place beside you again. She bowed her head, and crossed herself once, twice, three times. Her lips moved and you knew she was speaking in her other language, the one you didn't understand.

You stayed so long you thought your mother had forgotten what she'd told you on the way to church. *We won't stay for the whole service. It's too long for you.* You didn't mind. You were beyond being tired, or bored. You were sunk deep in the river of chanting as it washed through the church, through your skin and into the spaces behind your eyes. You knew it was like water, at one moment a trickle in your hands, at the next grown to vastness. You thought of the brown surge of water under the bridges of the Thames. Your mother was there, close to you, her body pressed against yours as the chant swelled and the candles guttered by the silver frames of the icons.

You came out blinking into daylight. It felt as if a whole night had passed in the church, and you were sure you'd been asleep, propped up and standing. You clung to your mother as she talked to people you didn't know she knew. Hands touched your hair, and you burrowed closer into your mother's side, wanting her to take you away.

She was wearing her best black suede shoes, but now there was a mark on them, where someone had stood on her toe. You watched her feet and knew she wanted to escape, too, but was standing still out of politeness. At last you were released and trotting beside her as her heels clopped on the pavement. The sun was on you both and your mother was smiling.

'Oh, that church!' she said. 'It's always so crowded, it gives me a headache. But soon the old people will start dying and then it won't be crowded any more.'

You looked secretly at your mother, who was forty-seven.

'How old are they, those old people?' you asked cunningly.

'Oh, they're old,' said your mother. Then she said, 'When I was a little girl I used to go to my grandparents in the country every summer. There was a little wooden church there which had been rolled over the mountains.'

'How can you roll a church?'

'I don't know, but I remember my grandfather telling me how all the men of the village had rolled the church over the mountains. He said, *If ever we need to, we can roll it away again, to a safe place.*'

You walked at your mother's side. You saw the church, packed with women in black, and the men under it, rolling it over the snowy tops of the mountains while the cantor sang, the priest blessed the people, and the old women groaned under their breath: *Euch, euch.*

'There was a wonder-working icon, too,' your mother added. 'People said the church could never be destroyed as long as the icon remained in it.'

'So the church is still there?'

'No, actually, I think it burnt down,' said your mother absently. 'We had a lot of fires, with all the wooden buildings. My grandfather's house burned once, and my grandmother tried to put out the flames with a soup-ladle.'

'With a ladle?'

'Yes.' Suddenly your mother came back to herself. Her voice changed to her daily voice. 'It's a long time ago, Louise, it doesn't matter. It's all finished.'

You are still walking along the sunny street. Your mother has been dead for twelve years, your father for fourteen. They never saw Anna. It was finished as far as they knew: one child, no grandchildren. They don't know what you have done. You walk in the ripple of wind and think of them: Daniela Maria Hapgood, Arthur George Hapgood. You think of your father in the tiny greenhouse he built for himself, weighing a bunch of black grapes in his hand. He showed you the bloom on them, and warned you not to touch it. The grapes were not quite ripe. When they were ripe he'd let you cut the bunch with your mother's scissors. He is a big, fair man, as clean and strong as linen. He can't understand the shadows inside you, so you put them away and make them invisible. He can't bear organized religion. When you go on a school trip to the Tower of London, he tells you that the National Health Service is worth a thousand times more than the Crown Jewels. *If you break your leg, is the Queen going to mend it for you?* He knows how to set a plant in the soil so it feels at home there. You're his little girl.

He'll be forgotten; both of them will be forgotten. Only you remember them now, in the way people need to be remembered. Their goodness has run away like water. Everything they touched has disappeared: the greenhouse is broken, the grapes eaten. The church has rolled away again, over the mountains. Only you are left here, in the muddle you've made, your child

29

separated from you, your flat strewn with sticky bottles which you're always meaning to put out for recycling. But you never do.

You stand on the shore, staring after the ship your parents have sailed on, but your toes sink into mud and there's a stench of sewage in the water. Their ship catches the departing light, but already they've gone below deck and they're considering the menu, seriously as they always do, because food is important and not to be taken for granted. They don't know that you're still watching. They don't know that you're walking along this sunny street after your trip to the plastic surgeon. Your mother thought you were beautiful as you were.

Five

You are with Anna, in the garden. It's a late November day, and Anna's wearing red woolly tights, a short navy skirt, a navy hooded fleece. You are wearing jeans and a cable-stitch sweater: Mum clothes. You want everything to be normal.

'I've been looking through your toys,' you say. 'Later on we'll sort out what you want to take to Dad's, and what you want to keep here. There might be some stuff you don't want any more, now you're a big girl.'

Anna stares at you. Her face is shrunken inside the blue hood. 'I want to keep everything,' she says.

Of course she can. If Paul doesn't want the heap of greying rabbits, the Barbie collection, the dozens of Barbie outfits with matching high heels which fall off and get stuck inside the Hoover, the six jumbo packs of felt-tips that never have any reds or yellows left in them, then you're more than happy to keep them here. But Paul said, 'Just pack everything.'

The day has come, the one you never reckoned on.

'Do you want to make me take it to court?' he asked you. 'You wouldn't win, I can tell you that, not with the brief I'd get. She was on the doorstep for nearly an hour, in the rain.'

'I thought Lola's mum was bringing her home.'

'She did. But there was so much traffic she just dropped her off. Anna said she could see the lights were on and she knew you were in. And the silly cow didn't wait. Why do you think Anna told her that? Because she didn't want her to come in and see you. Because she knew the state you'd be in. You've done it to her before, haven't you? She's come back from school and you've been drinking since she left in the morning.'

You didn't answer. There was nothing to say so you covered your mouth, so as not to say it and not to let out the whimpering that wanted to beg him not to do it. You knew he would do it, whatever you said.

'She was waiting on the doorstep. Anyone could have come by. She could see the lights and she knew you were there but she couldn't make you hear.'

'I was asleep,' you say. 'I've been having bad nights. I must have gone into such a deep sleep I didn't hear the bell.'

'Yeah, right, you've been having bad nights. And what do you think Anna's been having? Thank God she had the sense to go down to the call-box and get me on my mobile.'

And he'd had his key. He'd come in, with Anna, and found her. He had proof.

'And don't try to tell me it was just the one time. I've been asking around. I've been to the school. She's been late, some days she's not been in at all. There's been concern, that's what they said. Can you imagine me standing there and hearing that, there's been concern over my own daughter? This place is a pit. There isn't even proper food in the fridge for her, with all the money I give you.'

'We have our meals out a lot. Sometimes we have take-away.'

'Take-away! For Christ's sake, Lou, this is Anna we're talking about. Well, that's the end of it. I'm taking her. You can see her, I'm not stopping you, but she's living with me.'

Your face aches with the cold. You're kneeling on the stone flags of the terrace, and your arms circle Anna's waist. She stands stiffly inside them, not resisting you, but not yielding to you either. The last leaves in the garden are stiff, too, rattling in the cold wind. You feel as if you are falling off the edge of the world. Dead leaves lie in heaps in behind the pots, and the bare vines of creeper are flapping loose. You ought to put more nails in the walls, but you haven't got round to it.

You draw Anna close to you. 'Anna,' you say, 'guess what? I went down to Harrods and got you that Little Bear pyjama case.'

But Anna's face is still turned away. You know it's not because your breath smells: you've been using Gold Spot and Listerine ever since she rolled over to the wall when you bent to kiss her at bedtime.

'We could put your new pyjamas in there, and then when you get to Dad's you can cuddle the pyjama case in bed. It's like a teddy, isn't it?'

'I don't have teddies any more.'

'No, I know you don't.'

'Dad says I can choose the colour of my room.'

Her voice is small and cool. She will not break down, she will not soften in your arms.

'That's right,' you say. 'You can choose your favourite colours.'

'Will you come and see it?' She is tensed for your answer.

'We'll have to ask your dad.'

'And I'll be coming here.'

'That's right.'

'Mum?'

'What?'

'Mum. You won't move, will you?'

'Course not.'

'You said before, I was going to live with you always.'

'I know. But that's not fair on your dad, is it? He's got to have his turn.'

'And then you've got to have yours.' Her face has lightened a little. This sounds better than anything you've been able to tell her before. Taking turns: she knows all about that.

'I love you,' you say. She doesn't answer. It's wrong, it's too heavy, too emotional, grabbing at her like everyone's been grabbing at her these past weeks. 'You're my best banana. All the monkeys in the zoo are jealous of me. They want to come and live in my garden so they can see Miss Anna Banana.'

'Oh Mum.' She squirms, but a frowning little smile flits over her face. 'You're always silly.'

'Yeah, I am, aren't I? Not like you, Miss Anna Banana.'

'Did you used to call me that when I was little?'

'I used to call you Trouble when you were little.'

'I wasn't trouble. I was good.'

'Yeah, you were, you were good. You were the best.'

Suddenly Anna's arms are tight round you, her voice fierce in your ear. 'Don't ever say that to anyone else. Only say it to me.'

'Who else have I got to say it to?'

But that's wrong too. Why should she have to think about you being alone? She's got enough, without that. Quickly, you say, 'Listen, you've got my mobile number, haven't you? As well as the number here.'

She nods. 'I've written them down in my diary in case I forget.'

'You can always ask Dad. He's got them.'

You feel frozen. You need a drink but you won't touch one till Anna's gone. You keep the thought of it at the back of your mind, like the rescue that comes in the last five minutes of old Westerns, the kind you watched on Sunday afternoons when Mum and Dad were upstairs having a rest. They used to leave you a bottle of Seven-Up, and a packet of Iced Gems. Later on they came down warm and happy and Dad put you on his knee while Mum made a cup of tea with something a bit stronger in it for Dad. And you all ate a sticky fruit cake which Mum unwrapped, peeling off the greaseproof paper base and slicing it up so you got the bit with the most cherries. What's Anna got to remember, compared to that?

Don't think of what Anna's got to remember. Those afternoons cold and fuggy as old ashtrays. The light going, the promised trip to the park or the zoo once more failing to happen. Because everyone has a glass of wine to relax, don't they, and it's the weekend. And the level of the wine shrinks down the bottle as if someone else is sucking it up. For a while you're happy and Anna's happy, or at least you can persuade yourself that she is, apart from a wary edge to her laughter and the way she rushes off to get her maths book to show you when she sees you rummaging in the fridge for the second bottle. Because she still thinks she can distract you. You can even remember times when you poured a glass for Anna too, because it made it seem more normal, like something you were sharing. But she wrinkled her lips and wouldn't touch it.

And then it's late afternoon, darkening. *Mum's tired, Anna, she's got to have a little sleep.*

You don't know how long you've been asleep. Anna comes in with a pale cup of tea wobbling in its saucer. You grope up out of sleep but you know you can't stay awake. You feel too bad.

'Come and have a lie down with me, Anna,' you say, but she doesn't. You tell her to go and put on a video. *A Hundred and One Dalmatians*, she loves that, it's always been her favourite. Later you wake again and she's got herself into her pyjamas, even brushed her teeth.

'Night, Mum,' she says, but she doesn't kiss you.

The bamboo rustles. Anna leans in towards you. Her eyes are closed, her hair slips over her cheeks. You touch her cheek with your lips, and her skin is cold.

'It's better for you, Anna,' you say, because it's the truth and you know she's listening now, not resisting you. 'You'll have everything just the same. Your friends and school and all your toys. Dad's better at looking after you than I am, just now. Come on, it's cold out here. Let's go and find which of those old rabbits you want to take.'

'I wish it was like this all the time,' says Anna. You know what she means but can't say: *You talking to me, you remembering about my rabbits, knowing about my homework and how I like tomatoes hot but not cold. You staying there on the safe side of the tracks, being a grown-up. Not me watching you pee on the floor because you can't get to the toilet on time. Not me being allowed to watch videos all day if I want, and take money for sweets out of your bag. Not me seeing how frightened you are of what's happening to us both, and then grabbing me tight and trying to hug it all away.*

'It's better,' you say, stroking back her hair. You are not going to cry or do anything stupid before Paul comes. You're going to pack her bags with her and sort out the things she can't take but which Paul will collect another day. You're going to make sure her teeth are clean and her hair is brushed and she's got her homework diary with her. You won't slip: there's only an hour to go.

The day has come, the day you never reckoned on.

Six

After Anna was born, Paul began to work even later. He'd leave messages for me on the answerphone. Sometimes I thought he waited until he knew I'd have gone out, so he could leave those messages and not talk to me.

'I'll be back late. I've had to go to the Deptford site. Don't wait up,' or 'I'm going to Cardiff to chase a surveyor. I'll stay overnight.' He never remembered to say the name of the hotel, even after I said, 'What if I need to get in touch with you? What if something happens to Anna?' But he shrugged. He said, 'It won't.' Even though he was looking straight at me, I couldn't see into his eyes. I would lie awake thinking about it, and I'd start to frighten myself, and then I'd tell myself, 'Don't be stupid. You're imagining things.'

I saw a lot of Johnnie then. He wasn't supposed to be living with us any more, but even though he had the flat, our house was still his home. He had his own key, and he'd let himself in at any time of the day or night. It stopped me worrying about burglars, because every time I heard a sound I could think: 'It's Johnnie.' He'd come into the hall and prowl around, picking up my letters and listening to the messages on the answering machine. Paul's voice on the machine was so like Johnnie's that it must have been like listening to himself. I'm not talking about accent: anybody can change that. It's the grain of the voice, the thing that's there like the grain in wood when you cut it. You can get brothers who don't even speak to one another, but if you collected their voices from different rooms, they'd sound the same. Johnnie liked hearing Paul's voice. 'It's nice,' he'd say, 'the way he always calls home.'

Johnnie wants everything to be stable, except himself. That's why he liked our house so much, because it was thick with toys and clothes, and the cupboards were always loaded with food. He'd come in when I was alone and perch on the side of the bath and talk about nothing, making me laugh. He had a gift for that. Sometimes I'd have Anna in the bath, too. When I think of those times it's always about seven o'clock on a June evening. The sky's darkening, going bluer, and there's thick yellow dust in the shafts of sun. I always wished a shaft would reach right down into the bath, like a rainbow, but it never did. Anna used to stretch out her hand to touch it. Maybe there was only ever one long hot June, the year after Anna was born. I used Floris' Rose Geranium in the bath that year. I was extravagant. I ran the bath, washed myself, stood to let it drain and then filled it again with clean, clear water. Then I lay down and the water rocked around me. If Anna was in her chair she didn't like me to disappear inside the frame of the bath. After a while she'd cry and then I'd sit up and make faces at her and give her back her plastic octopus, then I'd sink back down again, into the water, down, down, until it covered my face. I had my hair cut short that summer. Johnnie liked it, but Paul didn't. Some men are funny about long hair. They think it makes you look more womanly.

'More womanly,' Johnnie said, 'but not as sexy,' and he flicked his hand along the wet points of my hair.

Johnnie and I never did anything once Anna was born. I don't know why. I felt as if we'd made up a story and now we had to live it. And yet I had Anna, and she wasn't a story. As soon as I had her I felt that she belonged in the house more than I did. But Johnnie isn't someone you can forget. I was aware of him, all my skin alive with it when I heard him in the hall, his footsteps straying, his fingers pushing buttons on the telephone, his hands unfolding my bills. He was fanatically curious. He wanted to know everything we'd been doing, me and Anna, even though it was never anything much. Maybe I'd shopped for a dress, or had Anna weighed at the clinic. It was the detail Johnnie was hungry for.

Sometimes, when I was lying in the bath, he'd put his hand on my breast, or run it down my belly. And I'd turn and rub my wet face along the inside of his arm, where his skin was pale and fine. But the water made it a different kind of reality, one we didn't need to worry about, or even think about once I was out of the bath. And there was Anna cheeping and laughing up at us from her chair. She loved Johnnie.

If Paul was away on business, I'd get dry and put on a dress. I love that time, when people are starting to come out for the evening, and the waiters are running in and out of pavement cafés scribbling on their order pads and then calling the order back into the kitchen. It's like the beginning of a play. With Johnnie you always felt you were part of it, walking on the stage as if you had the right to be there.

We'd wheel Anna out in the warm streets, through to the park. I could have got a babysitter but I never did, because I didn't want anyone else in the house. More than that, it seemed right to have Anna with us. I used to put some money in my purse from the pile of notes Paul always left for me, under his silver cigarette box, so we could go and eat somewhere afterwards. It would be about nine o'clock. Sometimes Anna would sleep, sometimes not. She never cried. I loved all the taxis going so fast, going somewhere, whirling people off to wherever they wanted to be. And in the park there were people doing t'ai chi and reading under trees, or staring into each other's eyes as if they knew they were in a play too. Then we'd go back through streets where the pubs were open and spilling on to the streets and there was a smell of beer from the vents. I didn't drink beer much but I loved the smell of it. The air was tired, like wilted leaves. Johnnie would push the pushchair.

We'd go in somewhere and eat. Johnnie didn't like fancy

places, he liked those little Italian restaurants which all buy their table-cloths from the same warehouse. They welcomed Anna. They'd warm her bottle for her while Johnnie poured Barolo into our glasses. I put Anna in the crook of my arm and wedged the bottle into her mouth and drank from my own glass. Johnnie watched us and said, 'You shouldn't be giving her a bottle. You should be feeding her from the breast.'

'Paul didn't like it.'

'Yeah, I know. He didn't like it. That's 'cos he wanted you all to himself. Tell you what I'd like, Louise. I'd like to sit in here with you opposite and you'd pull down that strap and feed Anna, and I'd watch you.'

'They'd chuck us out.' I said it quickly and I laughed, to hide the fact that what he said moved me so much.

'Course they wouldn't. Not in here, they know about babies.'

And it was true. When we came in they always smiled at Anna as if she was the most important person in the restaurant, and called her *bella bambolina*, and went off to sort out her bottle before they even took our order. They smiled at Johnnie too, and I knew they were thinking how young he was to be so serious and so good with the baby.

When I think back to those June days with Johnnie, I wonder why we were so good. There was I, lying naked in the bath, there was Johnnie. We were provoking ourselves, but what for? He touched my nipple, then he looked at me as the water slopped around me. It wouldn't have taken anything, but we held back.

That was years ago, and it's all changed now. Paul's left me. I shouldn't have bothered to go to that doctor. It was stupid. You do things like that to punish yourself, to rub your face in the facts. I knew as soon as I saw the look on the doctor's face that he had no respect for me. He was going to enjoy telling me he couldn't help me.

It's more complicated, anyway, than pretty or not pretty, young or not young. Paul still goes to bed with me; Sonia doesn't know that. He can't help himself, and I can't help myself, or at least that's what I tell myself. I go on believing in him, and he goes on believing in me. And he falls asleep afterwards. He always falls asleep, and I lie there and watch him for a while, then I get out of bed and make myself a cup of tea and drink it sitting in the window, while the people go by and Paul sleeps. I never have a drink when Paul's with me. I sit there, and I feel as if I'm dissolving.

Paul's left me, and now I have the house to myself. It's not too big for one person: we were always talking about moving somewhere bigger, but I loved the house so much we never did. I couldn't leave the garden. Although it's small, the house cost Paul a fortune, because of the position. He could have bought something twice the size in another postcode, but we didn't want to.

Look at my legs. Once I went to the front door without bothering to tie the sash on my dressing-gown. I'd been sun-bathing in the courtyard. And there he was, in his dark suit and his clean white cotton shirt that smelled the way his shirts always smelled. I smiled. Paul looked at me and I saw my dressing-gown had opened up without me knowing and there I was. And he didn't answer my smile or reach for me. He looked, and then he said, 'Cover yourself up.'

He used to love that. Him clothed and me naked, that was what he liked best. Me half-dressed, me undressed, me naked. He used to turn me around as if I was a vase. He used to like me to come to the door naked. That was before we had money, before there were always other people in the house, furniture coming and painters and interior decorators who know more about how you want your house than you do yourself. When you get money there are more and more things you have to have and have to do. You can't just drag a chair out into the garden when the sun shines: you have to have oiled teak chairs and tables, and a swing-seat with covers that need to go to the cleaners.

But before that, at the time I'm talking about, it was just him and me and the little grey street outside, where the day-time world was waiting. This was years before Anna wasn't born. Nothing had happened. Johnnie was still a boy. I'd stand inside the door. I wouldn't have had my bath yet and I could smell myself, and Paul on me from the night before. He'd fold himself round me as if it didn't matter about anything, not the dark suit nor anything. Then he'd pull the weight of my hair up in his hands then let it fall. And I'd feel the cool of it flickering down over my skin like feathers.

He went out into the day-time world, and I stayed. That was how it was, though I did work from home, typing stuff for him, and taking messages. We always wanted children, but it went on so long that we forgot 'having a baby' meant more than reaching a goal we'd set ourself. Paul wanted me to be pregnant but it didn't happen. I was small then, not thin, but small. He used to put his hands round my waist, or even my neck. It's a very strange feeling when a man puts his hands around your neck, and Paul is the only one I've ever allowed. I never flinched from him, or from the mirror. I knew there was no fault to find.

People say that drinking stops you knowing what drink does to you, like an anaesthetic stops you feeling the cut. If they see a woman in the doorway with her bags and her ankle socks on bare legs stuck straight out in front of her, and a trickle of dark liquid between her open thighs, they think, *She's out of it. She doesn't know.* They notice that her flesh is grey, mottled with purple and brick-red, but it's the way they would notice the colouring of a safari animal, not a human being.

You can feel pity. You can feel contempt if you want, and she can't stop you. I don't feel pity, because I know her.

And when she looks up and meets my eye I know she knows me. We're two of a kind, but you won't find me on any street. I've got a lovely house, and in the mornings the sun pours through the sticky windows on to the sticky glasses, and I think, 'I'll tidy up a bit later because Anna's coming,' but time doesn't work like that. I sit down. I've got my dressing-gown on and I pull it up to let the sun get to my legs. I lean back. I've always got a beautiful tan, I've got that kind of skin. I don't care what Paul thinks, I like my own legs. I stretch them out in front of me and let the sun soak in. Time slops round in my head, the minutes pulling away from the hours. I think of Paul and me, and Anna, and Johnnie.

Paul told me a story about Johnnie, the second time we went out together. I didn't understand that it was a story about Johnnie at the time; I thought it was about Paul. Johnnie is Paul's brother, but there are twelve years between them.

This was the story. Paul was living with his mother and Johnnie in a flat in Barking. Johnnie was a baby, about six months. Where their father was I don't know. He came and went a lot after Johnnie was born. He came back in the end, of course, after he got ill, for Maureen to nurse him. I found out about all that later from Maureen, Paul's mum, when we got to know each other.

It was night-time, and they were all asleep. Paul woke up first. He saw a line of light under the door. As I understand it, there was a kitchen with a bath in it, properly plumbed in but with a lid which came down over it except when you needed it. Then there was a sitting-room where Paul slept on a sofa-bed, and the bedroom where his parents slept, with the cot in it as well. The line of light was coming from the hall. His mother never left the hall light on. Then he heard a drawer open, and a clinking sound.

Maureen had silver-plated cutlery for a wedding-present,

and she kept it in that drawer. Paul used to polish it for her.

'You've no idea how little we had then,' Maureen would say. 'It was just after the war when we got married, and nobody had anything.'

More clinking. Paul was still half-asleep, and he thought to himself, 'What's Mum doing, getting the knives and forks out in the middle of the night?' Just then, he heard a man cough. Paul was out of bed, through the hall and into the bedroom in a second, and shaking his mother.

'Mum! Mum! There's a burglar in the kitchen!'

She was deep asleep, with the baby tucked in beside her. He shook her shoulder and she started to wake up, but just then Paul heard the door open from the kitchen on to the hall. He knew his mum kept a wooden door-stopper by her bedroom door in case of burglars, so he got hold of it by one end and pulled open the bedroom door. It was a big heavy mahogany thing, and you could beat someone's brains out with it. There was the man, just coming out of the kitchen. He had his back to Paul and he didn't see him for a minute, which was long enough for Paul to swing up the door-stopper and hit him with it on the back of the head.

It wasn't enough to knock him out, but the man went down on his knees and the silver spilt out all over the hall lino. Paul had the door-stopper up again, ready to smash him if he tried to rise. He was a big man. Maureen was out of bed snatching her dressing-gown round her, and the baby was screaming. Paul didn't dare move in case the man made a spring. He kept the door-stopper up. 'Get the police, Mum,' he said. Of course they didn't have a phone.

'I'm not leaving you here with him,' said Maureen. The man was big, and he was nasty-looking too. It turned out later that he'd done dozens of flats all round Barking, getting a ten-bob note here and a pack of cigarettes there. People didn't have all the TVs and videos they have now. So Maureen started yelling out to get the neighbours to wake up. She tried shouting 'Police!' but after she'd been screeching that out for a while she realized it wasn't going to work, so she changed to 'Fire!' After a long time there was a mousy little tap at the front door of the flat. It was Mr Berridge from downstairs.

'Is there anything wrong, Mrs O'Driscoll?'

'Yes, there bloody well is! Didn't you hear me? We've got a burglar in here.'

'Well, we heard some sort of a row, so we've been down in the cellar.'

There was a lot Maureen felt like saying, but she just told them to get the police. There was Paul, still holding the door-stopper while Johnnie screamed and screamed. Then some other people from the flats upstairs came down, and that was that. The man was sent to prison, I believe.

The first thing Paul did when the police came was to go into the bedroom and pick Johnnie up from the bed. He was so worked up he was shaking. Paul got him calmed down while Maureen talked to the police and went through her drawers to see if anything else was missing. And the thing was, they found he'd taken twenty Players from her bedside table, as well as a silver crucifix from her dressing-table drawer. So he'd been in there while she was fast asleep, with the baby tucked in beside her. It made Maureen shiver.

Paul held Johnnie, stroking his head. Johnnie was still hic-cupping out those big, reproachful sobs, there was sweat all over his head and his hand was clutching the sleeve of Paul's pyjamas. His knuckles were white. And Paul thought, 'I'll look after you, even if no one else will.' He remembers quite clearly thinking that. It was like a promise to the baby. His father wasn't there, you see, and his mother was fast asleep while the burglar walked around their bed, taking what he wanted.

Maureen hadn't got all that much sense, even when she was

awake. She tended to panic. Paul often came back to that night: the big man rummaging through everything they'd got, as if he had the right, and his mother asleep, and then Johnnie screaming and screaming.

When people tell you stories like that about their lives, when you first know them, you don't understand what it means. I thought the point of it was Paul telling me about the way he'd kept a grown man pinned to the ground, when he was only a boy of twelve. But, as I've said, the story was really about Johnnie, and about how Paul could never leave him, or give up on him. So in its way it was a kind of warning, though again, it took me a long time to see that. Perhaps that's why Johnnie could sit on the edge of my bath and we'd touch and float, but never fuck. Only the one time, and that was enough. Paul stood in for Johnnie in all sorts of ways, and Johnnie stood in for Paul.

I don't want to smell of drink when Anna comes. I'm still in the sun, though it's moved around a bit. I look at all the flesh of my legs. When you make bread you have to leave it to rise, in a quiet place, covered up. It stretches to the top of the bowl and knocks against the cloth. Dough. Then you knock it back and knead it some more and in the end you get bread. It's a long time since I've tried. I'm the dough bulging up against the cloth. I don't mind the fatness of women who are meant to be fat, with their tiny hands and their dimply wrists with threads in them, like baby wrists. There's a tightness in their fat, as if it's bursting with juice. It looks right. But what's happened to my body doesn't look right.

Paul pays the Council Tax and the upkeep. All my bills are paid. I don't bother with my cheque-book any more. I have the money Paul gives me, new notes in new envelopes. But then he's always preferred to give money in cash.

'That's what you do for your mistress,' I said to him, 'not for your wife.'

He was in my bed when I said this. It was the way his eyes went blank when I said 'mistress'. And that look of his travelled over me, up and down, and I knew the dressing-gown was gaping wide again.

I'm his wife. He may think what he likes, but he can't change that. He keeps coming back here. I'm his wife until we both die, and when we're dead I'll still be his wife, one flesh.

Seven

The room is hot and high. The radiator hisses, but otherwise it's quiet, even though there's a child in the room. She sits at a table, drawing. There are crayons and felt-tips scattered over the table-top, and discarded sheets of paper crushed into balls. The child bends down over her drawing, her mouth slightly open and her tongue poking out between her teeth. She is drawing with long vigorous sweeps of a black Conté crayon. She draws a hutch against a wall, a wired run, and a rabbit inside with its body flattened against the grass. She keeps getting it wrong. She keeps laying its head back like a hare's, and putting big startled bubbles of eyes on top of its head.

On top of the hutch there is a cat. It is striped like a tiger, too much striped, Anna sees now, but she likes the slash of black and white. The cat skulks forward and its whiskers lie back against its muzzle as it watches the rabbit in the run. Anna knows cats. She has sat in her mother's garden, her legs tucked up, her arms hugging her knees, watching the wild cats her mother says she mustn't touch. The drawing goes wrong again. Anna crumples it, and sweeps together the heap of discarded drawings, and stands up. But although she keeps crumpling up her drawings, she doesn't seem frustrated.

She goes to a chair, and picks up the Little Bear pyjama case which lies there. She holds it tight, rubbing its floppy body against her cheek, then puts it down again and sits on the carpet. Dark, ornate, highly polished slabs of furniture lean over her, like cliffs she cannot climb. The carpet is a thick-piled, dense maroon. Money's been spent here.

The walls are painted plain cream, and have the sheen of

hospital walls. Everything bounces off them: light, sweat, marks of hands that have splayed against them, trying to get out. They wipe clean every time. Anna thinks about the people who were here before them, and wonders if they had any children. They furnished this room to last. It flaunts itself: *I may be ugly, but look how expensive I am.* Paul has rented the house, while he makes up his mind what to do. It gets him down.

Anna stands up. She picks up the pyjama case again, and holds it like a stage prop as she walks noiselessly to the window. She's practised walking like this. The sill is too high for her to look out, or down, but she can look up. There are black branches, criss-crossing, and the corner of the fire-escape. There's the grey graininess of a London sky in midwinter. A ginger-and-white pigeon on the ledge looks back at Anna. She knows it well. It has a withered claw, and it stays up here, out of trouble, waiting to plunge down to the basement for scraps. No animals are allowed in the house: it's a condition of the lease.

Anna looks up at the sky for a long time. Its chill reaches for her through the glass, and she'd like to lean her cheek against it, but the sill is too high. She makes a circle of her forefinger and thumb, and looks through it. There is the sky, looking quite different now, framed, mysterious, with the black fingers of the branches walking across it like writing which Anna can't read. A message. Something is about to happen. Anna takes hold of the window-sill with both hands, tips her head back, and waits.

It comes. The sound she's been waiting for. Deep in the belly of the house a door opens, then closes. She knows exactly where he is. He's inside the front door, opening the inner door, closing it again. Taking off his coat, hanging it up. Frowning at himself in the big mirror, meeting his own eyes without needing to smile. The big mirror like a dark cup where you float to the top, surprising even yourself. He leans close to his mirrored face and adjusts his tie. He looks up the stairwell to the landing. He walks briskly across the silent, spongy carpet, to the foot of the stairs.

Anna hears another sound. Voices. Two voices, twining together. She stands quite still, the Little Bear pyjama case in her hand limp and grinning. Anna's face remains mute, like the face of her father looking into the mirror. She goes to the cupboard and gets out a doll, and a small steel comb which her mother used whenever Anna came back from school with headlice. Anna hasn't played with dolls for a year, but she sits down again with her back to the door, and unties the pale blue ribbons from the doll's plaits. The doll's hair springs out, a stiff, glistening bush of yellow. The metal comb goes through it, dragging the hair away from the bald patches on the doll's scalp.

'I know it hurts,' says Anna, 'but it's the only way I can get rid of them. Those chemicals give you cancer. Be a big girl.'

They're outside the door now. Her father's hand is coming up to grasp the doorknob. She waits for the sound of the knob turning in its socket, but it doesn't come. All she can hear is her own heart beating thickly in her chest. His hand will be on the cold brass. Then she hears the two voices again, mixed together like hot and cold water from a tap.

The door opens. It's cold, that's why the incoming draught makes her back arch. She lays her doll carefully on the carpet and turns.

'Anna,' he says. His eyes examine her. Beside him there is a woman in a slender, ice-blue suit. Anna's met her before, and knows her name. She is called Sonia, and one of her hands rests lightly on Anna's father's arm. She has long, white fingers, and on one of the fingers is an emerald surrounded by diamonds. It stabs out light as Sonia glances down at the doll's spilled yellow hair. Her slim, busy lips are still, and she makes no attempt to move towards Anna. Already her perfume has crept like smoke into Anna's mouth and nose.

Anna clings to the smell of her mother, not as she is now, but as she was. Her mother picks up baby Anna on a wet spring morning in the square and makes her dive down to smell the white bunched heads of narcissi. They smell of sherbet, fine and sharp. Anna's mother says, 'They're called Pheasant's Eye, fancy that.' Her lips are full and pale and they come close, then brush aside to touch Anna's cheek. Anna slips her hand inside her mother's white shirt, and nestles it into the warm crack between her breasts. Anna's mother laughs and says she's trouble.

That was a long time ago. Now Anna's mother leaks the smell of old alcohol. It's like nail-polish remover. It's on her skin and in the folds of her flesh as she presses Anna close. The smell of alcohol squirms and burrows into Anna. The funny smell is stronger than perfume, much stronger than spring mornings. Anna's mother has alcohol in her eyes too. Her morning face is dull and shallow as a puddle. She kisses Anna, digging at Anna's back as she squeezes her close, into the smell. Then, if someone else is there, they say, 'Give her a break, Louise.'

Sometimes her mother is Louise, but she can be Lou, Louie, even Lulu. She has no name that stays the same. In her mouth *Anna* is as big as a world you'd like to eat, but never can.

Anna's father is smiling, with Sonia's hand on his arm. 'You know Sonia,' he says. 'Listen, Anna. Sonia's going to marry me.'

The radiator hisses louder than ever. Anna folds her hands in her lap and looks up at her father.

'What do you say?' asks her father.

Anna moistens her lips and blinks. The ice-blue column of Sonia glitters at her father's side. Sonia smiles, and takes a hesitant step forward, so Anna smells her perfume more strongly. But as well as Sonia's perfume she smells her father's skin, and the cologne he splashes on his neck after shaving.

Sometimes she watches him while he shaves. There's no one else there, only the heavy, swinging door of his mahogany wardrobe, the slosh of brush in soapy water, the scrape of his razor. He won't use an electric razor. She watches him in the mirror. Sometimes he reaches behind him, fumbling at the towel rail, and she puts a white towel into his hand. The towels don't belong to them either, which is why they have other people's initials embroidered on their corners. Anna doesn't like using towels with FMB embroidered on them, so you can't help it touching your skin. She keeps thinking someone will burst in and shout at her: 'What are you doing, drying your arse on my towel?' Arse, thinks Anna. That's what Johnnie says: 'Get your arse in gear, Anna, we're going out.'

'When?' asks Anna. Sonia's features bunch together and sparkle. She is still smiling, but now it's clear she's not going to hug Anna. She made her step forward, and that was all. Her father reaches down and puts his big warm hand on Anna's head, as if he will press her into the earth that lies four floors down beneath the thick carpets, the regiments of stairs, and the cold, infested floor of the basement.

Sonia puts out her hand. She places her finger under Anna's chin and raises it so that they look into each other's eyes.

'She looks like you round the mouth, Paul.'

'No. She looks like her mother.'

He crosses to the window and looks out at the greyness of London. It's getting darker, even though it's the middle of the day. The sky is like paper that someone is colouring in, grey stroke by grey stroke.

'Tell her about the wedding,' he says.

Sonia takes his arm. 'I booked a table for one o'clock, Paul,' she says. 'Anna and me, we'll get together and have a proper talk about it another time.'

'All right. Listen, Anna. After the wedding you're going to a new house, a house in the country.' He looks at his watch.

'Ten to one, Sonia. You go on down, I'll be with you in a minute.'

But Sonia reaches into her handbag and brings out a narrow white package with a red ribbon tied around it.

'We were in the jeweller's,' she says to Anna. 'We saw this for you.'

Anna holds the package without opening it. A flush begins deep inside her, like a wave, and breaks on the pale surface of her skin.

'Aren't you going to open it?' asks Sonia in her quick, sharp voice, but she is still smiling. Anna pulls the end of the ribbon, undoes the paper, opens the box.

'There,' says Sonia. 'You can wear it at the wedding.'

'Aren't you going to say something, Anna?' asks Paul.

'Thank you.'

'Thank Sonia. It was her idea. She chose it.'

'Thank you, Sonia.'

Anna sees that Sonia is cross, but won't show it. Her face remains smooth, but her body stiffens.

'Where does she go to school?' she asks.

'St Ursula's. She's getting a good education.'

'Hmm,' says Sonia. Her beautiful, pearly shoes glide over the carpet. She stops, opens the door and says, 'There won't be anywhere like St Ursula's in Mexford Bridge. It's the back end of nowhere. Still, we'll have to see what we can do. Bye then, Anna.'

'Bye,' says Anna.

As the door closes her father turns away from the window. He comes over to Anna, bends down, picks her up in his arms. Her face is level with his face. He might say she isn't like him, but she knows that she is. She can read him as if he's herself. His dark skin, his dark hair, his dark eyes. The steady heat of him that makes her want to lean in and curl herself against his chest like a cat. She puts her two cold hands up, one on each side of his face, framing it. She knows he'll let her, because they're alone.

'You all right, Anna?' he asks.

She nods.

'This house, you'll like it. It's got a great big garden and a river down the bottom of the hill.'

'I like it here.'

He frowns and shakes his head slightly as if shaking off what she's said. 'You don't want to think like that. Anyway, we've got to move. The lease here runs out in April. We'll need to keep on somewhere in London, but we'll get a flat. Sonia wants something more up her street.'

'What about —' *School*, she makes herself think. *My friends.* Not the huge thing that can't be said. Every week a car comes and takes her to see Mum. Down the streets, across the park, through rows of lights flicking red and green. She nearly knows the way. As the car takes the corners she leans against the window and memorizes the route, shop by shop, street by street. If anything happened, she'd be able to walk there. 'Will a car be able to come and get me from the country?' she asks.

'What are you on about now?' He smiles indulgently, as if she's said something more childish than her age allows.

'You know. A car to take me to . . .'

One of his hands comes up and lifts her hands from the side of his face. 'You don't want to worry about that,' he says. 'I'll take care of all that.'

When he's gone downstairs to join Sonia, she picks up one of the balls of drawing and uncrumples it. The cat and the rabbit are both quite good. What's wrong with the drawing is that something's missing.

She picks up her crayon and draws in bold clear strokes the muzzle of a tiger, rising above the oblivious cat like the face of the morning sun.

Eight

It's a registered letter. Paul always sends them registered, so I can't pretend they've never arrived.

The postman rang when I was just out of the bath. I pulled my kimono round me and opened the door just wide enough to reach round and take the parcel, or whatever. But he didn't hand it over.

'I need a signature,' he said. Not the usual postman, but then they change all the time. Young and cocky, staring at my kimono. I was still damp from my bath and the silk was sticking to me. *Need a signature.* That's Paul all right. A signature to say we're not married any more, a signature to say nothing that belongs to him belongs to me any more. Except Anna. Even Paul hasn't been able to find a way to make me sign away Anna.

I took the letter and signed for it, then printed my name. I didn't want to read it straightaway. I was cold and I wondered if I ought to get back in the bath for a bit, but the water was blue and scummy on top, and I didn't like the look of it. I pulled out the plug and the suction wheezed. I've got to do something about that waste-pipe. It isn't draining right. There's no time like the present, I thought. I was still wincing away from opening the letter. I went and rummaged under the sink and there was the plunger, orange and a bit smelly, with black spots on the inside of the rubber. I fixed the suction cup over the waste-pipe and plunged it up and down. There was a spurt of old, evil-smelling air, then a cloudy clot of dirt came up into the bath-water. I did it again. The pipe farted and cleared itself. I fetched my rubber gloves and the bath-cleaner and when the water had run out I scrubbed the enamel all round until the surface was white and sparkling. It's quite a new bath, and it comes up beautifully. Then I got that stuff that takes limescale off chrome, and I cleaned the taps. I wished Paul could see it. He's always saying I don't take care of things, and I've let the house fill up with rubbish. Once he saw some sandwiches I'd forgotten about behind the armchair and he kicked the plate and said, 'It's a wonder you don't have rats, the way you live.' It was a chicken sandwich, dry, with a bit of mould on the outside. But nothing criminal. What I can't bear is when he looks at me as if I'm like that, too. Going bad on the inside, where no one can see.

I'm sitting in the armchair now, with the letter. I've got the clean, white bath in the back of my mind, to make me feel good, no matter what happens the rest of the day. I open the letter. It starts with words, not my name.

I'm getting married next month. I told Anna yesterday and she's already met Sonia, so it wasn't a surprise. We'll be keeping on a flat in London, but I've bought a place up in Yorkshire and that's where Anna will be living from now on. It's not doing her any good seeing you like this. She doesn't know where she is. I'm not going to let you spoil Anna's chances of a proper life. You'll be hearing through my solicitor about the arrangements for Anna.

I sit in the chair for a long time. A *proper life*. I keep thinking about it until the words come apart like stitches and don't make sense any more. On Anna's visiting days I'm always listening out for the car. It comes dead on time, Paul's good like that. I watch Anna through the upstairs window while she gets out of the car. All her movements are small and neat. She lifts her legs sideways and lets whoever's driving help her out like a little princess. Paul never drives her here. Then she stands on the pavement. I watch the top of her head, with the sun on her hair, until she moves, and then I run down the stairs so that I'll be at the door before she reaches it. I don't ever let her touch the bell. I fling the door open wide and there she is. Her little face is closed and polite, as if I'm someone else's mother fetching her from school. She's always pale.

When she goes it's a bit different. We get her coat on and stand in the hall, waiting for the sound of the car again. We don't say much, but by now she's standing close to me. Once, just as I heard the car slowing, she bobbed forward and kissed me on my stomach, through my jumper. It was so quick and light I nearly missed it, and then she looked down as if she didn't want me to see her face.

When we hear the car, I say, 'See you next week,' and she nods. The bell rings and I open the door, and she goes straight out without looking at me again. I go upstairs. I watch her climb into the car, with someone holding the door open for her. It's usually the same driver, because Paul is very careful like that. She sits back in the seat, he fastens the seat-belt. She never waves. When the car's gone I find myself standing in the middle of the kitchen, but I can't remember how I got there. I don't know what I want. I go to the fridge but I'm not hungry. I look at the row of yoghurt pots and the chocolate cake I bought for Anna, with one slice cut out of it.

We could make a cake together one day. She'd like that. I'll buy a cake-mix, one of those where you only have to add an egg. It's funny, she's only here for two hours but it seems like a long time when you have to fill it. She hasn't got her things here, that's what it is. Everything we do is stiff, like artificial flowers.

Need a signature. Not this time, Paul. I've signed everything else, but I won't sign this. I'll fight. I'll go to a lawyer, one of those ones with a picture outside of two stick people leaning forward over a table. They give a free consultation.

Isn't it strange how you think thoughts and they make you feel better, even though you know you won't ever do what you've promised yourself in your mind?

I stand by the fridge. I take out a packet of cream cheese, then I put it back. There's a bag of big red apples which I bought for Anna. She likes them, she likes biting into the shiny, tough skin. But these were woolly inside, no taste, you had to spit them out. I don't know why I've kept them. I don't fancy anything.

The thing is, I can't go against Paul. I know him too well. We're like two halves of a bone that's been broken and knitted together so the join's stronger than the bone was. And now he tells me he's going to marry Sonia, and I know I ought to be angrier than I am. I can't take it seriously, because it isn't real. Anna is real, and he's mixing her up with things that aren't.

He thinks I could stop drinking. He said, 'You could stop drinking.' His eyes burned into me. I knew he was angry because he thought we could go back and be as we were. He has hopes I haven't got any more.

There's a bottle of Martini, three-quarters full. It's very cold. I open it and pour out a glass, just a small one. It's oily on my tongue, then there's a bitter, herbal taste which ought to be doing me some good. It makes me tired, right down to my feet. I want to sit down. I pick up the bottle and the glass and go back to the sitting-room, but this time I don't sit in the armchair. I choose the sofa, in case I feel like putting my feet up. The Martini's moving round inside me already, getting everywhere. Nice. I get up again and find a lemon in the fruit-bowl. A bit wrinkled, but it'll do. I cut it into quarters and put them on a saucer. It looks good to put a slice of lemon into the Martini, as if it's a proper drink you might pour for yourself before going off out somewhere for dinner. I suck the last drops of the Martini from around the lemon quarter. It's a funny noise, and it reminds me of something. I fill the glass and the lemon bobs to the top. After a long time bits of fruit get sodden and they lie in the bottom of the glass no matter how much more you pour in.

I know what the sucking noise reminds me of. It's the noise of the bath water going out slowly, before I cleared the waste-pipe with the plunger.

The bath is white, clean. It smells of lemon bath-cleaner. I did a good job there. I keep it in mind.

With Paul, you don't go to lawyers. Not if you know what's good for you. Men don't make the money Paul's made without being quick on their feet. I've seen him run rings round Planning, round Environmental Health and the Inland Revenue.

Paul said I could have this house as long as I wanted. It's not in my name but I can have it as long as I behave myself. And the money every month. I've even got some savings: Paul doesn't know that. When Paul says 'as long as you behave yourself', he looks at me with that hot, angry look again. He's still appalled at what we've come to and where we are. He can't understand that I'm not appalled. I understand where we are, and I could look back and show you each step of the way that's got us here.

I behave myself. Drinking doesn't count. I see Anna. Anna comes in the car every week. I see her standing on the pavement, and I run downstairs so she won't ever have to ring the bell.

Anna doesn't look like me. She looks like Paul, that's why he wants her.

He's buying a place in Yorkshire. Anna won't be able to come in a car every week from Yorkshire. He's getting married. Well, I knew that was coming. He told me a long time ago.

'You can't do that,' I told him. I was laughing. I knew it was my moment. 'Marriage is for ever.' He knows that. I married Paul when I was very young and we've been through a lot of things together. I know things about him not everybody knows. I used to think it made us close. It took me a long time to understand that it was what was pushing us apart. He was trying to make everything better for us all the time, for me, for

Johnnie, for Anna, and there I was, stinking of where he'd come from.

'I'm divorcing you,' he said.

'Divorcing me,' I repeated. It wasn't unexpected. But divorce doesn't mean the end of a marriage. As I said, we still sleep together. Or rather, fuck.

'We'll still be married,' I said, 'in the eyes of God.' I said it to taunt him.

'The eyes of God,' he said. He stood still and looked at me. I saw how fast he was thinking and I saw the things he doesn't want anybody to see, about where he's come from and what he's done to get where he is now. I saw the idea of frightening me flick in his face, then sink down and swim away. He'll never do that. I don't know why I know, but I do, even though Paul is far from being a scrupulous man.

'I'll get an annulment, then,' he said.

'You won't,' I said quickly. 'They're not such fools as you think. You can't wipe out what's happened. We've got Anna to think of. What would that make her, a bastard?'

I knew he was listening, though he didn't want to. He'd got it wrong for once. He thought that when you'd got enough money you could do what you liked. Not that he'd send a wad of used notes to some Monsignor, that's not Paul's style any more. No, he'd put a new roof on a convent. But it wasn't going to work this time.

'You can divorce me,' I said. 'You can marry whoever it is you want to marry, if you like. *She* won't care. But you're not getting an annulment. You're not saying we were never married and Anna was never our child, that we both wanted.'

He was surprised, I could see that. It was a long time since I'd said anything he didn't want to hear, and made him hear it. I was clear in my mind as a glass of gin.

So we're still married. We're divorced, like I agreed, but we're still married in my eyes and Paul's eyes and the eyes of anyone else who counts. I don't bother about the eyes of God, it was just something I said to make my point. But thinking about it makes me tired now, like looking into the fridge at all the food and not being able to imagine eating any of it. I don't know how I put all this weight on. I don't eat anything.

I've never been to Yorkshire. It's a big house on the side of a hill, looking over a valley. High up. It'll be good for Anna. She'll go to school in the next village and she'll be able to play out in the fields and the woods, Paul says. It's all in the letter.

I'm not drinking. Just this glass, that's all. I'm going out later to look at some curtain material. In a little while I'll ring for a taxi.

Fields and woods. Don't make me laugh. I wish he was here now to say it to my face. What does Paul know about fields and woods? What do either of us know? There wasn't even a park, where Paul grew up.

I'll do something about it, once I've had time to think. After all, if I don't look out for Anna, who will? Her own mother.

There's a day nursery down the street. I see women arriving in the morning, with babies in car seats. The women are dressed for work, not for babies. They lean into the back of the car and I see their legs strain as they lift the baby out. So many things in their arms. The baby, the baby-bag, the handbag because they can't leave it in the car. They kick the door shut because they haven't got a hand free.

When they come out of the nursery they're always frowning. They move fast, climb into the car, slam the seat back as if they've suddenly grown taller, then take off. They're already late.

I tighten the sash on my dressing-gown, and think about getting ready. I can't seem to get myself dressed before the afternoon. I was reading an article in a woman's magazine yesterday, on how to manage your time. There was a chart to fill in, with everything on it that made up a proper life. Child-care, daycare, after-school, pre-school, dentist's appointment, supermarket trip, Christmas shopping, school run, eating out, mammogram, leg-wax, promotion, pension. Apparently Christmas shopping can be your main leisure activity for as much as three months.

It made me feel as if I was standing by the hole in an aeroplane's belly, waiting to jump. But I don't jump. I don't do any of it. Anna came with new shoes last time, but I don't know what size her feet are any more. I think, *What am I? I'm worth nothing*. But I can't feel it. I feel the same for Paul as I've always felt, and for Johnnie, and for me.

Nine

Anna stays behind after school. The others have all gone, walking the mile back to the village in a long noisy straggle, or crammed into cars. There used to be a school right in the village, but it closed down five years ago. People say there ought to be a bus, but there isn't. Anna drags a stool inside the store-cupboard, and reaches up to the shelf where jam-jars are kept. There are two small honey jars, smeared, dusty, but the right size. Anna rinses them in the classroom sink. There's only a cold tap, and the bottle-brush is thick with sludge from the mixings of thirty palettes.

She's Flower Monitor. That doesn't mean Anna has to bring in all the flowers, Mrs Fairway explained. Everyone can bring in something from their garden, and it's Anna's job to put the flowers in water, keep them topped up, throw away the flowers when they are dead and clean the jars again.

'What kind of flowers, Miss?' asks Emily Faraday.

Mrs Fairway gives her a sharp look. 'I've just said, Emily Faraday, any flowers you've got in your garden. Except your Dad's prize chrysanthemums, of course.'

Half the class titters. Emily folds her arms, just like her mother, and gazes back at Mrs Fairway. Her face is silky with insolence. She is exceptionally pretty, with the bouncing, white-curled prettiness that every ten-year-old can recognize.

'We haven't got a garden, Miss,' she says.

'Then you can take yourself out for a walk, my lady, and pick some berries or ivy leaves from the side of the road. There's plenty about.'

'I'm not bothering to pick stuff for *her*,' says Emily, just about under her breath. Fanny Fairway pretends not to hear.

The flowers have been in a bucket under the sink all day, thrust deep in the water, their thin stems tied with black cotton, their heads waxy, down-turned. They are snowdrops from Anna's garden.

Anna doesn't think of it as her garden. The garden belongs to the house, not to her or her father or Sonia. It is ancient, narrow and full of light, a terrace of grass and stone cut into the side of a steep black hill. It is backed by a retaining wall, and behind that the hill rears higher. Where the hill falls away from the garden there is another, lower wall, and then curious black railings, like spears. When you walk the length of the garden it's like patrolling the deck of a ship. The paving stones are worn by hundreds of years of feet, but Anna's shoes don't fit the smooth hollows.

Spring's early this year. Too early, everyone keeps saying, though Anna doesn't see how spring can come too early. The third of February, and there are blue-tits ripping at the fat buds of flowering currant. Rhubarb's already poking above the manure that's banked up over it in winter. Its leaves are a furled, acid yellow, its shoots transparently red. Yesterday Anna walked the length of the garden, alongside the house and the barn, then through the stone arch to the second terrace. On her left was the retaining wall, high, smoke-black. Under the apple trees the snowdrops were flowering. It was four o'clock, and already beginning to be dark down in the valley. But up here the light was clear, and the snowdrops shone white. Everywhere she looked, there were more and more, as if looking at them made them show themselves. They made patches of light under the trees.

She touched them, and turned their faces up. They were white and cold, closed tight as if thinking they were still deep in the black earth. They wanted a touch of winter sun on their petals to open them. Anna unpacked a tight bud of flower. The slender petals parted, showing their green inner veins. And then she wanted to close them, to have them back as perfect as they'd been, but they wouldn't close. The snowdrop hung, stiff and spoiled. Anna got up quickly and moved away from it, glancing up at the blind face of the wall as if someone might be looking out of it. A little farther off, she knelt on the grass, and began to pick snowdrops. When she had a bunch, she tied it with a stem of grass, and laid it on the paving stone. She'd find some proper thread to tie them later on. It didn't matter how many she picked, because the white crowd of snowdrops was as thick as ever on the bare earth. Their whiteness was cool, solid, flawless. They made everything else look like a mistake.

It was very still. She looked back over her shoulder. Across the valley the woods were now quite dark. There were streaks of green running over the sky, and high up there was the trail of an aeroplane. The knees of her jeans were wet from the ground. She stood holding her bunches of snowdrops loosely so as not to crush them. The steep rise of hill on the other side of the valley looked so close in this light that she could have put out her hand and touched it. The river was making its noise, loud after a wet winter. Sometimes she heard it, sometimes everything seemed to be silent, even though the river was always there.

The dark had got into the garden now. It lay heaped in the angle of walls. It swept the grass like a rising tide. It was nearly at Anna's feet. Her face calm, she walked back over the grass, placing her feet with care as if she were walking on stepping stones. She went through the arch, with the rhododendron tree on her right. It was rich with early buds, and it chattered with the harsh night noise of birds. You could see the splitting in the buds where crimson petals would come. Everything was too early, standing naked, waiting to be scorched by the frost that was sure to come.

In the store-cupboard there is a set of old comprehension books, with a chapter about Grace Darling in them. Anna sits on the floor, and reads.

'. . . the ferocity of the storm and the ravening waves almost swamped their boat, but Grace Darling and her father rowed on undaunted. They knew that they and they alone offered a chance of rescue for the terrified souls clinging to the wreckage. Grace was a girl of few words. She said a silent prayer and bent to her oar. No soldier going into battle could have shown greater pluck and determination than Grace Darling on that stormy night. She did not guess that she would become a national heroine whose name would be on the lips of men, women and children throughout the nation. There was no thought of fame or honour in Grace Darling's mind on that fateful night, as she rowed the lifeboat as well as any man. Stern purpose shone in her eyes . . .'

Anna reads to the end of the passage, then through the questions.

Why did Grace Darling become a national heroine?
Which honour was conferred upon Grace Darling in recognition of her courage?
Describe, <u>in your own words,</u> Grace Darling's thoughts as she rowed the lifeboat.
Choose <u>three</u> of the following adjectives which describe Grace Darling's actions: plucky, generous, foolhardy, dangerous, manly, courageous, prompt, headstrong, selfless, rash. *Write a sentence describing Grace Darling, using all three adjectives.*
Where did Grace Darling travel to receive her honour? (Note that 'receive' follows the spelling rule introduced in Chapter 4: 'i' before 'e' except after 'c'.)

There are eight pages of questions and exercises to three pages of story, and a black-and-white picture of Grace Darling in a long dress and a shawl, her hair flying, helping to push out the boat. One questions says, *Find three adverbs which describe the way Grace Darling rowed. Example: She rowed slowly.* Beside this, someone has written 'she rowed sexily' in pencil, and then tried to rub it out. Anna wonders if Fanny Fairway would miss one book out of thirty. She'd like to have that picture of Grace Darling. *Boldly, bravely, steadfastly, fearlessly.* Maybe she could tear it out. They don't use these books any more, but Fanny Fairway probably still counts them.

Anna fills the honey jars with water. She unties the black thread which holds the flowers together, and they spill on to the wooden draining-board, wet and fresh. She puts a few flowers into the water, but they look like nothing. Quickly, she picks up a double handful and crams the jar.

Anna's mother sits in the sun, her face loose, her hand around the stem of a glass. The glass sparkles. Every morning Anna's mother washes out her glasses in hot soapy water, then hot clear water, then cold. She has glass-cloths to polish them. She has to buy new ones all the time, because once they're dirty she never manages to wash them. But she still tries to keep her glasses nice. She says, 'You might as well shoot yourself as drink out of a used glass.' The line of her drink ripples round the glass.

'If you start thinking about what people think of you,' she says, 'there's no end to it.'

Anna's mother's legs are spread and loose, like her face. Her white thighs are parted. At the top of them there's the beginning of the forest that grows there. The curling hair is not the same colour as the hair on her head. The white thighs shift, the legs splay, the glass wobbles up to Anna's mother's lips. She drinks. There's a sweet, powerful smell. Anna crouches in the corner, picks up her comic and reads 'Minnie the Minx'.

'But *I'm* not going to shoot myself,' says her mother. 'I wouldn't give anyone the satisfaction.' She reaches down and picks up a white paper bag of sherbet lemons. 'Suck on them,' she says, 'don't bite them.'

Anna sucks. She shuts her eyes as the stream of sherbet and saliva washes round her mouth. There is a glassy crunch of sugar.

'You're as bad as Johnnie,' says her mother. 'He can't have anything in his mouth without biting it.' And she laughs as if what she's said is funny.

The snowdrop jar is still dirty. Anna rubs it. She's put all the flowers into one jar, and there aren't any left for the other. The caretaker's in Class Three, banging the chairs. In a minute he'll be here, shouting at her. 'Have you not got a home to go to?' She puts the jar on the window-sill. The snowdrops shine, but not as *strongly, bravely, boldly* in the classroom light as they did in the dark of the garden.

Anna runs up the road. Only another half-mile to home. The ponies in their winter coats look at her over their hay, as if they know something about her. She could take the path across the field, or she could go by the road, then the track. She'll do that. It means going by the big trees that catch the wind in their branches, and make it thunder. She looks up and down the road. It's empty, safe. Everyone else has gone home long ago. Anna thinks of Emily Faraday and Billy Arkinstall in their homes, tamed, made to take off their mud-cobbed shoes and help lay the table. But Billy Arkinstall's mum is evil. She chases Billy out of the door with a broom and shouts after him. That's why Billy lurks in the lanes, and hates Anna.

Anna walks under the trees and the wind lifts the hair up

from her head and whips it across her eyes. With each step she takes, more miles drop away on either side. She can see for ever now, over the network of little fields and walls winding up to the moor. There's the track the men go up at night, when they drink at the Golden Fleece, that keeps no hours. She knows about that, like all the children. They play cards for money and they take the short way back through the woods. They blaspheme as they stagger back, falling over tree-roots. They're men, but not like her father. They're rougher than him, but not as wild. She knows that. They'll go back to their work on a Monday morning, because they have to. They don't frighten her.

Here's the turn. The valley, the track down, the answering track on the opposite flank of hill. Stone-walled fields, fencing, pale, tearing sky, moor. She starts to walk down.

A spatter of sharpness hits her sleeve. She thinks it's the rain come quick, turned to sleet as it falls. Another spatter. Something hits her cheek. It stings. She puts up her hand. Little stones fall around her, on to the track. She thinks of animals kicking up stones, the soil spurting. Something laughs.

Someone laughs. Laughter brays out at her. A head bobs behind the wall, then another. Then they are down, hiding themselves. The silence hisses with wind as she stands stock-still on the track. Where the stone scored her cheek, it burns. Another hail falls around her but does not touch her. More laughter. The thump of feet, running away on the path back across the field, back to the village. She does not try to look over the high wall. She knows their faces, all of them. Billy Arkinstall, Jack Barraclough, David Ollerenshaw, JohnJo Dwyer. She doesn't need to see them.

Anna wipes back her hair, touches her cheek, examines the finger that has touched it. There's no blood. Ahead of her there are the beech trees, then the turn of the track, then the sharper turn down to the house. The boys have gone, and they won't come back today. Anna is free for sixteen hours and forty-five minutes. She fixes her eyes on the other side of the valley, where night's settling. There's where the men go late at night. They don't come back singing, they come stumbling into the tight-packed maze of the village again, past the streets and square and ginnels and the black, rearing church. They don't ever get away.

A shape stands, white-faced, at the stone stile ahead. It's David Ollerenshaw. They've fooled her. They thudded over the field so she'd think they'd gone back to the village. Then they doubled back, took the path further on, the one that comes out on to the track at the stone stile. They're waiting for her. The rest of them will be crouched behind the wall, ready to jump out at her. They've cut her off from the house.

Her thoughts beat fast. Run back to the village, up the track. Run into the shop. Mrs Barraclough will be behind the counter, looking at her, keeping a sharp eye. Anna hasn't got any money. She can't linger with one of Mrs Barraclough's plastic saucers, choosing from trays of fried eggs, pink shrimps, jelly babies and liquorice whips. Or run, run on, run fast, burst through the hands that stretch to catch her, and race on down the track, flying –

Still only David Ollerenshaw. The others aren't showing themselves. She sets her face and withdraws, deep down, to the place no one can touch. She walks on down the track as if she's walking on stepping stones, not looking at anyone or anything.

He comes through the narrow gap of the stile that is too wide for a beast, just right for a boy. No one follows him.

'My dad's got a dog,' says Anna.

'What kind of dog?'

'A black dog. A great black dog. No one can touch it, only me and my dad. He found it at the crossroads.'

'He never did. You're a liar. You haven't got a dog.'

'Listen,' says Anna, 'you can hear it.'

The wind whines in the treetops. The side of the hill is alive and moving, soughing with the wind that funnels along the valley.

'There,' says Anna. 'That's him. My dad sets him by the gate to watch out for me. He's so black you can't see him till he jumps out of the shadow. The only thing you can see is his teeth.'

'Your dad's never got a dog.' But the dog's there somewhere, not far away, and they both know it.

'It wasn't me that threw them stones at you,' says David.

'They didn't hit me, anyway.'

'It was Billy Arkinstall.'

'You were there.'

'They've all gone, anyway.'

'Why are *you* here, then?' says Anna, bold now, advancing a pace towards him.

He shrugs. 'I thought maybe a stone might've hit you. In your eye.'

Anna shakes her head.

'What did you want to go bringing so many snowdrops to school for, anyway!' he bursts out. 'Showing off.'

'I'm Flower Monitor.'

'Only because Fanny Fairway likes you, because you live in a big house.'

'She doesn't.'

'And you're always telling her you've finished your work before anyone else has finished.'

'The work's too easy,' says Anna, watching him.

'Easy for *you*,' he blusters.

'Easy for you, too.' She knows. She's watched him lick through a page of maths at twice the speed of anyone else. But when Mrs Fairway asks for the answers he doesn't put his hand up. He loses his homework, botches his calculations, gets a few things carefully wrong. His work's much the same as anyone else's by the time the teacher sees it.

'Well,' he goes on, more gently, dropping the playground indignation from his voice, 'even if you are Flower Monitor, you don't want to go bringing so many of the buggers another time.'

'All right,' she agrees. 'But Emily Faraday *has* got a garden. She was lying.'

'She's always lying.'

'Yeah.'

He says nothing for a while. She could go now, he wouldn't stop her. It's nearly dark, and she's supposed to be back before it gets dark.

'It was the Gytrash you were talking about, wasn't it? Not a real dog.'

She nods, though she doesn't know what the Gytrash is.

'I thought it was that. My dad's seen him.'

'Has he?'

'One night when he was coming back along the track. He waited two hours in those beech woods, so as not to pass him.'

'Did he?'

He looks sharply at her, suspicious. 'My dad wasn't drunk, if that's what you think.'

'Is it real, or is it a ghost? The Gytrash?'

'He's real enough. But only sometimes.'

'The Gytrash,' says Anna, tasting the word on her tongue.

'I'll be getting home now.' He turns away, into the gloom of the field. She watches. He's there, then he's not. She doesn't hear his footsteps, and neither of them calls goodbye.

Anna stands at the turn of the lane. Suddenly it's night, and all the lights spring out at the windows. The house looks like somewhere she'd like to live, if she didn't know what was inside. This is the best moment, standing outside, telling herself,

'That's my home. I'm going home.' She slips her hand into her pocket and touches the torn-out picture of Grace Darling.

Anna is in the park with her mother and Johnnie. Her mother looks up, sees catkins on the branches, points to them. Johnnie steps forward, puts his hands around Mum's waist and lifts her high above his head, so her face touches the catkin tassels. Anna sees Mum's feet in their high-heeled black leather boots rise up past her face, not kicking, but pointed like a dancer's. Johnnie holds her there for a long time. Mum doesn't stir. She leans back, her face in the tassels, her pale lips smiling.

'It'll be spring soon,' she says to Anna a bit later, as the three of them walk along.

'Will it? How do you know?'

'There'll be snowdrops first, then crocuses, then the daffodils. We'll come to the park to see the daffodils.'

'How do you know?' Anna wants to say. But they're smiling, they're swaying side by side, touching with every step they take. *First the snowdrops*, she says to herself, so as to be part of it.

'And then it'll be warm and you'll be out here in your shorts and a T-shirt.'

Johnnie whispers something in Mum's ear and she laughs.

'And we'll have a picnic under those trees.'

'As long as I can come,' says Johnnie.

'Oh yes,' says Mum. 'It wouldn't be half the fun without you, would it, Anna?'

Ten

Anna's father is at the window. He's high up in the house, in the attic bedroom which he has made his office. The place is wired up. A computer fan hums, a fax machine spews paper. There are files, mobile phones, printers. It looks like the home office of a successful businessman, except that the resemblance is too accurate. It leaves you wanting to open drawers and pull out books in case the shelves are false. Everything in the room shouts 'legitimate business'.

It's a property business. That's what Anna says at school.

'What's your dad do?'

'He's got a property business.'

One day they all had to write about what their fathers and mothers did for a living. It was Fanny Fairway poking her nose, everybody knew that. She had to ask, even if she knew anyway.

'My dad's a haulage contractor,' said Courtney Arkinstall. Billy scowled at her: she's his cousin.

'Don't you mean a lorry driver, Courtney?' enquired Fanny Fairway.

'She means a fucking haulage contractor,' said Billy, then sat looking at Fanny Fairway with a cool straight face, daring her to have heard. Later he grabbed Courtney as they were pushing out of the classroom. 'What did you want to tell her that crap for?'

Mrs Fairway's eyes lit on Anna. 'Anna. Your turn.'

'My father's got a property business.'

'A property business. Do you mean an estate agency, Anna?'

'It's buildings in London,' said Anna, in a deliberately childish voice.

'And your mother. What does she do?'

'She's a housewife,' said Anna. She smiled, she couldn't help herself. The wide, clear smile stayed, pinned to her face. She sensed Mrs Fairway's baffled anger.

'She looks after the house,' Anna went on. 'In London.'

Everybody was listening intently. They wanted the information, just as Fanny Fairway did, but they wanted the battle too. They weren't sure who they wanted to win.

'In London. Well, Anna, that's a long way away.'

'You can ask my dad, if you want to know any more,' said Anna. Fanny Fairway started slightly. A flush spread from her cheeks to her nose. She turned away from Anna.

'Now, we're going to make a pie chart,' she announced. 'Who can remember what a pie chart is?'

Anna's father stands by the window. It's dark now. Soft, yellow lights are coming on in the two cottages further down the hill. He watches them vaguely. His hands rest on the window-sill, palms down. He's waiting for something. The fax machine begins to spool out paper again, but it's not that. Anna's feet run lightly across the floor downstairs. He doesn't react.

The phone rings. Paul snatches it up, listens without speaking. After a few seconds he interrupts the flow. 'OK, OK, call me back when you're somewhere you can talk.' There are things he wants to say to Johnnie.

He waits again. Minutes pass. He goes back to the window and stares up at the night sky, where a pattern of stars is beginning to prick through. He can never get over the clearness of the stars here. It makes him realize why people have always thought stars were important. All that astrology rubbish that his mother used to read; but suddenly he can see that it began with something real. He watches the stars take up their places. He never uses his headlights coming down the track at night. Kills them at the top, coasts down in starshine. You buy a place like this, and it's only once you start living in it that you realize what you've bought. He was digging out the track in the snow all last winter. The weight of the shovel, the white blinding walls of snow, his own breath pumping smoke into the air. Little Anna coming out with a mug of hot chocolate, frowning with seriousness in case she slopped it. Giving it to him, still not smiling. Completely serious. He drank it off while she waited. 'Thanks for that, Anna.' And she nodded, took back the mug, said, 'I'll bring you some more later, Dad.'

The phone rings. His mobile this time.

'Johnnie.'

It's his brother again.

'How's it going?'

There's a noise of city in the background. He tries to picture his brother but the picture keeps breaking up. He can hear voices in the background, arguing. Nothing serious. One of Johnnie's places. Johnnie's voice is full, close to the receiver, flushed with something. He's been drinking.

'There's some stuff I need to sort out here, Paul.'

'What stuff?'

'For fuck's sake, it's nothing.' His brother sounds as if he wants to laugh. Or maybe he is laughing, with his hand over the receiver, his eyes glistening at someone Paul can't see.

Paul has a vision of his brother's thin, laughing face, and the complicity he can't get at to break. He wants to twist Johnnie's head off.

'I thought you were going to sort out Swindon for me, Johnnie.'

The Swindon site is a new one, derelict, plenty of potential. But the survey shows lead and cadmium contamination in the soil from a burnt-out glassworks. The surveyor rang Paul yesterday, wanted someone to go down and look at the site. They're getting figures on the costs of shifting soil. Johnnie's supposed to have gone down there.

'That's OK, that's all under control,' says Johnnie.

'Did you go down there?'

'Wait a minute.' Johnnie's put his hand over the mouthpiece. He's talking to someone else, sorting out some other stuff which has nothing to do with Paul.

'Paul? Sorry about that.' He's back, his voice near and moist in Paul's ear.

'Did you go to Swindon?'

'Chrissake, Paul.' Laughing now, humouring Paul. Who's the audience? 'Listen, you don't need to worry about the survey. I'm speaking to him tomorrow. I'll get it sorted. He knows what we want. I'm a bit tied up now, is all.'

Paul shuts his eyes. He feels grey and sweaty, like a hangover morning. Why do they have to go through this every time, say the same things, get nowhere?

Suddenly, for no reason, he remembers changing the wheel of a car. His first car. Not long after he'd got started in business. He was nineteen, which made Johnnie what? Seven. Their dad was upstairs with an oxygen cylinder by the bed. He'd been back home for months, the longest he'd stayed since Paul could remember. Mum was looking after him. He didn't want anyone else, he said, not any more. Only her and the boys. Did Mum believe that? Maybe. Paul couldn't say anything.

Mum was at Benediction. A hot late afternoon with Paul's first car drawn up outside the flats, stinking of oil and metal and hot plastic seats. The car was jacked up and Paul was taking off the wheel-nuts. Johnnie was standing there, watching. He didn't want to be inside the flat. Nobody wanted to be inside, with the noise of their father's breathing, the horror and pity of it grasping at them like hands round their necks, suffocating them. It was going to go on for ever, they were all sure of it, Dad propped up, a slit of his eyes showing yellow, a nurse or a neighbour or Mum by the side of the bed, the hiss of the oxygen, the scrape and draw of Dad's breath. Dad's chest was a cage, locked shut. Nothing could get in or out without going through the bars. And the bars were iron, they wouldn't open.

Paul got the spanner in place. 'Here, you do it,' he said to Johnnie. Together, they took off the wheel-nuts, changed the tyre, tightened the wheel-nuts again. Johnnie watched everything Paul did. His face was narrow with concentration, the effort of getting things right. Yesterday Johnnie'd gone out with Paul and had his thick, dark hair razor-cut. He thought he looked tough, but really he looked as if he'd just been born. His eyes were big and startling under the bare scalp, and his neck was pale. Paul'd wanted to stop the barber halfway through, but you couldn't do a thing like that. It'd only make you look stupid.

The job was done. Johnnie watched Paul put the tools back, then he asked, 'Will you teach me how to drive?'

It took Paul back. He remembered asking Dad the same question, one day they'd been changing the battery when Paul must've been Johnnie's age. They must have had a bit of money then: it was a nice car. That was before Dad started going away.

'Can I drive your car when I'm older, Dad?'

But Johnnie wasn't asking Dad about stuff like that. He was asking Paul. Under the stubble at his neck you could see the skin which had never had the sun on it. Mum was always saying how beautiful Johnnie had been, when he was a baby. 'Too beautiful for a boy. It's wasted on him.' Paul had thought that was just the kind of stuff mothers said. Now he looks at Johnnie and he sees it may be true.

'Will you? Will you, Paul?'

'Sure I will.' The words were on his lips, easy and American, making him a figure in the film of his own life. He reached out and ran the palm of his hand over the barbered fuzz on Johnnie's head. The tickle of the fuzz shot through him like electricity.

*

Johnnie's still there, on the other end of the phone. Paul's sick of it all, but he's got to keep up the talking, keep the link unbroken. Johnnie's screwed up on Swindon. He's not where he should be. At six o'clock he's in a bar and he's probably been there since the morning, if not the night before. He's with friends. When is Johnnie ever not with friends? Johnnie's one of those people you can't imagine in a room on his own. If you try to, you come up blank. There are always friends, and if there aren't Johnnie sleeps, like a stopped clock.

Johnnie's not that kid of seven with shorn hair any more. He's supposed to be Paul's partner, but he keeps screwing up because deep down he's not interested in Paul's kind of business, that kind of money. He wants the other kind. If he'd been anyone else Paul would have got rid of him long ago, but he can't do that to Johnnie. He can't believe that one day Johnnie won't suddenly see that he's being a fucking idiot, that Paul's handing to him on a plate everything Paul himself would ever have wanted. A share in a good business. Johnnie should have been in Swindon. But he's been sorting out his own business instead: Jackie and Ian Briscoe.

'They've been getting careless,' says Johnnie now. 'Ian's gone and bought a stupid car and thinks no one's going to notice.'

'Tell them to check the vacuum-cleaner bags,' says Paul. He knows all about it: Johnnie's made him know. He shakes his head, which swarms with knowledge he doesn't want. 'Don't let them get lazy. It's no good changing them and putting the bags out for the bin-men. Make sure they dump the bags in town somewhere, in one of the council bins.'

It's the little things that give you away. Vacuum-cleaner bags. Paul hunts down these stories like a pregnant woman hunts stories of birth. He has come across the trial of a couple who were convicted on forensic evidence from a vacuum-cleaner bag. The prosecution based its case on significant traces of cocaine found in an analysis of the bag's contents. It couldn't get them on anything else, but now they're doing fourteen years. Paul has never met the Briscoes, and will never meet them, but he knows them well. They're everywhere, like the mites that live on your eyelashes.

The Briscoes will have the right faces, middle-aged, respectable, dull. The kind that quack out the time of the next Neighbourhood Watch meeting when you bump into them in the street. They've retired early and bought a camper van, and they can't get enough of mini-breaks in Europe. Well, with the bargains you get on ferry crossings out-of-season, it makes sense, doesn't it? Cost you more to stay at home! Amsterdam one month, Brussels the next. They take a load of money with them. The money tucks away everywhere, nice, easy wads of it. In the wheel arches, inside the spare tyre. Used money that doesn't crackle. Money that's soft with sweat and grime, money that's been scribbled on by bank tellers and ripped going in and out of wallets. If you opened up that van you'd be looking at a fortune. They take out money, but they don't bring anything back. Their job is to take out the money and do the business. Other people bring the stuff back. Nobody knows anything but their own link in the chain. If you can flatter what they do by the name of anything as sweet and reasonable as metal linked to metal. Sometimes it breaks and the Briscoes have to fill their secret places with flat packets wrapped in heavy plastic. And then they've got to do a bit of weighing and measuring and that's where the vacuum-cleaner bags can get crucial. And the money's a problem too, after all the handling it's had. It's unlikely to stand up to forensic examination.

'Go to Swindon, Johnnie,' Paul says now. 'For fuck's sake. Just do it.' He looks up at the stars. Johnnie ought to come here, then they could have a proper talk. No good talking now, with Johnnie in the bar and his friends round him. If only Paul could get him away for three months, Johnnie would come back to himself.

'I can't. There's a problem here.'

Paul grips the phone, hears the surge of laughter and noise from behind his brother. A voice blurts in his ear, singsong and slurred. 'Bye-ee! I'm taking Johnnie home now.' More laughter, spurting up like vomit. They're laughing at him, thinking the whole world's there to be made a fool of, except themselves. They know nothing. He can't hear Johnnie any more. The voices are louder, arguing. Is that someone shouting? Was that Johnnie's voice? There's sweat on Paul's hand as he grips the mobile phone that can't connect him to anything that's really happening.

'Johnnie!' he shouts. 'For fuck's sake!' But the call crumbles. The phone's hanging loose, picking up background. Johnnie was on a fixed phone, not his mobile. He's gone. Someone picks up the receiver. He hears breathing, he shouts again, 'Johnnie!' There's a little laugh, then the phone clicks. They've hung up. The mobile sits in his hand.

Will you teach me to drive?

It's all right, Johnnie, I'll look after you. I don't care what happens, it'll be all right. I swear.

Is Dad going to die?

Yeah. I think so.

Why?

Look at him, Johnnie. You wouldn't want him to go on like this.

How old is Dad?

You know how old he is. He's forty-four.

How old are you, Paul?

You know how old I am. I'm nineteen.

All his brothers are on the end of the phone. Johnnie at seven, at twelve, Johnnie in the bedroom in Barking bawling his head off, Johnnie blotched and shuddering when his rabbit died, Johnnie tearless and pale, yawning with grief at their father's funeral, Johnnie at their wedding, dancing with Louise.

That's enough of that. It's gone.

How old are you, Paul?

It's all right, Johnnie. I'll look after you. It'll be all right. I swear.

There are other things. After five years, when Louise didn't get pregnant, he went for those tests without telling her. She didn't want any doctors or any mucking about, and she was so strong about it that he didn't press it. *If it happens it happens*, she said. *I'm not taking drugs and having my insides messed about.* But he read an article which said that for men it was simple. All you had to do was go along and wank into a test-tube. They even gave you a porn mag to make it easier. So he went to a clinic and told them he was concerned, he'd like a test.

We don't talk about sterility, they said, when he used the word. There were sperm, but not enough, and their motility was poor. It meant that natural conception was unlikely. It was still possible, but it was unlikely. He asked what other sort of conception there was, besides the natural, and they told him all the things that could be done.

He went away and he didn't tell Louise. He justified it to himself, telling himself that it was Louise who hadn't wanted to go for the tests. She was the one who said that if it happened, it happened. She seemed to have no cares about it, so he said nothing. Occasionally he thought of the false name he'd used at the clinic, and then he would get up from whatever he was doing, quickly, and walk away from it. Sometimes he thought of his sperm, like tadpoles hanging in a jam-jar back in junior school, a frill of them mouthing the glass, immobile.

Then she was pregnant, and when Anna was born, she looked like him.

Eleven

He didn't let me meet Johnnie till we'd been going out for nearly six months. Paul was twenty-one, I was nineteen. He was the handsomest man I'd ever seen. People don't say handsome now, but it was the only word for Paul. There was always something a little bit formal about him, a little bit old-fashioned. And then he was already wearing suits, when most of the boys I knew were in jeans. Beautiful suits. I knew a bit about tailoring even then, and I knew those suits cost money. The wool had a rich, dull sheen on it, the cut was sharp, but perfect. He always had a thing about pure cotton shirts. He'd never wear any of those easy-iron things. When I remember Paul at that time I see him at the mirror, tying his tie. He wasn't vain. He never preened. Everything had to be right, then he forgot about it. Or he seemed to forget. If we walked by a plate-glass window together, he never looked for his reflection. Dark suits, charcoal grey, white shirts, dull silk ties. He never liked anything flash. Kidney-shaped gold cufflinks, heavy for their size, and a gold watch. He bought them himself, as he got the money to do it, but they looked like the kind of watch and cufflinks that are handed down from father to son.

Except that Paul never had that kind of father, and he wasn't that kind of son. He bought seriously, going to serious shops as if he had a right to be there, and they took him at his own valuation. I didn't have the knack. I had to keep reminding myself: *If they were that classy, they wouldn't be working in a shop.* But I couldn't ever quite make myself believe it. My mother bought her groceries on credit when I was little, and we were always a week behind. I was used to the idea that shopkeepers and restaurant owners judge their clients, not the other way around. Although that's ridiculous, when you come to think of it.

I loved Paul's style. It was the way I was starting to dress myself, now I was earning. I think this is why Paul was attracted to me, at first. I didn't look like the English girls in their throwaway skirts and tops. I'm talking about the mid-seventies here. I *was* English, really, but my mother wasn't, and I'd watched her testing fabric between thumb and forefinger, looking at the seams to see how they were finished, checking the lining on a jacket in case it was cheap and would ruck when the jacket was dry-cleaned. Not that she bought much, because there wasn't the money. But what she bought was good. She taught me how to wash silk, and how to look after fine wool so it didn't lose its shape. When I was eighteen I saved up and had a couple of suits made. One was French navy, the other was black. Both wool, the best quality I could afford. I wanted them plain, and I knew they could be if the cloth was good enough. With a figure like mine, there was no need for the kind of cutting that draws attention away from bad points. There weren't any bad points. That was another thing about my mother. She wasn't English, so she would talk to me about my breasts and my hips and my waist. Just then, when I was eighteen, they were all perfect.

I can say this now, because it's gone. It isn't vanity, it's like talking about someone else.

I was wearing the French navy suit, with a little coral-coloured jersey, the first time I met Paul. I was out for the evening with a couple of girlfriends. We'd been to the cinema and we were having coffee afterwards. I can remember exactly where we were sitting. It was warm in the café, and I took off my jacket. The jersey was new and it was cashmere, short-sleeved. I'd saved for a month to buy it. You know how it is when you wear something that fits perfectly, so that you don't have to think about it. You can move just as you want, you can sit down or reach up for something and it will move with you.

I stretched out to take a cigarette from Mandy, and I saw a man watching me. I thought 'man', not 'boy'. He was twenty-one, a couple of years older than me. He was wearing a dark suit, and a dark-blue tie, and he was drinking an espresso. He was with a couple of men who looked as if they might be his brothers, though it turned out that they weren't. It was just that they were the same type, dark, quite well-dressed, *finished*. They didn't look English. But he was the one you noticed. I turned away from him, just a fraction, and lit the cigarette. I remember laughing and talking to Mandy and Sue with the extra concentration that probably never fools anybody. I felt a glow on me, as if lights were stroking my body. Everything was exaggerated: my jersey soft as a kitten, the coffee the blackest and bitterest I'd ever drunk. I swallowed the smoke from my cigarette, then narrowed my eyes as it seeped out. I thought that was so sophisticated. Of course I hadn't even looked at him, but I knew he was still looking at me.

I haven't seen Anna for eight months. When she was little I used to wonder what she was going to look like when she grew up. I remember her running through from the bathroom to the bedroom, naked. She must have been about two and a half. And already her body wasn't just a baby body, it was a little girl's body. And I remember thinking how her hips and breasts would swell and her waist would seem to grow small. And I wondered if she'd look like me. I thought about going to buy clothes with her, teaching her how to spend money on herself, and get it right.

He's got plenty of money.

Johnnie's not handsome, like Paul. He's much more ... troubling. The first time I saw the two of them together it was like a light going on. You think, 'So *that's* it.' And the whole thing suddenly makes sense. Who they were, where they came from, and why Paul was as he was.

Johnnie wasn't doing well at school. But that didn't matter, because Paul was making money now, and he was going to take Johnnie out of the crap primary they'd both been to and put him into a private school, one of those livery-company schools. And he did, too. Johnnie passed the entrance exam, no problem. He was a bright kid, he wasn't even lazy. He was just . . . easily distracted is about the best way of putting it.

Paul started going to Parents' Evenings. Fair enough, he had a right to do so, he was the one paying. I didn't think much of it at the time, but looking back it must have raised a few eyebrows among the teachers. Paul aged twenty-two, listening carefully to everything the teachers said, asking questions. Not quite the right questions at first, but he soon learned. Some of the teachers were twice his age, and Paul had never got past O-level. But he was the one paying their salaries, and he never forgot that. And more than that, he was quicker than most of them. I didn't go, not even when we were married and Johnnie was living with us. Paul never asked me. Johnnie was his affair. And I was pleased he took so much trouble over Johnnie. I wasn't jealous; I was never jealous. I used to think that if this was what Paul was like over his little brother, then he was going to make a fantastic father.

I haven't seen Anna for over eight months. I know Paul didn't take her away because he loved her. He does, but that wasn't the reason. He could have loved her, and left her with me. He took her away because he'd taken Johnnie away from his mother. It's the only thing he knows how to do, if he loves someone.

Anna writes to me sometimes, but she's not good at letters. I could go up there. I could take a room in an hotel and visit her. He wouldn't stop me. But I don't think it's what I should do.

Paul's been very, very clever. The most important thing is,

he's got self-control. It's as easy to lose money in property as it is to win it, because most people get too greedy. They want something more than the profit that can be made. They want something grandiose, a huge gesture fizzing up into the sky and taking them with it. This is what Paul says. The other thing that goes wrong is when someone can't deal with losses. You've got to be able to write it off, and never think of it again. You've only got so much energy, Paul used to say, you can't waste any of it on failures. Not even your own. I didn't understand the full force of what he was saying then, because I didn't understand then that failure is as much of a magnet as success. I do now.

Paul always had a plan. By the time we'd been married five years he was moving out of houses into derelict land. He didn't know anything about land contamination when he started, but he soon realized there'd be a lot of money in taking contaminated sites off local councils at low valuations, contracting out the decontamination, and then developing. He'd spend days with council officials, planning officers, environmental-health officers, clerks from Town Halls. Everything they told him, he used. He bought them, and used them, and each of them thought they'd given him no more than his money's worth. They didn't see the pieces adding up afterwards, or what Paul was able to do with them. He was making more money than we'd ever dreamed possible, but he never compared *now* with *then*. He wouldn't be dragged back. Paul's like that about the past. As far as he's concerned, you can cut it off and never think about it again.

Or he could have done, if it hadn't been for Johnnie. Johnnie was already starting to dip his fingers in the dirty water. Paul just couldn't believe it. Johnnie had had everything laid on for him. Paul didn't see how anyone could be that stupid, when it was so easy to be sharp, and rich, and safe. Johnnie'd had what Paul never had: he'd had father and brother, all rolled into one, and a future that someone else had already paid for.

I don't know exactly what Johnnie's doing now. I know Paul's still trying to keep him in the business. There's a car and an office and good money for Johnnie. But so far none of it has had any real appeal. Johnnie left the school as soon as he hit sixteen. The thing that upset me about that was the thought of all those teachers saying how they'd known all along. Thinking they'd got the better of Paul, in some way, even though it was their job to educate Johnnie. Two years later Johnnie nearly got caught. He sat across the kitchen table from me, smiling, and told me there'd been a complete fuck-up over manufacturing acid in a farmhouse in Herefordshire. He would have made a million. It was always a million with Johnnie: some glittering amount of money that you couldn't really pin down.

The next thing, he had an interest in a boatload of hash which was supposed to be brought into a little-known cove on the north Cornwall coast. So little known, as it turned out, that the skipper they'd hired couldn't find it. At the time Paul pretended to take the view that this was all part of Johnnie growing up and taking responsibility for himself, but I could tell he was beside himself. It was the way Johnnie would look at you with his eyes glowing like a kid at Christmas, and say, 'But it's immaculate, Paul! Nothing's going to go wrong this time.'

We let ourselves think he was like a child. It was the angle we looked at him. When you see a cat play, if you can call it play, you thank God it's the size it is.

Twelve

Anna and David are friends now. Nobody else knows. They meet in halfway places. 'See you down the beeches tomorrow,' one of them says, or 'I'm going up the river tomorrow. You want to come?' The spring wears on, buds thicken, catkins shake loose, and there's a smell like sherbet from tassels of flowering currant. The Easter holidays come and the weight of school drops away as if it's never existed. Anna forgets it; she's good at forgetting things. She wakes and hears the wind rushing in the branches, looks out and sees light and shadow racing over the land. She doesn't go up to the village in holiday time. Every morning she tells herself that it is more than two weeks before she'll have to see Emily Faraday or Billy Arkinstall, or sit itching with boredom while Fanny Fairway prates about the rainforest.

David's waiting for her, down by the river, on the stone bridge. They lean side by side watching the race of brown water from pool to pool. If they were younger, Anna thinks, they could make boats and race them downstream under the bridge. But they don't. They're ten, going on eleven. Anna's grown six inches in the last year, and under her brown knitted T-shirt there are the beginnings of her breasts. One is bigger than the other, but they're nothing to get excited about yet. There was a programme on Schools TV which all the top-class girls watched, packed tight into the staff room. It was about breasts and periods, and at the end every girl got a free plain-white box. Outside, the boys were rampant. Billy Arkinstall knocked a box out of a girl's hands and ran round the playground waving a stick-on towel.

'Stick your mouth up with it, Billy!' yelled Courtney, who'd fallen out with her cousin over money he'd borrowed and not paid back. 'They should put proper locks on the girls' toilets, instead of showing us a crap film like that,' said Emily Faraday. Anna had to agree with her. Using the school toilets was a nightmare, unless you had a reliable friend to hold the door shut for you. Sometimes the boys poured in, banging on the doors and shoving them open, tipping out the sanitary bins the school had been forced to put in when Mrs Faraday had come up to the school in pomp to tell them Emily had 'started'.

David and Anna standing together, watching the long, muscular ropes of current twist through the water. They watch the brown shadows, and the skulking-places of fish. David knows everything about the river. The spring sun is sharp on their backs. In summer there'll be no sun here, only thick, green shadow. The mill chimney stands at their back. Everything else has gone: the mill, the smoking chimneys, the chopping of wood for fuel, the harnessing of water, the pounding of metal-tipped clogs on the cobbled tracks, the flicker of innumerable fingers on the looms. The black-ribbed trees wait for their tide of green. Farther up there'll be bluebells, smoky-blue under shallow-rooted beech. The river is full of heavy stones, kneading the water into pools and fast, foaming passages.

'There's a pool you can swim in, farther up,' says David. 'I swam in it all last summer. But someone's dumped an old car.'

'How did they do that?'

'Pushed it up the track, shoved it over the edge. My dad says –'

Anna ceases to hear him. She's thinking about last summer. She wasn't friends with David then, and she didn't know about him coming to swim. What if she'd walked up the river some time, and seen him? She knows what he looks like in his swimming trunks, because they all get in a double-decker and go off swimming in Halifax once a week. But when she swam

90

in the river she didn't wear anything. She looked round and pulled her clothes off, and slid in. Once she was in it didn't seem as if anyone could see her, even if they pushed their way up the tangled path. She was so broken up with light and shadow it didn't look as if she had a body.

'– you have to watch yourself, 'cos the edges of the metal are torn,' David is saying.

Anna puts her hand on his sleeve. 'Hush.'

There's the whine of an engine in low gear, coming along the track that leads from the town, on the other side of the river from Anna's house. The children flatten themselves against the stone parapet for the car to pass them.

'Wow,' says David. 'Wonder whose that is?'

Spring sunlight glitters on the car's bodywork. It comes on slowly, growling, the wheels dug deep in winter leaf-slime.

'It's my uncle,' says Anna, flushing all over.

'Doesn't he know he can't get the car up to your house that way?'

The track from the river up to Anna's house is deeply ridged, ploughed by weather so that cobblestones stand out on end. God knows how long it's been since anyone mended it.

'Someone's told him wrong,' says David.

The car's alongside them, its scarlet flank inches from their legs.

'Johnnie!' yells Anna, 'Johnnie!'

He hears her. He turns his face on her, his flashing smile, his thin, hungry, beautiful face. He stops and leans across the passenger seat to open the door. 'Get in,' he says.

'You're going the wrong way,' says Anna. 'You'll have to turn round.'

'They told me the way in the town,' says Johnnie.

'They told you wrong,' says David.

Johnnie looks from one to another of them. 'We'll see about that,' he says. His eyes sharpen with yellow light. He shades them with his hands and stares up the track, at the spring-naked, brilliant side of the hill. 'Are you coming in with me?' he asks them.

David strokes the side of the car longingly. But he can't come up to the house. He knows it, Anna knows it, and it's never had to be said. And anyway this is mad, what Johnnie's trying to do. He can't force that beautiful car up the broken track. It'll be banged to bits.

'It'll take your exhaust off,' says David.

'I don't think so. I think it's going to be fine,' says Johnnie. He judges the bare, dazzling trees, the too-bright light. The track goes on up, gashed and buckled with winter floods. Johnnie puts the car into gear and touches the accelerator so the engine growls. He looks at Anna and she finds her hand on the car door, her body sliding obediently into the thick, creamy leather of the seat. The smell of the car rises round her, taking her into a separate world.

'Isn't your mate coming?'

'He can't. He has to go home.' She turns back to David with a baffled sense that she shouldn't be leaving him here. But of course he's all right. He knows every inch of this valley. It's his, not hers, even though she lives here. David is frowning, looking at the car, gauging it against the climb which he knows like the back of his hand. He looks grown-up. And Anna thinks, surprised, that David looks older than Johnnie, even though Johnnie's a man and David's only a boy. And he judges Johnnie in the same way as the track and the car.

'You want to put your seat-belt on, Anna,' he says. But before she can reach for the belt, the car's moving. Stones spurt as the tyres gouge into the track, and then David's face slides past, pale as winter.

'I'll have to speak to Paul about this track,' says Johnnie. His teeth are white, his lips laughing. But it's not really laughter, it's just the way of his face. How she wants to make him laugh.

It's like an ache that lasts all the time Johnnie's here. To make him laugh, to make him turn to her and his eyes light in that sudden recognition that tugs her into the circle of being his. As long as he's here, all she wants is to belong to Johnnie.

'It's not my dad's, this part,' says Anna. They are going very slowly, very carefully, over on the right side of the track. The crunching of the tyres sounds terribly close. They edge round the sharp bend.

'Jesus,' says Johnnie. 'I see what you mean.'

This is the steepest part, and the worst. Nobody ever drives up here. He'll go back, Anna thinks. He can reverse to the bridge and then we'll drive back into town along the track and come up through the village, and David can come too, for the ride.

'Hold on tight,' says Johnnie. He revs hard and a deep, animal sound of engine answers. The tyres leap. Little stones spatter and hit the wall. The car bounds, lurches, grappling the next ridge of cobbled stone. The tyres rasp like claws, then break off. The car jolts back into the rut it's dug for itself.

'Fuck it,' says Johnnie. He's still smiling. He presses down on the accelerator and the car churns against the ridge, tyres spinning, then falls back for the second time. There's a smell of rubber and hot metal. 'Ah, fuck it.'

Anna clutches her seat. The car judders, its front tyres grinding. Then the engine roars, and all at once the car springs. There's a grating sound of metal on stone. One front wheel is up on the ridge, the other whines at air. The bonnet flashes, rearing upward. To Anna it looks as if they are aimed for the tops of the bright, bare trees. Johnnie guns the engine again and the car surges up, zigzagging the next bit of rutted track.

'She fucking did it,' breathes Johnnie. He doesn't seem to notice the clamour of metal. Not letting the car breathe, he forces it on up the track, banging, juddering but steady, to the top where the rotten gate leans into the wall. And up, on to the slick tarmac Paul paid for, on to the track that belongs to the house. Johnnie stops the car, and the key comes out of the ignition with a slight, firm click.

Silence pours down on them as Anna lets out her breath. Johnnie gets out of the car, walks around to the back, bends down. Anna twists in her seat.

'Aren't you going to park down at the house?' she asks. Johnnie stands up, wipes his hands on a thick white handkerchief, shakes his head.

'Someone might steal it here,' says Anna.

Johnnie laughs. 'The exhaust's fucked,' he says. He looks so happy about it that she finds herself laughing too.

'Nice bit of driving, eh, Anna?' She nods. 'I'll teach you to drive,' he says, 'soon as you're seventeen. What are you now?'

'Nearly eleven.'

'You can practise on this track though. It's private. Listen, tomorrow we're going to have a lesson, Anna. Just you and me. How about that?'

'OK,' says Anna, in her smallest, most pressed-down voice. If she shows how much she wants it, it won't happen.

They walk under the beech tree, past dark, high walls, down to the house. Johnnie stops by a pool of water, collected in what looks like a stone sink set in the wall.

'Don't put your hands in there, Johnnie! You've got oil on them.'

'What's the matter with you? It'll wash off, won't it?'

'That's our drinking water. It's the water for the house.'

'Bloody hell, Anna. What, you mean you come out here with a bucket?'

'No, it goes through that pipe there. It's spring water.'

'You really drink this stuff? It's got to be filthy. Out in the open air and everything.'

'Dad says it's cleaner than tap water in London.'

'Is it? OK, Anna, you put your hands in. Give me a drink.'
She dips her cupped hands in the water. It's cold, with an
end-of-winter coldness that lasts well into spring.

'It's soft water,' she says, trailing her fingers through it.

'All water's soft.'

'Not like London water.'

'London water's the best in the world. It's been through
some class kidneys. Here, Anna, wouldn't you like to go back
to London?'

Anna looks up. 'No.'

'Not even to see your –'

'No. I like it here.'

'She gave me something for you.'

'She didn't. You never saw her.' But she wants to believe it.
He watches the struggle in her eyes. 'What is it, Johnnie?
What've you got?'

'Aha.'

'It isn't anything. You're just saying it.'

'I've got it here in my pocket –'

She springs, her wet fingers quick as wires.

'Hey, leave off that, Anna, you don't get anything like that.
What about that drink of water you were going to get for me?'

'I'm not getting you anything. Not till you tell me about
Mum.'

'Go on. Please.'

And suddenly she softens. She scoops up a double handful
of water and holds it out to him. He leans forward, ducks his
head, sucks up the water. His nose is wet.

'You look like a horse drinking, Johnnie.' But she gives him
more, and the rest of it sparkles down between them, on to
the green-furred cobbles. It's always dank this side of the house,
facing into the hill, bounded by walls.

'Yeah, you're right. It tastes nice.'

There's no sound behind them, but at the same moment

Anna and Johnnie turn, and there is Paul, at the top of the three stone steps that lead down into the house. His look isn't for Anna. It grazes her, it embraces Johnnie. Then the two men stand off, without touching or greeting one another.

'Where's the car?' asks Paul.

'Up at the gate.' Johnnie nods, indicating behind him.

'Why don't you bring it down to the house?'

'It's OK where it is.'

'Let's have a look.'

Her dad knows. He heard the car coming up from the river. Maybe he could tell from the sound that the exhaust's broken. Her dad knows about things like that. But he wants to make Johnnie show him. And suddenly they are standing together, the two men: her father, her uncle, but before that they are brothers, and that has nothing to do with her. She slips past them.

It is late. The wreck of a meal lies on the table, the candles are stubs, the iron stove holds a heap of red coals. The air is thick with cigarette smoke. Paul leans into the candle flame to light another Marlboro. Sonia has gone to bed. Outside the frame of candlelight the rest of the room hangs in shadow. Flagstone floor, stone walls and fireplace, long, dark wooden table. The windows look out over more stone, the flagged terrace that's the boat-deck of this house slung into the side of the valley, high above the river, the mill chimney, the distant town whose street-lamps are too far off to pollute the night sky.

'Are those real owls?' asks Johnnie suddenly.

'Course they're real. What else would they be?'

'Don't ask me. Sometimes things that sound too real, they're not real, if you know what I mean.'

'Yeah.'

'Wouldn't like to be something they've got their eye on.'

'They lock on,' says Paul, 'like missiles. It's war out there.'

'It was you told me I ought to come up here and sort my head out.'

'Well, you did,' says Paul. He looks at Johnnie, with his hair cut short again, because that's the fashion. Too short for Paul's taste. 'And now here you are. Do you like it?'

Johnnie stands, stretches, glances behind him at the black space of window. 'You ought to get some curtains up, Paul. Anybody could be looking in.'

'There's no one to look in.'

'You ought to get a dog.'

'I'm getting a dog.' Paul pauses for effect. 'Cocker spaniel.'

'*Cocker spaniel!* I said a dog.'

'I don't want one of those.'

'A Dobermann.'

'I don't need any of that.'

'What about Anna?'

'Anna's all right.'

'Even when you're away?'

'She's not on her own. Sonia's here.'

'Sonia!'

'It's not London. Sonia's fine. I moved your car, Johnnie.'

'What for?'

'Because it's a stupid car. People don't have cars like that round here. People don't *need* cars like that round here.'

'It's a good car.'

'Then why treat it like shit? It's down by the barn.'

Johnnie yawns again, his arms up, his fists knuckling childishly on each side of his head. He smiles at his brother, his softest, most beguiling smile. 'It's only a car,' he says. 'If it's fucked, I'll get another.'

Paul's mouth aches with what he mustn't say. Say the wrong thing to Johnnie and he's off, the lid comes down. He doesn't hear you any more, he doesn't even see you. You're just a shadow blocking the way that's lit up for Johnnie.

'Come up to the attic. Come and see my new toy,' says Paul.

'You been buying another computer?'

'No. Better than that.'

They climb the wide, shallow stairs to the first floor. Funny how the silence of people sleeping is almost like a sound. Anna, Sonia. Their doors are shut. Anna has never been afraid of the dark. The house is noisier than the London house, even though it's miles from anywhere. There's water: the river, the streams that run to it down the hillside. This valley leaks from every pore. The boards creak like Paul thinks a wooden ship must creak at anchor. Back and forth, back and forth, as if someone's walking, walking, all night long. There are mice. All old houses have mice. There are two or three cats to keep them down. Rats in the barn, though there's nothing for them in there now. Just a big, cold space. A real barn's never cold. He ought to do something with it.

Up to the next floor, open the door in the wall. The staircase to the attics is narrow and bare. He hasn't bothered to carpet it, because he likes to hear footsteps. He doesn't want anyone coming upon him silently. Johnnie behind him, breathing. Then the three doors in front of him, each one plain and small. He takes the right-hand door.

'What are the other rooms?' asks Johnnie.

'That's my office. I knocked out the wall.'

'Where are we going, then?'

'My observatory,' says Paul. He snaps on the light.

'What's that?'

'It's a telescope.'

'Christ, Paul, you could be a Peeping Tom on Mars with that thing. When did you get it?'

'Last Christmas.'

'What's it for?'

'The stars.'

'You mean you're into astrology?'

'Astronomy.'

Johnnie touches the telescope. The cylinder is five feet long.

'Russian,' says Paul.

'It's a big bastard, isn't it?'

'It's the minimum. Anything less, you're just playing around.'

The walls show the geography of the sky. They make it fixed. They will never match the wheeling of the earth, the sweep of the planets, the dumb explosions of the stars.

'It's all moving,' says Paul. 'All of it. Even the sun's moving.'

'The sun? I thought it was the earth that moved.'

'Yeah, the sun as well. The whole galaxy's turning on its axis.'

Johnnie turns on Paul a look that Paul knows well. Not exactly disbelief, more an unwillingness to know more.

'I should've done more maths at school,' Paul goes on. 'Did you know, they predicted exactly where Neptune was going to be, before anybody discovered it? Just through mathematics. So when they found it, it wasn't only finding a planet. Because the maths worked, then it meant physics worked all through the universe. Which they didn't know before.'

'That the sort of thing you're doing, then, with the telescope?'

'They discovered Neptune in 1846.'

'Oh. Right.'

'I told you, I don't know maths. I couldn't work all that stuff out.' Paul's charged anger fills the room. Johnnie says nothing. He knows Paul, and he knows that anger. Paul's bought the telescope, bought books, charts, software. Found out enough beforehand so he won't show himself up in front of the guy in the shop. He's a fast learner. Too fast not to come up slap against the things he doesn't know and can't understand, not without going back to basics. And he won't do that. *My observatory*. Johnnie knows that it's only to him Paul ever says the words that give flesh to his secret dreams. Sonia probably thinks he's up here plotting how to screw the Customs & Excise.

'After they discovered Neptune, they knew there was another one.'

'What?'

'Planet. Another planet.'

'You going to let me have a look through that thing? How do you look up it?'

'You don't. You look down here, through this eye-piece, down into the lens. There's a mirror at the bottom that sends you right along the cylinder.'

Paul slides back the attic window. The telescope squats, waiting.

'I can't see anything.'

'Get out of the way, you don't just look down it, you've got to adjust it. Don't touch that band, it's on a permanent setting.'

Johnnie gets out of the way. His brother frowns, fiddles. 'The instructions were crap,' he mutters. 'All written in Russian.'

'How'd you read them, then?'

'Well, not in Russian as such. But it might as well have been. All the thinking was done in Russian, plus they parked some English words on top of it. There. There you are. Don't move it. Just look straight down.'

Johnnie looks straight down. A wobble of light, much too big and sharp, swings towards him. He blinks. He wants to shut his eyes. He looks for long enough, then straightens himself.

'Fucking unbelievable,' he says politely.

'What've you got?' mutters Paul, settling over the eye-piece again. 'Oh yeah. Good. That's the Bear. Ursa Major.' For a long time, it seems to Johnnie, he remains transfixed. Occasionally he makes a tiny adjustment to the band. At last, reluctantly, he draws back.

'Sorry, Johnnie. It should be you looking. I can do it any night.'

'That's all right. What's Sonia think of all this, then?'

'She's never been up here.'

'You're kidding.'

'No. She's never been up here.'

'What, you don't let her? There's a big invisible *Keep Out* sign at the bottom of the stairs?'

Paul frowns. He crosses to the window to shut it, but his attention is caught by something. A sound. Voices down in the wood, carrying clearly on the night wind. The moon's up, sinking away from fulness. Near-gibbous. There are clouds coming in from the south-west to clot the purity of the night sky. And those voices. Clear, but not clear enough to make words. Shouting drunk.

'I thought it was all quiet in the country,' says Johnnie.

'They're on their way back from the pub.'

'It's half-past one in the morning, Paul.'

'They don't keep pub hours round here.'

Johnnie's at the window. The closeness of his brother's body always disturbs Paul. *Johnnie was a beautiful baby.* Johnnie has a way of touching you, leaning into you as if the normal spaces between people don't count for him.

'I'm knackered,' says Johnnie.

'You need to get away,' says Paul. He finds himself speaking fast, in the voice that never works with Johnnie. Why is it he can't learn? He hears himself going on. 'Listen. You stay here a month. That stuff you're doing, you think you're on top of it, but you're never on top of it. It's on top of you. Finish. We've got the business, you don't have to do any of that stuff. Listen, two more years and I'll make you a full partner. Half-shares. How's that sound? You stay here a month. You've got to get out of it, Johnnie.'

'Not now,' says Johnnie. His voice is stifled. 'It's not the right time.'

'It's never the right fucking time. It never will be. Not till you're doing fourteen years. Everybody thinks they're magic till they get caught, Johnnie, it's not just you. Everybody thinks they'll just do one more job, then they'll finish. And they never, ever do. Not till someone finishes it for them.'

'It's not that.'

'I know.'

You're frightened, Paul thinks. A Dobermann's no more use than a cocker spaniel when it comes to that kind of frightened.

'I made a mistake,' says Johnnie suddenly, in a light voice that sounds as if it's on the edge of laughter.

'Course you did,' says Paul.

'No,' says Johnnie. 'I mean a real mistake.'

Paul says nothing. He puts his hand on Johnnie's shoulder. In a rush Johnnie turns to him, clings as tight as the kid with the shaven head did the night the breathing finally stopped. Mum got up from the side of Dad's bed and wound her rosary into his dead fingers. Paul takes his brother in his arms. Under the cotton shirt Johnnie is burning. The near-gibbous moon races through cloud, the planets move. The galaxy turns on its slow axis, pulled by a gravity no stronger than the one which drags Johnnie from his brother's arms.

Thirteen

Paul can't sleep, so he watches the stars. He thinks about all it takes to make a gas cloud become a supernova, and about the volatility of everything that looks stable through his telescope. His mind is full of the words he's learned, in order to have words for what he sees. The facts are polished with language. That's what he never understood at school, when they talked about vocabulary. Education is about getting new words because you need them. Neutron, ring nebula, helium flash, planetesimals. Things like that can't exist in your mind until you know the words for them. Imagine people knowing all the words for the growth and death of a star, even though they'll never see it. The cycle is too long: human beings are nothing beside it.

The words Paul's learned press up against his lips, but he never speaks them aloud. He reads, then writes things down in a red notebook, but he never turns the pages back to look again at what he's written. He watches planets swim through space into the grasp of his telescope. They are public, yet as private as dreams. He doesn't speak of this, not to Sonia, not even to Johnnie, though when he brought Johnnie up here maybe the thought was at the back of his mind that these words might be shared. And not to Anna. It has never even crossed Paul's mind to show the stars to Anna. Why should she care? He never did, at her age.

'*I made a mistake.*'

'*Of course you did.*'

'*I mean a real mistake.*'

Even the sun's middle-aged, and it's seen everything. Johnnie thinks I don't know, but I do. Of course I do. It's my business to know what he knows. You put such things out of your mind. You use words that don't educate anyone. You say, 'He's sorted.' You say, 'I took care of him.'

And to yourself you say, *black hole*. You can never see a black hole. That's where everything changes, where stars die, where even the laws of physics don't work any more. Light cannot get out, because these are outlaw places where the bandits of gravity have taken over. Paul smiles.

He won't sleep now. He might as well stay up, and cat-nap between five and seven. That's got him through a day before now. He's awake, and the stars are awake with him, both of them seizing their time. Downstairs, Johnnie's sleeping. He sleeps like the dead, always has done. Or so he says.

Paul remembers another place, and another time. After their father died, when Mum sat in the kitchen of the flat in Grays. Her hands flexed and unflexed on the white embroidered cloths she laundered each day, starched, ironed, and placed back on the table. She didn't seem to notice her own fingers plucking the lace edge on the cloths. The skin on her knuckles was dry and swollen, like the flesh around her eyes. She had wept the colour out of her face, and the clarity of her eyes was dull with a scurf of salt.

Paul was off making money. He had his flat in Notting Hill, and his car. He had tailors calling him sir. The city was his now, and he was part of it. No more tubes and buses, no more waiting in queues, no more watching other people spend money and get respect. No more going home at night to the flat in Grays. He came on Sunday afternoons, when he could, but he hated it. Most of all he hated his mother's grief, the noise of which seemed to fill the rooms of the flat, even when she was most silent. Her hair lay flat and dank against her scalp. He gave her the money but she would not go out and get it done.

Every time he came she wore the same dark skirt, pale blouse, dark, loose cardigan. Being his mother, she washed them fanatically often, so the wool of the cardigan was pilled and matted. He could not bear the way she would wear tights when she went out of the house, and yet sit indoors, in front of him, with her legs bare and her exposed veins twisting down the inside of her knees. And she would sigh huge unconscious sighs, and then swallow them.

'For Christ's sake, Mum, have the operation. You've only got to ask. You can get it done private without waiting.'

And the kitchen was dirty. Not so anyone else would notice, but by his mother's standards it was dirty. There was a layer of dusty grease on the hob, a jam-jar of sodden tea-bags leaked on to the worktop, and the rubbish bin overflowed with take-away packaging. And there was his mother, with her razor eye for bad housekeeping, sitting in the middle of it.

He took the rubbish out. He brought his mother the cleanest banknotes and she accepted them without question. She was tired, and she didn't want to know. She rose, and put the notes behind the clock. She still talked about going up west, and he thought, *She means, where I live.* But he knew she'd never come.

One night he stayed. He can't remember why now; perhaps she asked him. More likely he was just tired. He slept in the room he used to share with Johnnie, which was Johnnie's now. It was the noise that woke him. Johnnie's soft feet on the carpet, to and fro. Then a rubbing sound that Paul couldn't identify.

'Johnnie? What you doing?'

Silence.

'Johnnie?' Paul sat up and snapped on the bedside lamp. His brother stood, staring, caught, his thin body shielding itself. He was in his underpants. The sheets were pulled off the bed.

'What's the matter?' Then Paul saw the dark stain on the mattress. 'Here, you'll catch cold. Get in my bed,' he said.

'I'm all right.' Johnnie defied him, as if it was Paul's fault, as if it would all have been all right if Paul hadn't woken.

'Don't be stupid. Get in.'

Paul pulled back his own bedcovers. They didn't have duvets then. His mum had these harsh, thick blankets she'd used since she was married. They pressed you down into sleep like heavy hands. Paul got out of the bed and gave Johnnie a gentle shove towards it. 'Go on. I'll get this sorted.'

It was then that he saw his brother was shaking. Johnnie was skinny, with the kind of skinniness boys have before their hormones pack muscle on to them, and his shoulder-blades stood out like wings.

'Have you had a wash?'

Johnnie nodded.

'All right. You go on, get in bed, go to sleep. I'll sort this out with Mum.'

'Don't tell her.' It jumped out of his mouth.

'What's it matter? All she's got to do is put the sheets in the washing-machine. It won't kill her.' He'd bought the washing-machine, and a dryer too, because he couldn't bear the way his mother still laboriously pinned her underwear on to wire racks, out on the balcony, for the wind to rip at them and belly out her shabby bras and knickers and nightdresses.

Paul felt anger like a taste in his mouth at the thought of his mother sitting there in front of her snow-white table-cloth, lost, crisping the edges of the lace between her fingers, doing nothing, knowing nothing about Johnnie's sheets. She looked as if she was waiting for a photographer to come along. Like a refugee whose family had all been killed. As if she hadn't got anyone left, when there was Johnnie sleeping in the bedroom.

'Don't.'

'OK. Listen. I'll go and put these in the machine now. I'll tell her I spilled a cup of coffee over the bed if that makes you happy.'

Johnnie nodded. Slowly, he sank on to Paul's bed, let himself fall back against the pillows. Paul drew the blankets up under his brother's chin. 'There.' He touched Johnnie's cheek, and Johnnie turned, as if by instinct, towards the touch.

'All right?' said Paul.

'Yeah.'

Johnnie's face was tired and hollow in the sideways light flung by the lamp. There were stains under his eyes. Must have been getting up like this night after night. And she hadn't noticed. Or she'd pretended not to notice, so she wouldn't have to do anything about it. Her at the table, her friends coming in with their patter and their headscarves. The priest taking his tea and stirring it till the sugar gritted on the bottom of the cup, while he said that it was all for the best, after so much suffering. The mass cards his mother kept on the sideboard and would not take down. She would read them aloud to herself at night, her voice low, but not low enough. As if Johnnie wasn't there too, in the bedroom, just through the wall. She ought to know you could hear everything through those walls.

'Fuck it,' Paul said.

'What?' Johnnie's eyes snapped open.

'Nothing. Go to sleep.' Paul sat down on the side of the bed. In a minute he'd sort those sheets out.

'Listen, Johnnie. Tomorrow we're going to go out and I'll get you a load of new sheets. Brand new. We'll put them in here, in the cupboard. Mum doesn't have to know. Any problems, you just put a new pair of sheets on. And when you want a new mattress, you give me a bell, all right?'

'All right.' Johnnie's eyes were shut, sealed tight. A smile fleeted across his face, and he looked like a child. Christ, thought Paul, that's what he is, he's a child.

'Wha' bout the sheets?' Johnnie muttered out of his cave of sleep. 'Wha'll I do with –'

'Put them out for the bin-men. It's your business, no one

else's. You run out of sheets, I'll buy you more. All you got to do is tell me.'

The smile again, stronger, firmer. Then it vanished, like water poured on hungry soil. Johnnie slept.

Paul sat still. He could hear the traffic growling far away, on the flyover. It was late, but he no longer felt like sleeping. In a minute he'd get up, turn Johnnie's mattress, re-make his brother's bed, and take the sheets to the kitchen. He could turn the washing-machine on, then the dryer, and have the sheets done by morning. These machines were almost soundless.

Mum hadn't believed the clothes would come out clean. She thought if a washing-machine didn't slosh and rumble for forty minutes, then spin like a jet engine taking off, it wasn't doing a proper wash. Paul didn't tell her that it cost twice what she'd have paid for the machines she peered at in Floyds on the High Street. That's what money does. It buys you easiness. It doesn't sound much, being able to carry on talking when your washing-machine's on spin. Just a little thing, like having a car that doesn't break down, like having the heating on with a window open because it's nice to be warm and still have fresh air. What they don't tell you is how all those little things add up, and what they add up to are the smooth, easy faces of people who've always had money.

When Paul bought a cashmere sweater, the salesman said, wrapping it in tissue-paper, 'There you are, Sir. The first of many.' He knew it was the first, because of the questions Paul asked about taking care of cashmere. Then he went on, 'In our experience, once a customer has got used to cashmere, he doesn't go back to wool.' Paul'd looked at the man sharply, quick for the covert mockery that might be there. But there was nothing: the man was serious.

Paul could buy sheets for Johnnie, throw them away and never notice it. He had a gift. He could make people do things. He could think ahead, he could organize. He could work like a snake-charmer on the greed of others. Money could not help finding him. He knew that: he was at his high-water mark. More importantly than that, he knew something none of the others knew: that the tide which was flowing with him would suck him back down if he let it. Not many people seemed to understand that. They got grandiose. They believed life had let them into a secret. No one else seemed to hear the hard, clear voices Paul heard, that told him he'd got to hold on to his money, plough it back, look for the next thing which no one else had thought of yet. Money makes money. You don't have to be stupid, you don't have to be greedy, you just have to want things and not be distracted. All you have to do is to let money go to its work, flowing as fast as it can away from the filthy hole in the ground from which it came, flowing fast and cleaning itself as it goes. The money-for-nothing miracles of crime were nothing compared to the miracles of capital, which Paul came to understand before he was twenty-five. He was walking on water.

Paul never felt more sure of himself than he did that night, as he watched his brother's face relax into deeper and deeper unconsciousness. He felt as if he had hunted down that peace for Johnnie. A passion of protectiveness stirred in him, raw and sweet. He promised himself again, as if Johnnie was new-born, that nothing would ever hurt Johnnie any more, after the long labour of coming to this point, here, now. No one was ever going to harm him while Paul was there to prevent it.

But there was nothing for Johnnie here. She didn't even cook for him any more. Johnnie knew where her purse was, and she let him rifle it for money to buy doner, pizza, burgers, fish-and-chips. It was a miracle if she bestirred herself to buy a bag of oranges. 'Vitamins, Johnnie. They're good for you.' But Johnnie wouldn't eat the oranges, and they shrivelled in the dish.

The only time she went out was to daily mass. Paul felt a

spasm of hatred against the church as he thought of his mother dipping her fingers in the holy water, crossing herself, leaving a spatter on her cardigan. The smell of stone and stale candles made him gag. The women in their cardigans with their hands cupped like holy hamsters to receive communion: how he hated them, too. They clacked round his mother with their sympathy and they frowned at Johnnie when he banged into the flat with the greasy parcel that was his dinner. And Johnnie was taking money from her, too. She'd never let Paul near her purse, she used to have the sense to know that was the first step. *If you want money, you wait till I fetch my purse. No going down in my bag.* She had standards for everything then.

Only with Paul could Johnnie be safe. He let his mind play on the thought of all that was to come, and the way he would lift Johnnie out of this room, take him beyond the memory of their father's breathing that still struggled through these thin walls. Their grandfather had lived to draw his pension for three years; their father had died twenty years off retirement age. The world had never opened its legs for them, but for Johnnie it would be different. From time to time Paul reached out his hand, and stroked his brother's hair.

Fourteen

In the morning the stars are wiped out by the sun. Sonia sits at the long, freshly polished table, her back to the brilliance of the valley, the black trees, the sharp, lemony daffodils. She chooses to sit with her back to the sun, in this room where the crush of spring light is like narcissus petals packed into papery buds. Light searches the table, the flagged floor, the heavy oak settle. Sunshine makes a nebula around Sonia's pale, smooth head. She is writing a list in her firm handwriting, pausing every so often to summon up in her mind the world she's pulling into shape.

Johnnie sits opposite her, a coffee cup propped in his hands, his eyes above it clear and wide. His hair is damp, his face glows after cold water. Sonia takes in the sight of him, and is unimpressed. So few women are unimpressed by Johnnie that he has not yet developed a technique to deal with Sonia. Sonia wears a narrow tunic, the tint of rotting blackberries, over a narrower skirt with a side-split that rises to six inches above her knees. She will not wear anything unless it permits her a cat-like fluidity of movement. Sonia has perfect knees which she shows just often enough to remind you that they're there.

'Where's Anna?'

'Outside. Gone to feed the cats.'

'Cats? You got cats? That doesn't sound like Paul.'

Sonia shrugs. 'There's rats all over the place. You've got to keep them down. The cats aren't pets, they live in the barn.'

'Cats,' says Johnnie. His eyes pretend amusement, but Sonia can see he doesn't like the change. 'How about a cocker spaniel, Sonia?'

'Anna'd like a dog,' allows Sonia. She takes out the first cigarette of the day, taps it on the table but doesn't light it.

'But she won't be getting one,' says Johnnie.

He's gone too far. Sonia's face smooths over as she removes herself behind the regularity of her features. She glances sideways, over the landscape which flashes with spring light.

'Don't go putting ideas into Anna's head, Johnnie,' she says. 'She's all right the way she is.'

'With you looking out for her,' says Johnnie. The offensiveness of his words doesn't seem to affect Sonia at all. She smiles, as if they know each other too well for her to bother to reply, then she lights her cigarette and draws in the first, tarry mouthful of smoke. At the prickle of it in her throat her eyes close with pleasure. They sit in silence, Sonia smoking, Johnnie staring into his coffee cup.

'Nice coffee, Sonia,' he says at last. 'I thought all you'd get up here was Nescaff.'

'It's not Nova Scotia, Johnnie,' says Sonia tartly. Johnnie's face shimmers with amusement as he picks up her annoyance at being parked up here, two hundred miles from London, to look after Anna.

'Bit quiet for you, though, isn't it?'

'I'm taking riding lessons,' says Sonia.

He bets she knows she'll look good in the clothes. Women like Sonia, with small high breasts that look hard even though they've got to be soft, small waists, tough little blonde faces, they look good in those dark tight clothes. Also, up on a horse, Sonia will be looking down on everybody, which is the way she thinks things ought to be. What a cow. All the same, you've got to give it to her, Sonia doesn't moan. She looks around, works things out, gets the best out of them. Johnnie can respect that. She'll have Paul paying for a horse before you can say knife.

'What about Louise? She been up here yet?'

'She won't be coming up here.'

'The kid ought to see her own mother.'

'That depends on what kind of mother she is, doesn't it?'

Johnnie stares at her, foxed. The words seem to have too much echo. Who the fuck knows what kind of mother anyone is.

'She's her *mother*, Sonia.'

'Like your mum was your mum.'

Johnnie's silenced. He'd like to tell her to fuck off, she knows nothing, who does she think she is, talking about his mum that way? But he can't. Sonia's earned her right to speak. Every month Sonia takes a train to London, and then another train to the residential home outside Horsham. Sonia taxis out into the brilliantly green Sussex countryside, where the best crop now is old dears whose families have got enough money to keep them in comfort. The residential home might as well be on the moon for all his mother knows. When she gets up from her chair in the TV lounge, she still walks the invisible pathways of the flat in Grays. Stove to table, table to cupboard, cupboard to sink. Her hands carry burdens no one else can see. She wipes, she lifts, she takes hot dishes from the oven. Then it all vanishes, and she stands bewildered between one chair and the next, her incontinence pads sagging between her thighs.

Sonia visits. She takes grapes and boxes of Milk Tray which his mother devours. Sonia doesn't bring flowers any more, because the smell of them upsets Mum. Breathe in the perfume of a narcissus and she'll be restless for hours, back and forth with the invisible housework. Sometimes she's not right for days. Paul and Johnnie wonder what Sonia finds to say to their mother, but they don't ask and Sonia says nothing. Again, you've got to give it to Sonia. She goes on their behalf, and she absolves them all. Lots of women wouldn't bother, especially when all his mum seems to want to know is when Louise is coming. She always liked Louise.

'Anna's all right,' says Sonia now, quietly but emphatically.

'She been having riding lessons as well?' asks Johnnie, to bring some lightness into the conversation. Ignoring him, Sonia starts to gather the cups and plates. She likes everything neat, Sonia does. The débris of last night was whisked away before Johnnie came down. The row of Bosch kitchen equipment starts to purr as soon as Sonia gets up, dealing with dirty washing, dirty dishes, wet clothes. Just because you live in the country, Sonia says, there's no need to carry on as if you've dropped out of civilization.

She holds the door open with her hip, balancing the pile of china. It's funny how he doesn't find Sonia attractive at all, but he can't help thinking how well every part of her body works. All her movements follow on from one another. She transfers the weight of the door to her elbow, slides the load of china around the door, then passes through the doorway without so much as a clink. It's all right for Sonia. She never looks caught out, at a loss, lost, trapped, frightened. He swerves his thoughts away. He hasn't come here to think about stuff like that. He turns towards the window where even the dazzle of morning sun can't show up a smear on Sonia's glass. The door opens again, behind him. Sonia, back again.

'Paul's up in his office all morning. He said he'd got a load of phone calls to make.'

Don't get in our way, she means. *Don't come here undoing everything I've done*. She knows Paul wants him here, but she's not having it. Sonia can be realistic about him, where his brother cannot.

'I've got to get off anyway. Things to do. I'll say hello to London for you.'

'Don't go without seeing him.'

'I'll have a look round and find Anna first.'

He wanders out into the garden, across to the railings. He stares at the landscape, but there's nothing of interest to him.

And the sun's too bright. He can't work out why Paul's come here. Johnnie thinks with longing of the drive back into London, the moment when houses and cars thicken and the brick laps round you and things start to happen. Here, anyone can see you coming for miles, because there's nothing in between.

He finds Anna in the barn, crouched over a cardboard box.

'Hi.'

She jumps, moves instinctively to cover the box with her body.

'What you got there?'

'Nothing.'

Her face is fierce. For once she doesn't want to please him. He feels it as a small, precise shock, and he doesn't like it. Immediately, instinctively, he sets out to win her back. There's a pile of logs in the corner of the barn, and he rolls out one of the thickest logs to a safe distance from Anna, and sits down. He can't see into the box from here, and she knows he can't.

'You never asked me about that letter,' he says.

'You were mucking me about.'

'No, I wasn't. Would I do a thing like that to you, Anna?'

Her face stiffens with annoyance as she turns away, back to her box.

'I know you're not going to give it me. Anyway, I don't want it. I'm busy.'

Johnnie reaches into his jeans pocket and pulls out Louise's letter.

'Here you are. Your mum said there was something inside it for you, so mind how you open it.'

In one movement she's up, beside him, snatching the letter from his hand. She looks at it, turning it over, assessing the thick, blank envelope.

'Aren't you going to open it?'

'In a minute.'

'All right. Show me your kittens first.'

'How do you know they're kittens?'

'I can hear them, can't I?'

'You're not to tell!'

'I won't tell anyone.'

Slowly, easily, he gets up from the log and strolls to the box. Just as he thought, they are blind and new, a writhing knot of furless kitten flesh.

'Ugly little bastards, aren't they?'

'They're not ugly. This is what they're meant to look like. Don't you know anything about kittens?'

'Where's the cat?'

Anna hesitates. 'She'll come back later.'

'You sure? Anna, you've been feeding them, haven't you?'

'What if I have?'

'You can't do that. She won't feed them if you do.'

'She wasn't feeding them anyway,' says Anna flatly. 'David, he's my friend, he says she was too young to have kittens. It did something wrong to her insides, and she won't come near them. He's let me borrow the dropper out of his chemistry set to feed them with.'

Johnnie puts his bare hand down into the stir of kittens. They sense him and their sealed-up faces squirm against his fingers for milk.

'They look bloody awful, Anna. You're not doing them any favours, you know.'

'They'd be all right if I could have them in my room, then I could feed them in the night.'

'Yeah, but you know, Anna, they don't feel anything. That's why people drown them when they're like this, before they get any feelings.'

'*You're not to tell my Dad.*'

'All right. All right. I said I wouldn't, didn't I? Listen, have you got a kiss for me before I go, or can't you think about anything but those kittens?'

'Are you going, Johnnie?' And her face is as he wants it to be, empty with disappointment. 'Are you going now?'

'Yeah. Got to get back on the road.'

'What about your car?'

'I'm leaving it here. I've got a hire car ordered down in town.'

Her black eyes sparkle. 'Can I have your red car?'

'Yeah, all right.'

'Really, Johnnie?'

'Plenty more where it came from.'

'Wow.' The intensity of her pleasure is no less for vanishing almost as soon as it came. 'You're lying.'

'No. You can have it till your dad sells it for me.'

'I knew you didn't mean it.' She stoops, picks up one of the kittens and the dropper. Carefully, kneeling over a saucer on the floor, she squeezes the dropper until the tube is full of milk, then applies the glass tip to the kitten's mouth. 'See, he's drinking.'

But the milk trickles down the sides of the kitten's mouth as it squirms in Anna's hand. Frowning, she rubs its mouth with the glass tip. More milk spills out.

'You're drowning the poor little bastard, Anna.'

'No, I'm not. He's just not hungry. I got mixed up – he's the same one I fed last time.'

'Anna,' he says. 'Anna. They're better off dead. You know that, don't you?'

He wants to help her. He wants to cut short the hours she'll spend in the barn, dropping milk all over them, kidding herself it's going in, then watching them die one by one. That's if a rat doesn't get at them first. He'd drown them for her himself, if he thought she'd let him. But the way she's kneeling there, bowed like a little old woman over her cardboard box, Johnnie knows it's no use to argue. Time to go.

'For Chrissake, Anna, will you stop mucking about with those kittens and come and say goodbye to me?'

'I don't want you to go,' she says, looking down, speaking as if to one of the kittens.

'Come here.'

The kitten's back in its box, the dropper on the saucer. Anna's thin arms are tight around his neck, wrapping him close, and her breath is warm and light under his ear. He smells the rodent smell of the new kittens on her, and milk, and her own clean hair. He lifts her to him and she wraps her legs around his hips and clings there. She's getting tits. Anna. Think of that. It doesn't seem five minutes since she was in her pushchair. And he shoves the thought away, because it makes him feel old. Thin, spidery Anna with her eyes shut and her mouth whispering fiercely, 'You never stay. You always go away.'

'Here, what's this? I want a proper goodbye.'

The arms tighten. 'Goodbye.' He feels her breath. Then 'Johnnie –' But she doesn't say it. Yesterday he said he'd give her a driving lesson, but today she knows better than to ask.

'Back soon, eh?'

'Yeah.'

'You read your letter when I'm gone. It's nice to have a letter from your mum.'

'All right.'

He peels her off him. 'You look after those kittens for me now.'

She drops to her knees, bends over the box again as if it's the only thing that interests her in the world. She won't look at him again. He doesn't push it. With Anna you don't want to go too far, or you might reach an edge you can't see until you're right on top of it, with the ground wheeling away miles beneath your feet. He takes one more look at her, at the black, soft, straight hair sliding forward and concealing her face. He thinks of saying something, then thinks better of it. Johnnie leaves her then, going out through the dusty bars of light that fall from the barn's high windows.

Fifteen

You take the letter into the wood. You sit on the knotted grey root of a beech, and open it. You open the envelope, shake it, and fifty twenty-pound notes fall out. They are oily and stuck together, and at first you aren't sure if they are real money or play. Maybe Mum has forgotten how old you are, and thinks you still play shops with plastic oranges and play money. But you peel one off and hold it up to the light, and there's the metal strip. You count the notes aloud. Mum has sent you a thousand pounds.

A thousand pounds. You could buy your own second-hand caravan and haul it down in the woods, by the river. You'd have a set of camping pans which fit into one another, and a Calor gas stove. The caravan would have a step and you'd sit on it, eating sausages. There'd be nobody else there, except maybe David. You'd cook him a sausage, put it in a burger bun and ask if he wanted ketchup with it, or mustard. And when it was dark, you wouldn't care. You'd shut the door tight, and you'd listen to the river until you fell asleep. Anyway you'd have a dog that would bark if anyone came near, as well as the cats to sleep on your bed.

You lean back and shut your eyes. Inside the wood it's so still that it feels warm. You put your arms round your knees and squeeze tight. Your mum has sent you a thousand pounds, but it's ages since you've seen her and you are not sure you can get a picture of her face in your mind any more, not even just before you go to sleep at night. You don't try, in case it doesn't work. You can look at a photograph any time, but that's another thing. In the photographs Mum is young and smiling, and you are in her arms. Both of you smiling, and knowing nothing about what was going to happen, like two strangers.

You'll read the letter in a minute, then you'll get up and go back to the barn and feed the kittens again. This time they'll suck properly. They're getting fatter, anyone can see that. You hug your arms around your knees, then roll up the leg of your jeans and explore a ripening scab with your finger. That's where you fell and gashed it in the lane. When you lift the scab the skin under it is shiny pink, but you know it hasn't healed in the middle yet. You think of pulling it off anyway, and of Johnnie going down through England, back to London. He never stays. He says he will, and then he goes away. You roll down the leg of your jeans.

The letter's in your lap. Your mum has written it in big, clear writing, the kind that helped you two years ago, before you could read grown-up handwriting. But you don't need it now. If Sonia leaves one of her lists lying around, you can read it at a glance. You wonder if it would be OK to tell Mum this, so she could write in her normal writing from now on.

Dear Anna

Everybody ought to have some money of their own and then if they want to go anywhere or do anything they can. Put this away in a safe place.

I had a dream about you last night. You had a Dalmatian puppy and you were playing with it. Maybe one day when you're older and you can take it for walks and look after it yourself, you and I can have a puppy. But you'll have to buy a book, because I don't know anything about dogs.

I might be going away on holiday soon for some sun and fun. If you want to come with me, why not ask Paul? We could get an apartment.

Well, not much to add as everything is the same as usual with me. Thinking of you lots, love you loads,
with fondest love,
Mum XXXX

You fold the letter carefully, just as Mum folded it, and put it back in the envelope. You put the money in your lap and look at it for a while. It wouldn't be OK to tell Mum about her writing. You think of what Mum has written about sun and fun, as if you are five years old.

You weigh the banknotes down with a stone for safety while you search for the smallest, driest twigs, and add to them a handful of beech-nut cases from last year. You heap them in the centre of a little ring of stones, then you balance more twigs in a wigwam. It is a perfect shape for a fire, but you haven't got any matches. You don't want to go back to the house and get caught by Sonia and asked to do something.

'Anna, are you there?'

You're not frightened. You know it's David, coming down the wood on the path from the village. You'd half-planned to meet, but with Johnnie and then the kittens, you forgot. You glance behind you, where the notes poke out from the stone, but you don't move to cover them.

'I thought you'd be here. What're you doing? You can't light a fire in the woods.'

'It's not lit. I haven't got any matches.'

David bends down and examines the fire. 'It's too small. It won't burn, even if you get it lit.'

'I've got some stuff to put on it once it starts burning. Have you got any matches?'

'I've got my lighter.'

David smokes sometimes, but you don't. He takes out his Camel lighter, and snaps the flame. It jumps up, and he snaps again and again, absorbed. 'You light the fire,' you say. You keep your back to him as you remove the stone, and pick up the money.

'What's that, Anna? What're you doing?'

You take a note, hold it in finger and thumb above the unlit fire. 'Go on. Go on. Light it.'

'You can't burn that. It's money.'

'I can do what I want with it, it's mine.'

'Look at it, you've got loads of the buggers, how much've you got?'

'A thousand pounds,' you say.

'Give it here.'

You hand it to David. He riffles the edges of the notes, then counts it carefully. 'Where'd you get it?'

'My mum sent it.'

'From London?'

'Yeah.'

'She must be rich.'

'She isn't. My dad gives her money. She said she wanted me to have it, in case I wanted to go anywhere.'

'You mean leave home?'

You shrug. 'Maybe.'

'She wants you to go and visit her, that's what it is, cause she's your mum. Why don't you go? You could buy a ticket.'

You crouch by the twigs, adjust the wigwam until it's perfect. 'I can't go,' you say.

David doesn't ask why not. He says, 'This is the most money I've ever held in my hands,' and then he puts it back where you'd laid it before. He snaps his lighter so the flame jumps up, its blue core stretched, then snuffed.

'I'll light the fire if you want,' he says. 'But I've got a better idea.'

'What?'

'We'll burn one note, and we'll bury the rest. We'll mark this tree, then we'll know where it is. No one'll find it, even if they see the mark.'

'OK.'

'I've got a packet of crisps. We can wrap the money in the crisp bag.'

You and David champ the crisps one by one, matching sizes so each of you takes a large crisp, a medium-sized, a small one. When they're all gone, you wrap the notes in the greasy bag, and fold it over. Scuffing with your heels, then digging with your hands, you make a hole in the earth, and lay the crisp packet down. It begins to unfold, bulging out of the hole you've made.

'You'll have to dig deeper,' says David, and he gets a stick and pokes out the earth between the grey roots of the beech. You wedge the packet in as deep as you can. You cover it, bury it. The soil brushes off your hands easily, then you scatter leaves and twigs over the burial place. David sears the flesh of the nearest tree with his lighter flame, to mark it. There's one note left.

'Light the fire now,' you say.

The fire is small, quick, hot. The flame makes a rattling sound, like a whistle that won't blow.

'Go on,' says David, and you offer a corner of the note to the flame. The fire swipes it, nearly touching your fingers. You drop the burning note among the twigs and watch it writhe.

'We must tread it out,' says David. 'It's dangerous to start fires in the woods.'

He gets a handful of earth, throws it on and tramps it down until the fire is mashed. The note has completely disappeared.

'There,' he says. There's a streak of carbon on his face. 'It's gone.'

'I'm glad,' you say. 'I wish we'd burned the rest.'

'You know where it is,' says David, and smiles. It's like when people say, *You know the way to your mouth.*

You look at each other. You've done something people don't do. You've burned money with the Queen's head on it.

'Have you got a fag?' you ask.

He gives you one. You hold the tip to the flame of the Camel lighter, and then when it's lit you hold it loosely, burning between your fingers, the way Sonia does. But you don't want to be like Sonia. You shift the cigarette to your other hand, although you're not left-handed. You take a puff of smoke, let it out, do it again. You're smoking.

David says, 'You don't want to start smoking, Anna.'

You say, 'Like I'm really going to,' in Courtney Arkinstall's voice.

'I'm trying to give up,' says David. You know he means it. 'Cause I don't want to have a cough like my dad's.'

You look at him with his pale face and the freckles that splash on to his skin as soon as the sun comes out after winter. His eyes are squeezed narrow against the smoke. They're the only real grey eyes Anna's ever seen. Grey eyes and nothing-coloured hair, like rain. He's narrow and calm to look at, like a cat watching out of the window and seeing things nobody else sees. You want to see those things too. You want him to show them to you.

Sixteen

I wrote her a letter. I wanted her to know why I didn't come and see her. I don't think Anna would ever believe I didn't want to, but then she's been away from me for a long time now. I haven't kept her thinking I'll come at any minute and take her away with me.

I've never been north of Birmingham in my life. I would have gone, but not to Sonia's house. I don't dislike Sonia and I don't like her. I never think of her. She thinks she's married to Paul: well, let her. I know the truth.

I could write a book about what Sonia doesn't know. First, she doesn't know that Paul is still married to me. Second, she doesn't know that Anna is still my daughter. Third, she doesn't know that giving birth to Anna was like shitting a pineapple, and Paul was there all the time, much against his original inclination, but he stayed, he sponged my face, he held my knees still when they wouldn't stop shaking.

There are times when you think your life has changed for ever, and it can never go back to the way it was. That night in the hospital was one of them. By the time Anna was born it wasn't night any more, it was morning. The midwife left us to have a few minutes with the baby before they cleaned me up. Paul went to the window, looked out. He said, 'It's raining,' then he came back to the bed and knelt down beside it so his face was level with the baby where I was holding her wrapped in one of those towels that have the hospital name printed on them. She was fast asleep. He didn't touch her. He just looked and looked, for a long time. And I said, 'We did it,' and he nodded. There wasn't room for questions, because all the answers were wrapped up in my arms.

Paul was wiped out. So tired, and younger-looking than I'd ever seen him, even when we first met. Paul's one of those men who've never let themselves look young. He always had to look older than he was, so people would take him seriously.

He didn't touch her. I remember that quite clearly. I think he was frightened, that's all it was. There was this new person in the room with us, and we didn't know her. It shouldn't have troubled me, because there was plenty of time, but it did trouble me. I felt as if he hadn't reached out and claimed her. It pressed down on me, even then in the moment that she was born. I had my knowledge of where she had come from, and it pressed down on me. My mother would have said that it trod on my tongue. It stopped me saying to him to all the little senseless things I wanted to say to someone, about the beauty of her and how I couldn't believe it. How there was nothing else in the world like her, and we had made her. It trod my tongue down, because it would have been a lie.

I wish he had touched her. I wish he'd held her. I wish I'd put her into his arms. He's claimed her now, but not in the way it should have been, with both of us there and knowing it was right.

I could hear the rain, now that Paul had told me it was there. We were on the fifth floor of the hospital, in a private room. The wind threw rain against the windows, then let it go so it streamed down the glass. It rained all the five days I was in there. I used to lie and watch it. I wasn't going to feed Anna myself, because Paul didn't like the idea of it when I was pregnant. Lots of men don't. But after he left that morning I told the sister I'd changed my mind, I wanted to try. She was pleased with me.

Paul came in twice a day, though he never stayed long, because he had a thing about hospitals. And he was busy with the flat he was buying for Johnnie. He didn't know how I could stand it, being there all the time, and I didn't say that I enjoyed it. It was a little world of its own. I used to take Anna along the corridor to the lounge where the other mums watched TV. I liked having a private room, but I wanted to talk about Anna and my nipples and stitches and all that stuff you can't imagine not being disgusted by, until it happens to you.

Paul used to come in and talk about money. I knew it was because there was no one else he could talk to about it, not freely, as if he was wandering about in his own mind while he talked. His business associates knew the bit they needed to know, and no more. He kept them in the dark deliberately.

He'd just lost nearly all the money he'd put into a property company called Bluebell Securities. He didn't let on exactly how much for a while, but I knew it was a lot. Paul didn't say much about it. What was gone was gone: he was always very pragmatic like that. But he was angry with himself because he'd been completely taken in by this man, Christopher Ross. Chris Ross. We'd been to his house, been out with him and his wife for dinner. Chris paid. He had everything: the voice, the car, the house, glossy-looking kids and his wife in designer jeans, white linen shirt and just one heavy diamond on her left hand. I quite liked her. She was nice to me about the baby, but she was so on edge that you couldn't really relax and talk to her. I didn't understand why, at the time.

We all went for a weekend in Paris, and stayed in a little grey hotel off the Boulevard St Germain. I loved it. There was a courtyard with tubs of flowers. They were mostly hydrangeas, with big, loose white flowers that spilled over the sides of the tubs. Then there was another courtyard inside, dark and secret, with a goldfish pool and spindly metal chairs and tables. Everyone in the hotel was very quiet and correct, and they didn't bother you. I didn't feel like going out much. I was perfectly happy to sit in the chairs and order coffee and read the magazines that were piled up in the salon. All the latest issues, French *Vogue* and English *Vogue*, French *Elle* and English *Elle*. One thing I really enjoyed about being pregnant was that you could look at pictures of beautiful, slender models without any sort of worry that you ought to be looking like that.

Paul went out with Chris and Alicia. They showed him everything, took him to all the restaurants everybody wants to go to in Paris. I was glad he was having such a good time. I thought it was great that for once he could mix business with really good company: friendship, almost. Chris spoke brilliant French and he was always teaching phrases to Paul, and saying how quickly Paul picked it up, that he had a real gift for languages and he ought to develop it. I sat there daydreaming by the little pool where the goldfish tickled my fingers if I kept them still enough, and I thought maybe we'd come here lots of times, and we'd look back on our first visit, with Chris and Alicia.

Paul learned a lot through that. He knew all about real villains, but he was still a bit naïve when it came to crooks like Chris. Both of us learned a lot, really. I realized it had nothing to do with money or education or background. Chris *had* to con you. It was much more important to him than sex, or even money, though you'd have thought money was the whole point of it. It wouldn't have mattered if you'd given Chris a million pounds, the next day he'd have started again. He *had* to have that moment when he knew he'd got you to trust him, and he could do what he liked with you. In a way he really did love you, just for that moment, because you'd let him have what he wanted. That second day in Paris, you'd have thought Paul was his brother.

We never went back to Paris, which was a pity, really, a whole city spoiled like that.

*

I don't hate Sonia. I feel sorry for her if you want the truth, though she'd never believe it. She looks down on me all right. Anything to hide from herself the fact that she's frightened, deep down, of all that me and Paul have had, and she'll never have.

I sent Anna some money with the letter. I told her to put it away in case she ever needed it. I meant, don't think because I don't come to see you that I'm not your mother any more. I made sure I wrote the letter in the morning, when I was feeling all right. Where's the use in upsetting her?

People think if you're a mother who doesn't have her kid living with her, then you must be some sort of devil. They think there's a reason. But I love Anna. Sometimes I think about the other mums in the hospital, and how we talked about everything. We knew we were all going back into our own lives, so it didn't matter what we said.

No. It wasn't really like that. The others were already making plans to get together after they got out. Get the babies together, have a coffee and a laugh. But I said nothing, because I knew with Paul it wouldn't work. He never wanted me having friends round to the house; not what I would call friends. People he was doing business with, yes. And their wives, too, so sometimes it could look almost like friendship. Couples coming and going and laughing. Like it did with Chris and Alicia.

I remember Paul, in Paris, going out through the courtyard with them, and waving back to me. When he came back he told me all about where they'd been, and what they'd eaten. I knew he'd have been watching Chris without seeming to, so he wouldn't make any mistakes. He sat on the side of the bed taking off his shoes and we were laughing and feeling great, as if we'd bought Paris all for ourselves.

But it turned out it was Paul's hundred thousand pounds Chris and Alicia were after. At first I said to myself it was just Chris, and she didn't know. I wanted to believe that, because she was nice to me about the baby. But I knew it was both of them, really. Alicia was part of what made people trust Chris, and they both understood that. He knew it happily, and she knew it unhappily, but that was the only difference between them. They were a couple of Judases. They should have stuck to money, but they had to mix it up with love.

I used to talk to Johnnie more than anyone. He was the closest friend I ever had. I could tell Johnnie anything. Paul didn't like it, because he wanted Johnnie to himself. That's why he bought the flat. It took me a long time to understand that. I thought he was jealous because of me, but it was the other way round. He was jealous because of Johnnie.

For a long time it frightened me, and when I'm not careful it still does. On a bad night, I keep seeing Anna in my arms in her yellow shawl, wrapped up tight the way the midwife taught me. And then I lift her up and put her into Paul's arms. Then I look from his arms to his face, and I see it isn't Paul, it's Johnnie. The way he's holding her isn't right, and I'm afraid he's going to drop her, so I hold out my arms to have her back. And he says in a voice which is half Paul's, and half Johnnie's: *You gave her to me. You can't have her back.*

Seventeen

That flat for Johnnie. The first time Paul went into it there was nothing. It was empty, with the smell of air that's been in prison. Flies on the window-sills, fag-ends on the floor. It'd been empty a long time. Nobody else'd seen what Paul saw, that this area was going to come up. The flat was a repossession. Paul had an instinct for changes in property values, the way other people have instincts for a change in the weather. He didn't know himself how he did it. He knew things. Information clung to him like dust on static. He knew when a sink school got a new head and suddenly the word was out among the parents that things were changing. He knew which way planning committees were bending over the route of a new road. He could have licked his finger, held it up in the air and told you which way the money was blowing. Except he didn't tell you. He bought.

The flat smelled of failure. Paul knew that smell and he hated it. He wanted to wipe it out. He didn't tell anybody else what he was doing, not even Louise. Buying another property, that was nothing to her. At the time he was going through with a deal to buy up fifteen ex-council flats. They had asbestos problems which made them unsuitable for direct sale to tenants. A job lot. He knew the problems and knew he'd sell the flats for three times what he'd paid, once the asbestos was sorted. The surveyor had done his bit, making the most of things, putting a spin on the costings.

This flat now, though, Johnnie's flat, this was something different. Plaster mouldings, cornices, beautiful wide floorboards under the cheap, felted carpet. There was a narrow kitchen, a bathroom with a cracked acrylic bath.

He wanted the place empty. He wanted it clean. He started coming to the flat every day, as if he was visiting a woman. The work went fast, with men diverted from the council flats to steam-strip layers of wallpaper, make good the walls and paste them with lining-paper. There was some replastering needed, not much. Most of it only wanted a skim. He skipped everything in the bathroom and kitchen, and started again: white cast-iron in the bathroom, plain, pale wood in the kitchen, new cooker, new fridge. Not that Johnnie cooked, but it all had to be there. He bought Italian tiles, hand-made, so you didn't come out with a dead block of colour staring at you across the room.

The place was taking shape. He paid the men a bonus and sent them back to the flats. He wanted to sand the floors himself, paint the walls, choose the rugs and sofa and bed. He was spending two or three hours there every evening, more at weekends. He told Louise he had a lot on, what with the flats and the negotiations on a former bonded warehouse with planning permission for conversion. For once, he didn't give a fuck if he got the warehouse or not. He was back where he started, making something out of nothing. The floors were as good as he'd thought. He hired the machine and sanded and sealed all through the flat. He'd forgotten it could be like this, the sun moving across the big empty windows, the jar of coffee and the jar of sugar, the cans of beer in the fridge. He had the radio on and he ate take-away sitting on the floor, his legs stretched in front of him, a fresh pack of cigarettes on the window-sill. It felt like home.

He spent an evening brushing the walls down, after the sanding was finished. This was the way he'd been when he started out, with the first house he'd bought, borrowing the money from Charlie Sullivan because no bank would look at him then. Charlie screwed him, and thought Paul was too green to know he was being screwed. That was his mistake. Paul worked all the hours God sent on the pissy little bedsits, the plasterboard partitioning, the crap plumbing and the electrics that hadn't been touched in forty years. He knew what he was after. Three two-bedroom flats, one of them a garden flat which could be sold at a five-thousand premium. The garden was a junkyard of broken concrete, old tyres, a dumped fridge, a dumped washing-machine. Paul didn't even look at it. There would be plenty of time for that at the end.

He borrowed more money off Charlie for labour and plant hire. He saw the smile Charlie didn't quite hide. At night he woke and counted the speed at which the debt was growing, then he got up and drove to the site and got working. There was always something that could be done. He knew what the kind of people who were going to buy his flats would want. He could see them as if they were standing in front of him with their wallets open: it was his vision. They wouldn't have much money once they'd signed the mortgage agreement, so they didn't want to buy work. They'd want everything to look finished, but they wouldn't notice detail the way he did. He could get away with cheap pine doors that were wrong for the house, as long as they were lime-washed, but there had to be a power shower, and as many work surfaces as he could cram into the narrow kitchens. He made sure Charlie came round to look at the house when it was at its worst.

'It's a big job you've taken on here, Paul,' said Charlie.

'It is,' said Paul. He let his fingers play with a cigarette. He cleared his throat. 'You don't need to worry about your money, Mr Sullivan.'

'I don't,' said Charlie. 'I never worry about my money. I know when it's safe.' And he showed his teeth again, in the way he thought was a smile.

The flats were done in seven months. Paul painted every

wall himself, in airy, neutral colours. He ran a 50 per cent wool, 50 per cent polypropylene carpet in a warm pinky-beige through all the flats, and in a darker shade down the common stairways. He carpeted the garden, unrolling slabs of green turf on to the cleared, levelled earth. And then the final touch: a huge terracotta pot full of trailing geraniums, visible from every window. He tore out the front garden with its mean privet hedge and sickly lawn, had it brick-paved for three cars. And he saw Charlie driving past, slowing down, looking hard. A dull, classy-looking terracotta paint on the front door, brass door furniture, plain white paint everywhere else. It was time to sell.

Paul was lucky. Property went on up, hand over hand, all the months he spent on the flats. Looking back, he felt frightened at the risk, but at the time he knew, he just knew it was right. Even when he felt dizzy calculating Charlie Sullivan's interest, there was never a doubt in his mind that he'd be able to pay it back. No, his doubts about Charlie Sullivan were of another kind.

And the buyers came, just as he knew they would. Young couple after young couple. He thought of them as young, though they were older than he was, but they were young in a way he'd never been. He wore a dark suit to meet them when the agent brought them to the house. He was slow, measured, a little reluctant, as if the privilege of owning one of these flats was something he was loath to part with. He didn't need to think about how to play it. There was one way, the right way, the way that was going to work. They looked at what he wanted them to look at. It wasn't real looking, anyway: it was a sort of grazing over what they knew from the first moment that they wanted. The price was right. High, but not greedy. And they could see, just looking around at the new electric sockets, the new radiators, the sparkling taps, that there'd be nothing more to pay. The work was done for them.

All three flats went in a week. He picked cash buyers. When

the money came through he went round to Charlie Sullivan to pay him off. He wasn't going to pay an extra day of Charlie's interest.

Charlie greeted him warmly. 'Nice job, Paul. Didn't I tell you you were on to a good thing there?'

'I've got your money, Mr Sullivan.'

He counted it out in front of Charlie Sullivan, note by note. Thousands and thousands and thousands of pounds. But less than half of what he'd made, and by now Charlie knew it.

'There's something missing,' said Charlie at the end, after he'd signed off the debt.

'Is there, Mr Sullivan?'

'It's what we call goodwill, in the trade. I've given you your start, Paul. You need your goodwill if you're going to get on in a business like yours.'

'You do, Mr Sullivan. I'll be back tomorrow.'

'You and me should be partners,' said Charlie, turning his back.

Money buys all sorts of things. Paul knew that now. He went to a club where he knew he'd find the man he wanted.

'I want you to do something for me,' he said.

'What's that, then?'

'It's a little bit of veterinary work. You know Charlie Sullivan?'

The man rested his cue on his forearm, let it sway and balance there. 'Yeah?'

'He's got a little dog. Cocker spaniel.'

'I've no objection.'

'I want you to get hold of it.'

'Could be tricky.'

'Could be a very fair price.'

'What's a fair price?'

'A grand.'

'A grand for Charlie Sullivan's cocker spaniel? You're barking.'

'I don't want it. I want you to break its legs.'

'What, all of them?'

'That's right. Then put it somewhere he'll find it. And you write something I tell you on a label and tie it on its collar. Very fond of his cocker spaniel is Charlie, or so I hear.'

'How'll I get at it?'

'He leaves the dog in his car when he goes shopping.'

'Listen, mate, I'm an animal-lover, me.'

'You can give the money to the RSPCA then, can't you?'

'What do you want me to write?'

'Goodwill.'

And now he was doing up the flat for Johnnie. It felt good. He'd forgotten how good it felt to make something out of nothing. Every time he loaded a roller with paint, his mother's flat in Grays grew fainter, like a moon in daylight. Everything was gone, all the dirt and crap and disappointment. It was perfect. He'd paid for Johnnie's flat in cash, he'd already paid off the men who worked on it, he'd bought and swept and cleared and let the light come in. It was a start: the start he'd never had. Doing it for Johnnie was better than doing it for himself.

All the time he worked, in some part of him, he thought about Johnnie opening the door and seeing it for the first time. It was unlucky to think about things like that too much, because they never worked out the way you pictured them. He knew it. He wasn't after gratitude, anyway. Sometimes, in Paul's mind, he'd drive Johnnie to the flat, stop the car, get out as if it was a building Paul was interested in, that's all. And then he'd open the door and somehow he'd get Johnnie to go first up the stairway, and then he'd snick the key in the lock and push the door wide so all the light poured through into the hallway. And he'd stay there, holding the door, watching while Johnnie went on in. He wouldn't say anything.

Other times Paul thought it would be better to let Johnnie come alone. He'd hand Johnnie a piece of paper with the address on it, toss him the keys. 'Go on, go and take a look. It's yours. Anything you don't like, we can change it.'

He painted the walls in shades of white. The place looked bigger than ever. He bought a couple of rugs, one for the bedroom, one for the lounge. He bought a huge bronze-framed mirror and hung it over the fireplace. He went looking at chairs and tables and sofas; he even lay full-length on beds in John Lewis, bouncing a little, feeling the give. Then he thought of something better, and wrote a cheque and put it in an envelope with Johnnie's name on it, in the middle of the dark green Chinese rug. It was time to go.

It was time, but he didn't want to let go. He kept finding little jobs to do. He went out, bought dusters and Windolene, cleaned the mirror. He tidied away the coffee jar, wiped the spills of milk inside the fridge. It was getting silly. Then he just stood, watching the dark come.

As soon as Johnnie stood in the flat, Paul knew that he'd been stupid. The best part was always going to be before Johnnie came, why hadn't he realized that? Johnnie'd been on his way out somewhere when Paul called. He hadn't wanted to let Johnnie know what was going on.

'There's this flat I need you to see, Johnnie. It's got potential. It'll only take half an hour.'

'I can't, I've got to meet this guy at four. He's Dutch, he's only over here till tomorrow morning.'

'Hasn't he got a mobile?' Because they all had fucking mobiles, Paul knew that.

Johnnie's eyes flickered minutely. No one else would have

noticed. Paul had to give it to him, Johnnie thought as quick as fish swam.

'I can't muck him about, Paul.'

'Half an hour. That's all it'll take,' Paul persisted, letting go of the weeks and weeks, the smell of paint and sanded wood and sealant, the smell of yeast coming up from a beer can when the aluminium tab tears. Letting go of big shadows on pale walls, and the slash of cars going by through the rain, and the noise of someone whistling which he heard before he knew it was himself. Letting go of the warmest, most secret pleasure he'd ever given himself: giving it to Johnnie.

Johnnie knew about gratitude. He knew what was wanted and he did it all, inside half an hour. Paul looked back from the doorway as they went out of the door, and there were the keys which Johnnie had forgotten to pick up. But the white envelope with the cheque in it was gone.

'Here, Johnnie,' he said, 'you forgot these.'

That flicker again, that fast look in Johnnie's eyes as he juggled with giving Paul what he wanted, just as he always gave everybody what they wanted, as long as he was with them. And then Johnnie looked back, too, over his shoulder, into the flat that was as fresh and bright as a nursery for a new baby. He looked at the flat, then he turned to Paul, his face six inches away, his eyes warm and eager, bright as new money. And Paul knew as if the words were written on the wall that Johnnie would sell the flat. He said quickly, lyingly, 'There was a problem with the title. It'll take a while to get the deeds transferred into your name. But it's yours, you know that.'

He calculated that Johnnie wouldn't check it. It wasn't Johnnie's kind of information. But against his will, without knowing the words were going to come, he heard himself ask, 'You like it?'

And Johnnie said, 'It's got class.'

'That's right,' Paul said. 'You can make anything you want out of it.' And he watched Johnnie closely, to see if he'd got the message. *Listen*, he wanted to say, *you see what I'm giving you?*

But he didn't. He thought of the cheque, already translated into something else in Johnnie's imagination. He knew he'd been stupid, but there was no way of wishing it back.

Eighteen

Anna kneels by a patch of raw earth. She pats it down with the palms of her hands. At her side is a pile of flowers: twigs of forsythia and flowering currant, wild daffodils. She begins to stick the flowers into the earth, making the shape of a cross. Above her head a blackbird bobs and sways on its branch. She frowns, shoves back a wing of hair, then packs the spaces between twigs with loose yellow flowers of forsythia.

The sun warms Anna's pale neck. She sits back on her heels and looks straight up at the clear sky. She peels off her sweatshirt, rubs her bare arms against her face, snuffs her skin, licks it. An early bee swings low, staggering through the spring air on its first flight. Johnnie's gone. She still has the letter from her mother, warm and soft with the warmth of her body. The paper doesn't crackle any more. She's always known that open-ing letters and getting messages means trouble.

The dead kitten lies under the earth where no one can see it. It was still and stiff this morning, rolled away into the corner of the box. For a moment she didn't recognize it as a kitten. She thought it was something else that had got into the box. When she picked it up it was stiff and light. Its eyes were still shut, so she didn't have to close them, the way she had read in books that you had to close people's eyes when they died. Suddenly the touch of it made her skin crawl. She dropped it behind a pile of logs, and ran off to get a cornflakes box to bury it in. But the box was much too big. Inside it, the kitten looked like an unwanted give-away toy. She fetched scissors and cut the box down until it was just big enough for the kitten, then she made herself settle it inside, on a bed of folded tissues.

She folded more tissues on top until no one would know there was a kitten in the box.

The spirit of the funeral goes out of her halfway through. With David there she could have kept it up, but on her own it's flat. Even the cross of flowers is only something she's thought up and now has to finish. The kitten's gone. The rest are going to die now, one by one. Johnnie was right, it was better to let them die before they knew they were alive.

Anna shivers, and reaches for her sweatshirt. She puts it on, but it's cold from lying on the earth. She sits back on her heels and surveys the bare, flowery soil. It looks stupid. Quickly she stands up, and with her heel she grinds the flowers into the dirt.

Johnnie's gone. Paul makes phone calls, sends faxes, e-mails. In the wake of Johnnie's going, he needs to feel his money move. Roy can go down to Swindon instead of Johnnie. He should have gone in the first place. Paul should never have given the job to Johnnie, who knows nothing of heavy-metal contamination and cares less. The surveyor was all set up. Stupid. It cuts at Paul, because there's nowhere else in his life he'd do anything like that. Only in that place which belongs to Johnnie.

His computer screens swarm with figures. He likes e-mail. You know it's there, but you can choose just when to do something about it. People call him all the time, letting him know they've done what they are meant to do. Some he'll answer, some he'll leave for a while, some have to learn that what they've done doesn't require answers. His expectations are high. He doesn't go around slapping people on the back for doing what they're supposed to do. But he knows when to give praise that's like a message, showing he knew all along, he was aware of everything. Business, it's a matter of rhythm. If you've got it you don't need to keep thinking about it. When Paul finds himself doing something without knowing why, he just does it. He'll turn up on a site, not knowing quite why. Follow his nose, drift here, drift there. See whose eyes are watching him, who looks anxious. There are plenty of fiddles and he knows them all. But more important than that he knows which ones to let through, and which ones to come down on like a hammer. Nobody frightens him. There's nobody he can't do without.

He sits back with a sigh. Everything's OK. His business of profits and secrets is intact. He rubs his fists into his eyes and swivels the chair round so it faces the window. Then he stands. The huge landscape unrolls inside the oblong of his window, making him dizzy. You could never buy a view like this. You could never turn it into property. You could despoil it, that's all. He thinks of the scarred and stinking land he buys cheap and sells dear, where gasworks have stood, and factories. Carving into clean green ground, that's where the money is, some developers say. That's because they've got no imagination.

He looks down. There she is, so strange from this height that he almost fails to know her. Anna. He watches as she walks slowly along the path, her hair blowing, her head bent, her arms couched, carrying something.

She went into the barn expecting to bury the last kitten. But the kitten in the box is alive. It keeps on being alive. The others are gone, flipped into their quickly dug holes. She couldn't do any more funerals when they died so quickly, all within an hour of the first.

But this one is alive. Anna challenges it. She won't conjure the end of the dropper into its mouth. She lets the little thing squirm until it finds a blob of milk shivering right at the end of the glass bulb. Suddenly the milk isn't running out of its mouth any more. The level in the glass tube shrinks, pulse by pulse, as the kitten swallows, sneezes, swallows again.

Anna heaps the box with cotton-wool, stolen from Sonia's

careful store-cupboard. She knows it isn't safe to leave the kitten in the barn any more. Now that it's really alive, that's when a rat will get it. She waits, checking the paths. Everything is silent in the pale sun. Sonia's car isn't in the drive: Anna thinks she's gone riding. Head down, body curved over the top of the box, she scurries from the barn to the back door.

Away at the stables, Sonia rides a white horse which she has learned to call grey. In her boots and jodhpurs she looks much as Johnnie has imagined, but he hasn't imagined the way she's laughing at something one of the other riders calls across to her, nor has he imagined the way a strand of her pale hair comes loose and strokes her cheek and her neck. Shadows fly over the paddock where Sonia is learning to ride. The big, mild mare, chosen for her lack of temperament, seems suddenly to understand every turn of Sonia's thoughts, and change it into movement. For the first time, Sonia rises to the trot, and there she is, circling the paddock, cheeks bright, eyes fiercely ahead, intoxicated.

Nineteen

I'm not saying I didn't expect him. Johnnie, I mean. It never seems strange when he comes, it seems natural. He fits in. There's only me to fit in with, I know, but two people make the most difficult jigsaws.

'Johnnie,' I say. He's standing in the doorway with the sun behind him. He has his own key, just like he's always had his own key, wherever I've been. And he looks as if he's just stepped out of a storm, even though everything's perfect. Leather jacket, soft deep-blue cotton shirt, jeans. Johnnie knows how to wear his clothes.

So I say, 'I've been thinking of plastic surgery. I've been to see a surgeon, but I wasn't very impressed.' He just laughs.

'Have you got a drink?' he asks. That's nice. Johnnie would never, ever, rub your face in it. As if to say that he knows you must have a houseful of drink, because drinking is what you do. And as it happens I haven't had a drink all morning, so I say, 'I was going to make some coffee. I'll put you a brandy in yours.'

Which I do. It's easy to tell there's something wrong, but I say nothing. We sit down, me on the sofa, him on the wicker chair Paul hates, that creaks every time you open your mouth. I put the brandy bottle down beside him.

'You don't need plastic surgery,' he says. 'You shouldn't change yourself.' His face is completely serious.

'I want to recapture my lost youth,' I say.

'You might as well take a carving knife to yourself,' he says. He drinks the coffee steadily, quite fast.

'I know; I'm not going to do it,' I say. 'The consultant put

144

me off. I thought that if he couldn't take the trouble to hide what he thought of me, then he might be careless all round.'

'You don't care what people think of you, do you?'

'Not really,' I say, without stopping to think whether it's true or not.

He looks pleased, as if I've confirmed something he wants to believe about me. He wants me to be careless. Lucky I didn't add that I care what I think of myself. That's what eats at me.

'Did you see her?' I ask.

'Course I saw her.'

'I meant, did you give her the letter?'

'Yeah. And the money was still in the envelope, in case you were wondering.'

He looks dead tired. He reaches down, unscrews the top of the brandy bottle and knocks a splash of it into his coffee. But drinking's not really Johnnie's thing.

'How was she?'

'All right.' He smiles. 'She's got some kittens.'

'My God, I bet she has. Not much else for her to do up there.'

'It's not Nova Scotia, Lou.'

A bit of an odd expression, but I let it go.

'What did she say?' I ask.

'She sent her love.'

I look him over. Johnnie'll say anything sometimes, if he thinks it's what you want to hear.

'It wasn't real plastic surgery I was thinking of,' I say, 'just liposuction.'

'What's that?'

I stretch out my arms as if I'm hugging a whale, then slowly bring them in. 'They suck your fat out and make you slim.' But as I say it I realize this is one of those days when I don't feel fat at all. I feel sleek and rich, like a whale who can beat anything on earth once it gets into the water. The only problem comes when it beaches itself. It isn't just missing the sea, or not being able to move. The whale can't carry its weight out of water.

'Don't do it,' says Johnnie. He stands up and rubs his hands down the side seams of his jeans, a funny gesture, nervous, not like Johnnie at all. He's always so easy in his skin and in his clothes. 'She wants to see you,' he says. 'I can tell she does.'

'Did she say so?'

'Not in so many words.'

'What about Paul?'

That's something else we do. We talk about Paul. Or at least, I do. With Johnnie, Paul is real, still here, still part of my life. And I'm still part of his. When you come to think of it, Johnnie is the only person I can really talk to about Paul.

'Still making money,' says Johnnie.

'Don't knock it. He's been very good to you.'

Johnnie shrugs, more like a twitch, throwing something off. 'Listen, Lulu, I'm going away for a while.'

He hasn't called me that for a long time. It goes back to when Anna was born. He used to call us Annie and Lulu. He'd come in with his arms full of stuff, flowers and toys which were way too old for her, a big box of glacé fruit for me because he knew I loved it. He'd dump it on the bed and ask, 'How's my Annie?' and after that, 'How's my Lulu?'

He was very good with the baby. He was never frightened of her, the way Paul was. Then I thought about it and I realized this was because Johnnie didn't think Anna was his responsibility. He was always playing with her. Anna wasn't a laughing baby, but Johnnie found out that if he swung her up and balanced her on top of his head, that would always make her laugh. Unwilling, wheezy laughter as if she didn't really know how to do it but she couldn't help herself. Paul used to watch them, and he'd have a smile of pleasure curling on his lips, but I was never quite sure.

'Don't go,' I say to Johnnie now. I look straight at him. I

play a lot of games with Johnnie, but this isn't one of them. 'Listen,' I say, getting up from the sofa, 'you sit down here. Get the sun on your face while I make some fresh coffee. I can do you a meal if you like.' But he won't change places with me.

'I'm all right,' he says. 'But I've got to go.'

He's frightened. It's not hard to tell that. He's mucked something up and in the field where he's been playing that's bad news. I feel a tight pain in my stomach, as if I've eaten something bad. I pour a little of the brandy into a glass for myself, and sip at it. The tight place begins to loosen. Johnnie's watching me.

'I thought you said you were making coffee.'

'I am.'

It was such a little drink and now it's gone. I pick up the bottle and take it with me to tidy it away. I bang around in the kitchen getting the coffee-maker ready and trying to find where I'd put the coffee.

'It'll be in the fridge,' Johnnie says. Suddenly he's in the kitchen doorway. 'You always keep it in the fridge.'

I put down my glass and swing the fridge door open. There it is, the top folded over and fixed tight with a peg. Sometimes I astonish myself, how organized I am.

Johnnie says, 'Why don't you go out more?'

This isn't the kind of thing Johnnie and I talk about. I get busy measuring coffee into the coffee-maker.

'I don't like the traffic. This part of London's a nightmare.'

'You can walk to the park from here,' he says.

I think of Anna. The park is a child's place, and I don't go there any more. I think of Anna when it was nearly dark, with her face shining out of her hood, on the swings, swooping up into the dark so I could hardly see her. Then back again, down, to the touch of my hands.

'Push me harder,' she said. She never yelled and screamed

when the swing flew up, she wasn't that sort of child. In the winter the park has a smell I can't describe. And Anna's skin, cold and sweet as fruit, not like our skin.

'I don't like the park,' I say to Johnnie. 'Tell me where you're going.'

'Abroad,' he says.

'You going to give me a bit more detail?'

He smiles. 'You're better off without it,' he said.

'In case Paul asks?'

'In case anybody asks.'

'Well, he is my husband. He's entitled to know.'

'Lulu, he's married to Sonia.'

'That's a pack of cards.'

'You mean a pack of lies.'

'No, I don't,' I say. I know what I wanted to say. Paul and Sonia, they've bought this big stone house in Yorkshire, twice the size of our house in London. And they've got Anna there. But that doesn't make it the truth about what's happened between us all. 'It's a house of cards,' I say. It's the best I could do with the brandy swirling in my head. 'You don't know about marriage, Johnnie. You've never been married.'

'I know about you and Paul,' says Johnnie.

'You know too much,' I say quickly, sharply. Then I remember myself and turn straight to Johnnie. 'You know I'm right, don't you? He's my husband. Anna's our daughter. You're my brother-in-law.'

'Yeah,' says Johnnie. He let the word out in a long, tired breath. 'Yeah. Don't have another drink, Lulu. I need you to stay here.'

'I'm here.' I sit down. 'Listen, Johnnie, I went to see your mum last week.'

He looks so weary. I almost say to him, *Don't keep talking here. Go on in my bedroom, lie down and I'll put the quilt over you. Have a little sleep. Don't worry, I'll still be here when you wake up.*

I love daylight sleep. First of all there are the hours it eats, that you never have to live. Yet all the time you're aware of time passing, and you hear the noises of outside like speeded-up music. Traffic thinning then thickening again, children on their way home from school, doors slamming. And even right in the middle of London the birds sing fiercely at dusk, so you know when to get up. I could keep Johnnie safe here, between my Egyptian cotton sheets, under my quilt, deep in the bedroom with the blinds drawn down and the inner door locked as well as the outer. But I know as well as he does that doors don't mean anything, or locks either, if you're really in trouble.

Johnnie's eyes are almost closed. If you didn't know him you might think he was completely relaxed. Then he says, 'I've got debts.'

'What sort of debts?'

'The kind I can't pay.'

'How much?'

He shrugs, as if he doesn't know. I'm thinking fast, about my bank account and what's in it now I've sent the grand to Anna. About the flat and what it's worth.

'You ought to tell Paul,' I say.

'No.'

'He'd help you.'

'I've had enough of his money. That's why I'm going away.'

'Don't be stupid.'

He opens his eyes a little, gives me a cat-like, squeezed smile. 'It's not just the money anyway. There's other stuff.'

There always is, I think, but I don't say it. I think of the way knives cut and the flesh doesn't seem to notice it for a moment, then all at once the blood wells up. I must have been mad, thinking I could let some man cut me. I feel sick at the thought of it now. I want the results without the pain. I'm a bit like Johnnie, that's my problem.

'How was Mum?' asks Johnnie.

'There's a new nurse she likes. We didn't talk much, we just sat. That's what she prefers.'

We sat in the conservatory. The people who run the home are wonderful with plants. There was gardenia, and big troughs of hyacinths. It smelled like heaven. I was a bit worried about Maureen because she doesn't like certain flowers. They upset her. It's as if, with some of her senses going, others have developed until they are sharp as razors. But she was smiling and her hands lay quite still and loose in her lap. I hate it when she washes her hands, over and over, as if the job's never done. And then she reached out and covered my hand with hers, as if she knew me. As if she hadn't forgotten anything.

'She was all right,' I say. He doesn't go and see her, but he likes to hear about her. 'Listen,' I say, 'I'm going to make you something to eat before you go.'

Twenty

I send Johnnie out to the French bakery on the corner, for some bread. I want to keep him here for a bit longer, but when I look out from the window and see him walking away down the street, I'm suddenly sure he won't come back. The back of his head looks so final, like an extra in a film, pushing forward through a crowd.

Now the street is empty. I pull up the lower sash window, and lean out. There are white patches on the trunks of the plane trees opposite, where the bark's peeled off. They're clever trees. All the poison goes into the bark, then they get rid of it and grow a new skin. There'd be no need for plastic surgeons, if we could do that. I look up at the London-coloured sky. Then a car goes by, a new black Saab.

That was Johnnie's car. A black Saab, turbo. When Anna was a baby he used to come and take us out for the day in it. Johnnie had time on his hands, and we never saw Paul from seven in the morning to seven at night. If then.

One day we went to the sea. It was grey and quiet, the kind of day that seems like nothing when you look at it from inside a house, but it's beautiful once you are out in it. The beach was pebbly and I sat Anna up on a rug and let her put stones in her bucket, then take them out again. She didn't try to put them in her mouth: she was always good like that. Then I lay back and the whiteness of the sky felt like sun on my eyelids, even though the sun never came out all day. Lying like that, low down, it was warm. I could feel myself falling into sleep. I was always ready for sleep, because Anna still woke at night.

I felt Johnnie's shadow swoop down and block the light, then he said, 'I'll take her for a walk.'

He slung her up on his shoulders and she twisted her hands into his hair and held on tight. She loved it. Anna was a serious little baby, but she was laughing up there on Johnnie's shoulders. I squinted and watched them walk off, Johnnie loping along to make her bump up and down and laugh more. He was going to show her the sea. She hadn't seen it before. I closed my eyes and I could hear them through the distant noise of water: Anna's voice cheeping, Johnnie's deep. He sounded young too, like her. Sometimes I forgot with Johnnie how young he was. I must have fallen asleep, because when I next looked up there they were beside me, Anna bolt upright with the straight back babies have, eating an ice cream, and Johnnie smiling. I was surprised at myself, falling asleep when Anna was with someone else. I hadn't been worried for a second, and I was always worried over Anna, even when she was with Paul. It felt as if they were both my children, and I loved them just the same.

Then we went back. Johnnie hadn't had the car long, and it was too powerful for him. We drove fast, but I didn't mind that. Anna was asleep in her seat in the back. We went past a harbourside pub that backed on to the water, and Johnnie said we ought to stop for a drink. I didn't want to disturb Anna so he brought the drinks out and we stood by the car, watching the water. It was nearly dark, not quite. He wanted to get another but I said no, we ought to get back. I was worried in case Paul came home and we weren't there. I think Johnnie must have been angry about that, though he didn't say anything. We got back in the car, and he turned the lights on and all at once it was night, with the lights of the harbour behind us and the pub ahead. It wasn't a real car-park, just the quayside, with no barrier between us and the water. But we weren't parked right by the edge. I was relieved, though I didn't say anything.

We were about ten yards from the edge of the quay. Johnnie revved the engine. He looked at me. I thought it was one of those 'We're off again' looks, so I smiled, and then he smiled back. And that was it. Nothing. No reason.

Johnnie put the car into reverse and pushed his foot down on the accelerator. I didn't see what he was doing but I saw the way the other cars shot away forward instead of backward like they should have done. I was thrown back in the seat. I saw the lights as if they were being sucked past me. I was too frightened to scream. And then he stamped his foot on the brake. The car was big, it was heavy, it was powerful. Even so I could see what might happen, what would surely have happened with any lighter car. I could see it slewing round, the wheels losing the quayside, the body of the car grappling then falling and all of us with it, sliding down deep under the water and into the harbour mud that never lets go.

It didn't happen. The car stopped. Johnnie stopped. He put on the hand-brake and turned off the engine. But I wasn't looking at him. I was twisted round, reaching for Anna. She'd woken, and I could see her eyes shining even though there wasn't much light. Her face was clear, not frightened, not crying. I was halfway over the seat and grabbing at the release catch. I had her out of her seat and clutched to me and I was out of the car in one movement.

The back wheels were a few inches from the edge of the quay. What I thought was, *Why didn't they put something there?* It was as if I was afraid to blame Johnnie, or really believe that he could have taken such a risk, with Anna in the car. I held Anna tight and I looked down into the water. It was rocking, so you saw the tremor of light on top of it. You couldn't see past the surface. The water looked as if it was calming itself.

I thought if I could look down far enough, if I could see inside the water, I'd see myself. I'd be looking up, but the weight of water would press me down. If it wasn't for those few inches of quay behind the wheels, that's where we'd be. I couldn't feel Anna, even though she was in my arms. I was shivering. It had so nearly happened, and I couldn't shake off the feeling that the fall we'd nearly fallen was the truth. I could feel the plunge and the cold water closing round us. Somewhere under the water there was the car, and Anna's car seat with the straps swaying like weed.

There are some moments when you know more than you can understand. You could call it a vision. In the vision I saw Anna, but she wasn't with me any more. She was somewhere else, somewhere safer, without me.

Johnnie had got out of the car too. He looked at me, his face blank and bright in the neon. I said, 'Get the car back on the road, Johnnie, and we'll go home.'

We drove home, Anna sleeping, Johnnie silent. I think he was waiting for me to say something, but I didn't. I wanted to be home with Anna in her cot, and me in a deep bath, washing the day off. But I knew it wouldn't come off. I was stained by it, and Johnnie too. All the things we hadn't said, and all the silent lies we'd told, to Paul and to ourselves. And to Anna too. I thought of her face all the way home. She would have kept on believing in me even as we all went down into the water together.

I'm still at the window, playing that day through in my head, when I see Johnnie coming back with the bread tucked under his arm. He doesn't know I'm watching. He stops under one of the plane trees, takes his mobile out of his pocket, gets a number. His face is tight and frowning. He waits, but nobody answers. He stares down at the phone for a long moment, then pushes it back into his pocket.

I cut the bread, and lay the cheeses out. Johnnie's looking over my shoulder, and he can't believe how empty my fridge is. It always used to be packed with everything he liked. I used to make fresh vegetable and fruit purées for the baby, and my own tomato sauce. The cheeses are a bit old, but they still look all right. Sometimes it gets to about six o'clock and I can't remember if I've eaten anything all day, or not. I don't get hungry.

I pour us gin-and-tonics. I wish I had some lemon, but I'm no good with lemons. I forget about them, and they go dead on me in the fruit-bowl.

'Nice gin,' Johnnie says, putting down his empty glass. I pour some more and it goes flashing down the side of his glass. He hasn't touched his food.

'You should eat, with a journey in front of you,' I say.

'I'll eat on the boat,' he says, absently, as if he doesn't know what he is saying.

'Where's the boat going?' I ask.

He smiles at me, a *You think you've caught me out, don't you?* smile.

'I haven't made my mind up yet,' he says. 'I might go to Denmark.' I can't think why he'd be going there. Well, I can. There've been enough boats in the past, with Johnnie. 'Don't look like that. It's a ferry,' he says. 'We sail from Harwich tomorrow morning.'

'They used to go from Tilbury,' I say, remembering.

'That's all finished.'

'I liked Tilbury.'

I did, too. My dad used to take me down there, to show me the river. We watched the boats going out, slipping out on a cold, greasy November day, in the fag-end of the afternoon. The river's wide there, and strong, and brown. It's rucked up with currents like a dress a girl's worn all night, and come home in.

I stood with Dad and watched the tide turn. He told me it went out past Sheerness and Shoeburyness, past Sheppey and Canvey and the Isle of Grain. I used to listen to him with half my mind while I watched rubbish and orange boxes spinning round on the current.

'That's on its way out to sea,' he said. 'It'll get smashed up in the shipping lanes.'

I looked down and there was weed and polystyrene and rags of plastic bobbing in the water. It went in and out, in and out, but never far enough out. Like breathing. Like what Paul told me about his dad breathing. It would never escape. There was mud under the wall and it looked velvety soft, but it stank.

Dad said that was how he found our terrier bitch. He saw her swimming downstream, a little bitch miles from home, paddling hard. She was snapping at the current as if she thought she was in a fight. She wasn't ours then, of course. Dad knew someone who kept a boat down there, and he got the engine going and brought our terrier back. Bloody silly thing to do with the tide on the turn, he told me, to make sure I'd never do anything like it. I wasn't with him when he found our terrier, and I always wished I had been. He got her into the boat. She was still snapping at him but when he laid her down on the planks at the bottom she seemed to know that he wasn't going to hurt her. She shivered and shivered, until he got her back in to land and rubbed her dry on a bit of sacking.

When he got her cleaned up she was a nice little bitch. Nice nature, too. She never snapped at us in all the years we had her. Most likely someone had chucked her in. It was the way she was swimming that got him, as if she thought any minute she'd find a grassy bank and scramble up and dry herself and go off home again. She had no idea that someone had dumped her in the dirty old Thames, hoping she'd be dragged out to sea with the rest of the junk nobody wanted, and drowned. I like to think of my dad going after her. Mum said it was stupid and irresponsible: it was the only time I heard her shout at him. *You might have been killed, and then what would I have done? It isn't just your life you have to consider, it's mine and Louise's.*

I used to watch the cranes poking into the sky, and the sun hiding in the fog, and wonder if we'd ever find another dog to be a companion for Sheppey, but we never did.

Isle of Sheppey, Canvey, Isle of Grain. I can hear Dad's voice now, saying the names. He told me how big the river looks when you're out in the middle of it, and about the pilots who guide the big ships down the river. He said the mudbanks and sandbanks and currents changed all the time. *Look at the strength of that current, fighting the tide.*

'You won't stay there long,' I say to Johnnie. 'In Denmark.' I pour us another gin. Gin is the most beautiful thing to watch when it's flowing. It's like water, only more alive.

'I'm not coming back,' he says.

I feel as if he's dropped something in my lap, heavy as a gun wrapped in grease and newspaper. I believe him as soon as he says the words, even though I don't know what's behind them. And I'm terribly afraid. I know I've got to keep him here, but I can't think fast enough. Even to me, my voice sounds slurred as I say, 'You mustn't do that.'

'I've got to.'

'Is someone looking for you?'

Johnnie stands up, swirls his drink in a circle round his glass. He's working out how to tell me about a tenth of what there is to know. I don't want to hear it. Being told lies makes me tired, and anyway it's a waste of time when the important thing is to stop Johnnie going off. I know enough about how certain people behave when you owe them money not to need any further information. I wish I hadn't had the second gin.

'Listen,' I say, 'I've got an idea. I'll go with you.'

'You can't do that.'

'Why not? Course I can. I haven't got anything to keep me here, have I?'

He looks at me, the thoughts clicking up fast.

'I've got some money,' I add. 'Not a lot, but I can get hold of five thousand. That ought to take us somewhere worth going.'

'What would Paul say, if I got you mixed up in all this?'

'What's he going to say if you go off to Denmark and never come back?'

'I'd sell the flat,' Johnnie says, 'but it takes time.'

'You don't need that much money. All you need is to get away somewhere for a while and calm down and work out what you're going to do. And it's easier to do that if you've got someone with you.'

I was going to say 'someone you can trust', but it sounded such a cliché that I couldn't bring the words out. Also, I know Paul will have run me down in the trust stakes. I have got to be very careful, or Johnnie will be off and out of the door. I am not quite sure how long he's been here. Things slow down when you've been drinking, or else they speed up.

'We'll go to Brighton,' I say. It feels like an inspiration. 'We'll go to Brighton for a few days, and we'll keep our heads down while I get the money organized.'

'I don't want to stay in an hotel. It's too public.'

'We'll get a place of our own. This time of the year we can get a holiday let, there'll be no problem.'

I'm thinking so fast it's like a dream. In my mind I have the blinds drawn down and the answering machine winking, and we're already on the platform at Victoria.

'Just let me put a few things in a bag,' I say. And he's looking at me and his face is changing and growing softer, less certain. He doesn't quite dare let himself hope yet, but soon he will. He'll believe that I know what I'm talking about, and that I can get him out of all this mess he's got himself into, and then when he wants to he can start it all again. I smile, as if to say, *It'll be fine.* And he wants to believe me so much that he smiles back.

'I've always liked Brighton,' I say. 'Make us some black coffee, Johnnie, while I get my things together.'

I go into my bedroom and start pulling drawers open. I can't believe how excited I feel. For the first time in years I want the black coffee. I want to be sober. I know I am smiling.

Once, when I was cross with Anna, a long time ago, she said, 'Be happy. I don't like it when you look at me with that face.'

She made me laugh. We were all curled up on the sofa together, and she sang me a song she'd learned at school, one I didn't know. She kept twining her hand in my hair: she loved that. Then she said, 'I dreamed you lost me.'

'I wouldn't do that. Mums don't lose their children.'

'Sometimes they do.'

'It was only a dream.'

She had her legs tucked up in my lap. She always had long, narrow feet, ever since she was born. I couldn't get shoes to fit her in the shops. We had to order them. I tickled the sole of her foot, and her toes curled round my finger, and she was laughing. I knew how nervous she was, and how hard she took life sometimes. But I could still make her happy, and that was a wonderful feeling.

Twenty-one

Seven o'clock. A perfect morning, still and pale. The West Pier floats in mist on a flat silver sea, and beyond it the Palace Pier catches a stroke of early sun. Down on the path that runs across the lawns two whippets dance round their owner. He stands with his arms folded over his chest, waiting for them to calm down and crap on the grass. He's poised on roller-blades, his arms folded over his chest, naked but for his shorts.

It's only April, but the air is warm as you step out on to the balcony in your kimono. A freak early summer, filling the beaches with bodies. People lie in the lee of the breakwaters, getting up sometimes to look out to sea, their hands over their eyes, smiling. The whole beach shares that secret smile. *You wouldn't believe it was April, would you?* It's a gift, a string of days which you'll always remember. You buy the papers, and all the mischief of the world has been pushed off the front pages by the sun.

The whippets leap around their master and he pushes off, one blade, then another, with the perfect balance of a clergyman on ice. He's going fast. Round by the bike path, down on to the promenade and still gathering speed.

You used to roller-skate from dawn to dusk, tightening the metal nuts in the metal plate on the base of the skates, knotting the laces that snapped when you tugged them too hard. Those roller-skates were crude compared to the technology they have nowadays. Look at him, almost out of sight. But you loved it, on your skates all day so that when you had to take them off and come indoors you found yourself skating along the kitchen lino.

It was lucky getting this flat. It wasn't the first one the girl at the letting agency thought of as she scrolled down her computer screen. There was a modern flat in a block near Churchill Square, but you didn't fancy it from the photo. Too like London. *It's on the sixteenth floor*, she said, *you'll have fantastic views*. Or down the other end, they had a second-floor flat in Marine Parade. Or this –

This. Where you are now. The flat belonged to two sisters who died, one after the other, in June and August of last year. The heirs don't want to sell yet. They're waiting for property prices to rise, and they're going to have some work done on the place, too, at the end of the summer. Meanwhile here it is, with most of the old ladies' clutter moved out to reveal the big high rooms, the marble fireplaces, the walls in their various shades of white. You've got a kitchen and a sitting-room facing the sea, and the huge bedroom the sisters shared. But it's a new bed, the letting agent assured you, knowing that you would think of the sisters dying there one by one. A king-size bed anchored into the centre of mirrors, marble, and a sheet of window looking over the complicated backs of houses.

You've taken the place for a month, paid in advance. You paid in cash. You've got sets of keys for the outer door and the three locks on the inner door. The old ladies were careful with locks and spy-holes, and the flat is on the second floor, so it's not overlooked. It feels as private as a nest in the side of a cliff.

After she'd finished showing you everything, the letting agent stood in the middle of the sitting-room, looking around. Suddenly a doubt seized her. You saw it and thought it was about you. Johnnie wasn't there, he was waiting in a café down the road, with the newspaper. You both thought it was better if he didn't have anything to do with the letting people. 'There's just the two of us,' you said. Did you look like the wrong sort of tenant, were you too eager, could she tell how much you wanted the flat?

She couldn't. 'Now you come to look at it,' she said, 'there's not much furniture in here, is there? But we could always bring you along a few more chairs, and another sofa.'

'No,' you said quickly. 'No, it's fine. We like the space.'

You like what has been taken away. There's no sense of former lives here, only of a flat like a ship's prow pointed over lawns and sea. It floated there in the lovely white morning while the letting agent stood with her clipboard and computer printout.

'The kitchen's pretty basic, I'm afraid.'

'We'll probably be eating out most of the time.'

The French windows were open. The letting agent showed you how to operate the complicated Edwardian brass rod fasteners.

'If the lock slips out and you can't get it back in, give me a ring. We've got someone who goes round fixing things. Don't try to do it yourself, because you can't get these replaced for love or money.'

You stand on the balcony and the long sleeves of your kimono stir in the breeze, brushing silk over your arms. You like this kimono which covers a multitude of sins with grace. Here you are, you and Johnnie, holed up in this beautiful flat. You touch the hoary eleagnus in a black tub, which the old ladies must have grown. Beside it there are neat pots of feather-pink geraniums, put there by the agency. The girl told you how hard it is to keep flowers nice here.

'Even in summer, it only takes one salt-storm. We have a contract with a garden centre, so any problems, they sort them out.'

The old ladies would have tapped their barometer and brought the pots in at night if it was falling. The barometer is still there, on the kitchen wall. You've already tapped it this morning and it's steady, at *Fair*.

*

When the sun comes round the corner of the balcony, you go back into the kitchen, leaving the French door open wide. There is food in the fridge, and you take out a packet of frozen croissants, then turn on the oven to preheat. You'll make breakfast in bed for Johnnie.

He's sleeping more than he's awake. Even though he goes to bed at nine, he sleeps on in the morning, like a thirsty man drinking a long glass of water, gulp by gulp. He wants to get away from everything, even from you. You can understand that, and it doesn't bother you. You guard his sleep. In the morning you slip quietly out of bed, feeling for the kimono that's rucked up in the duvet like a silk rag. You tiptoe out, leaving the door slightly ajar so you won't have to wake him if you need to come back to the bedroom for anything. In fact you prefer the early mornings on your own. You're used to solitude, and now that you've got someone in the next room, Johnnie drifting through his own solitude of sleep, there's nothing to fear. You've got him to plan for now. There's the luxury of thinking, 'Later, we'll have breakfast,' or, 'When Johnnie wakes up, we'll go for a walk along the sea-front.'

You do go out. At first he didn't want to.

'No one knows you down here,' you said, but Johnnie wasn't sure.

'There's a lot of London people down here. You don't know who you're going to bump into.'

'Put on your sunglasses and get a baseball cap,' you suggested, and to your surprise he took it seriously, and sent you out to buy a baseball cap. 'One with Nike on it or something.'

'I never thought I'd see the day,' you said, as he put it on. Baseball caps weren't at all Johnnie's style. He didn't like being laughed at, but he never went out without the cap.

The croissants smell good. You put them on a tray with apricot jam, two plates, a pot of coffee and two beautiful pale-yellow coffee cups which you bought yourself because you couldn't stand the ones the agency had provided. You think for a moment, then go back on to the balcony, pick two pink geraniums, put them in a little glass of water, and place them on the tray.

Johnnie is asleep. You put the tray down noiselessly on to the bedside table, and stand looking at him with the mixture of pity and envy you always feel for people when they're sleeping. He's huddled up, his face in the pillow. He's got away where no one can follow him. But he likes having someone sleeping with him, because he has bad dreams and when he wakes up from them he doesn't know where he is. Every night you tell him, 'You're in Brighton, remember?' He sits bolt upright, staring, and demands as if it's a matter of life and death, 'Is it morning, or is it evening?' 'Hush,' you say, 'it's the middle of the night. Go back to sleep.'

He'd carry on sleeping like that all morning if you let him. And why shouldn't he? Well, no reason, except that you're here with coffee and croissants. Or more than that, because of a feeling you don't articulate to yourself. It's the feeling that keeps you polishing the glasses from which you're only going to get drunk again, that makes you scrub the bath no one else is ever going to see, and pat skin-cream into the loose flesh of your upper arms.

'Johnnie.'

'What is it? What's the matter?'

'Nothing's the matter. I've brought you your coffee, that's all.'

He relaxes, turning so that he lies back on the pillows with his eyes shut. 'What's the time?'

'Time you were up. It doesn't do you any good, lying in bed half the morning.'

He squints at the watch on your arm. 'It's only nine o'clock.'

'Yes, but it's a lovely day. I've been sitting out on the balcony. Just think, in April.'

'We're not on holiday, Lou.'

'Why not? We're not working, as far as I can see. We've got plenty of money. Why shouldn't we be on holiday?'

He takes a croissant, splits it with his thumb, and loads it with butter and apricot jam. He doesn't drop a crumb. Just like Paul, they both have that cat-like neatness. You like watching him eat, and it doesn't seem to put him off. He takes three croissants, one after the other, and three cups of coffee.

'Aren't you eating, Lou?'

'No. I'm trying to lose a bit of weight.'

Because suddenly it seems worth trying. You can change gross slabs of flesh back into curves. You can release your face from the fat that pushes each feature slightly out of shape. You aren't meant to be like this. It's just a mistake that happened when you weren't looking. If you try you can get yourself back.

Johnnie rests on white pillows, with white sheets crumpled round him. You kick off your mules and lie down too, beside him, staring up at the white ceiling where there are echoey shadows of sea-light. You shut your eyes and it feels as if the bed is moving. You've always wanted to sleep outside.

You say to Johnnie, without opening your eyes, 'When I was a kid I used to dream about having a bed outside, and going to sleep in it, and nobody being able to see me. In the playground, or in the middle of the park. Whenever I wanted it, there it would be, and I could just climb in and get down under the covers.'

He doesn't answer. You settle yourself more comfortably, wriggling deep into the bed but not touching him. You've slept together every night in this bed since you came to Brighton. The time seems endless, in the way holiday time does, until you come home and your two weeks snap shut like a telescope.

You don't touch him. You feel tender and exposed, as if you've been ill for a long time and you're just coming back to life. Johnnie's the same, recovering from something you don't know about and don't want to know about. Neither of you has the energy for anything more. What you want is the taste of morning bread, like a miracle, and the smell when boiling water spatters on ground coffee. You want to spend long hours absorbing this view of the tide coming in, or going out, or lying slack at low water and exposing the stretch of hard sand that lies below the pebbles. You want to watch tiny, far-away children lug their buckets to the edge of the water and back to the holes they've made in the sand. You want to be too far away to know if they're laughing or crying.

You hear the sea all night long, far away, but as close as the blood punching its way around your bodies as they lie separate in the big white bed. You lie awake, and Johnnie sleeps, or pretends to sleep. You think of Anna. Two nights ago the wind got up and you heard a gull through it, sounding like a child who is hoarse with crying. But you knew you'd never left Anna to cry, not once. You could swear it. And you felt rather than saw Johnnie in the bed, at your side. For the first time you thought that Johnnie should be awake and listening too. He should hear that voice that sounds like Anna's, worn out by crying, and he should listen and listen for it to come again.

But of course you didn't wake him. You lay there hoping that the wind would die down. You wanted to get out of bed and slip through to the kitchen and have a drink, just one, to steady yourself. And then you'd be able to hear that the wind was simply the wind, and nothing more.

But you didn't move. You lay there, telling yourself that tomorrow the needle on the barometer would rise when you tapped the glass, and the sea would be shining.

'Or I used to pretend the bed was out in the country, in a field somewhere, with long grass and flowers by the hedges. The grass would be flowering too, and bowing down every time there was a breeze. And I'd lie there all day long, and watch the birds flying and the clouds going past.'

Johnnie grunts, and subsides deeper into the bed. You roll over and thump the pillow by Johnnie's head, on a rare impulse of violence towards him.

'Come on, you idle bugger. Time to get up.'

Twenty-two

For the first time, David's come up to the barn. Anna thinks it's safe. Sonia heads off up the track soon after ten every morning, and she's away for hours, learning to ride. At first there was the threat that Anna would have to go too, but not any more. Sonia disappears with a tight, secret face, saying to anyone who wants to listen, 'If I don't put the hours in now, I'll never get anywhere.' It's better without her, and Paul doesn't seem bothered. Some days he goes away, to London or to Leeds, and even when he's at home he's upstairs in the office most of the time, leaving the house light and free for Anna. She makes her own lunch, fish fingers and Stringfellows out of the freezer. Sonia's given her five pounds to go up to the village if there's anything else she needs, and left her the phone number of the stables in case of emergency. Sonia has a sense of responsibility, unlike some.

Anna keeps the number in her jeans pocket, along with the letter from her mother. She clears a corner of the kitchen table, blobs ketchup on to her plate, and eats in luxury. The place is getting messy, like a real house. Anna drops chips on the flags, and lets them lie there. Sonia is always talking about rats. That's why she cleans so much, because she's afraid of them.

'You could come up to our house for tea,' says David. 'Mum said I was to ask you.'

'I can't. I've got to be here, because of the kitten.'

The kitten's doing well. David reckons it'll live, and he knows about animals. He holds the little thing firmly and looks into its eyes, its nose, its ears. He says it's male. It'll be a tom-cat. Anna keeps its box in her room at night now, just under her bed, where she can reach down and touch it. In the box she's put a fur collar that belonged to David's great-grandmother. Kittens thrive if they can rub theirselves up against something soft, David says.

'You can make a lamb think anything's its mother, as long as you put a sheepskin over it.'

'I'll cook tea for us,' says Anna. 'I've got sausages in the freezer, and Sonia's not going to be back till nine tonight.'

'Is she up at the stables?'

Anna nods, putting fresh hay into the kitten's box. 'Yeah, she always up there.'

David can't tell if she minds. Sonia's not her mum, anyway. *She'll be getting a good ride up there*, his dad said last night, watching the Land Rover lights sweep over the shop wall opposite as Sonia slowed for the cobbled bit of the street. He went to the window and watched her tail-lights disappear. They never drew the curtains in their front room until they went to bed; nobody ever had, in this house, because they had nothing to hide. *She's been up there since eleven o'clock this morning.* And his mum shut his dad up, because David was there doing his football cards, but she laughed as well. Her face looked pink and plump, like it did when she came out of the bathroom in a cloud of scented steam, with her hair wrapped in a turban. *Don't begrudge me my one bit of luxury*, she said when Dad told her you didn't get any cleaner in ten inches of water than in four.

'They won't last,' his dad said. 'They'll be off.'

His dad was always sure, like that. David was proud of his dad's sureness, though it could be awkward. It made them different: it was like keeping the curtains open at night. Once you'd started you had to keep on, because if you suddenly drew your curtains it was worse than having them shut in the first place. His dad didn't need to talk to anyone else before he knew what was right. *They'll be off.* That meant Anna, seen off by rightness of the village.

'There's a fair on at Copstone next Saturday,' he says now to Anna, instead of saying anything about Sonia. He unsnags the needle claws of the kitten from his sweatshirt.

'Give him to me. Put him on my shoulder and I'll hold him like you do.'

He lowers the kitten gently. Not on Anna's narrow shoulder, where it might slip off, but on to the soft brown-and-yellow sleeveless T-shirt she's wearing. He'll put the kitten inside the curve of her arm. The kitten wriggles, and he's afraid of dropping it. The back of his hand brushes Anna's arm, which is warmer than he'd thought it would be. He's touched the close, pale skin on the inside of her arm. He flushes, and bends over the kitten.

'I like your T-shirt,' he says in a sudden, thick voice. He didn't know he was going to say anything, but Anna looks up and smiles as if she's not at all surprised, as if it's just what she wanted him to say.

'He's a lot stronger,' says Anna. 'Look at him trying to climb up on my shoulder.'

'Careful, he'll fall off.'

'He won't, I've got him.'

There's sun through the barn door, warming the air that's packed with old scents of grain and hay. David's got the sun on his back, and it shines full on Anna. There are tiny, glistening hairs on her bare legs and arms, which he's never seen before. She doesn't notice him looking, because she's got her head twisted round to watch the kitten as it struggles up her T-shirt, getting its claws caught in the cotton. Then she looks at David, laughing, saying, 'Look at him!' Her face glows with joy. He knows she believed the kitten would die, and now it hasn't died, but is alive and likely to live. Soon she'll be flaking fish for it, making pom-pom balls for it to chase, teaching it to catch a plastic mouse. *I'll have to teach it how to be a cat, because it hasn't got anyone else to learn from.* She's keeping a notebook to record the kitten's progress. Cats live a long time, more than seventeen years sometimes. *That means we'll be twenty-seven, nearly twenty-eight. Do you think we'll still know each other? I think we will. I don't know why, I just feel sure of it.*

But David has been nearly eleven years in the world, in the range of his father's big, sure voice. Joy is dangerous, like matches in woodland. *They won't last. They'll be off.*

Paul is up in his office, working. He doesn't know how to stop, even when he's possessed by a fear which feels more like an illness than an emotion. His limbs ache from sleeping badly. His eyes hurt, and in the bathroom mirror they stare back yellowly and malevolently, as if they're hiding bad news. He coughs all the time, a hard, nervous cough.

'I think I've got flu,' he said to Sonia at breakfast. She flicked him one of the brief, hostile glances he was getting used to.

'Go to the doctor if you're worried,' she said with an indifference that made him know for a second what it might be like to be old and sick and married to Sonia. He almost smiled. Imagine counting on Sonia to push your wheelchair round for you. He wasn't such a fool as that any more. He knew what she was up to. He knows Sonia, and he knows the precise degree of cold irritation she feels for him. He is making his own betrayal too easy. He's selling Sonia short on the range of emotion which she has a right to expect.

'I never go to doctors,' he answered, and picked up the sheaf of post and went off upstairs with it. The look on his face had stilled her for a moment. He'd felt her quick recalculations: had she gone too far? But he didn't look round, and a little while later the sound of the car told him she'd decided it was all right, she was safe for today.

The post is still on the table. He turns his back on the computer which will be full of messages. *You have mail.* He'll deal with it, even while he's unable to stop thinking about

Johnnie. He's eaten up with Johnnie, every fibre anxious, waiting, aching. And at the back of it there's the cold thought that everything he's done makes no sense, if Johnnie can walk away from it. Johnnie's been walking away ever since he first got involved in a scam with stolen mountain bikes, when he was fourteen.

Paul walks from room to room, comes up against a door or a window and stands there, frozen, unable to think how he got there or how to start again. Sonia's out of the way: let her go. When he looks down his telescope at the stars they say nothing to him. He watches each one brighten in its turn, like the eye of a fox in the night. But you can't break the patterns they make.

He thinks of phoning Louise, in case she knows something, but every time he picks up the phone he puts it down again. She won't know anything.

He lies on his bed and Johnnie's image stares at him from the ceiling, the nose knocked sideways and the mouth too swollen to speak. But the eyes stare straight at him and they're full of strange satisfaction along with the pain and fear. *This is what you wanted*, Paul thinks, and he knows it's the truth. Why else would Johnnie be so fucking inept?

He'll get down to London again. He'll make more enquiries. He's been too cautious, not wanting the word to get around that he's looking for Johnnie. He'll even go and see Louise, just on the off-chance. If she knows where Johnnie's gone, there's no way she'll be able to keep it from him.

He'll sell this house, he'll sell the roof over Louise's head if he has to, he'll do anything. It doesn't matter what it costs, because he can make it again. He can use up his fortune and make it all over again. He has the muscle, groomed for use. He has persistence. He used to think everybody had the qualities he had, it was just that they didn't use them, but by the time he was twenty-five he knew it wasn't like that. He's seen a room full of faces light up at the energy of his wanting, seen them turn to him and be glad. And that's something Johnnie doesn't understand. Johnnie thinks he knows a lot, because he found out very early that there's no such thing as safety, only a frayed rope over a drop. He can't stop himself putting more and more weight on the end of the rope. If he had a knife he'd cut it, strand by strand, even if it was himself dangling there, because not to be able to trust yourself is the biggest thrill of all.

Twenty-three

'I used to play on the penny slot-machines there,' you say, pointing at the West Pier. A cloud of starlings whirls around the end of the pier, then settles while another darkens the approaching sky. 'They must be roosting on the pier.'

It's early evening. The light's deepening to a richer blue, but why does it have to get dark so early, when it's as warm as this? The time and the weather don't fit. Half-naked children are still playing at the water's edge, or huddled in towels with hot-dogs. *Don't know when we'll get another weekend like this. This might be our summer.*

You and Johnnie stroll along, licking ice-creams from Marrocco's. You've turned back on your walk now, towards the piers and the town. Young men with hard bodies and hard eyes bike down the centre of the promenade, keeping well clear of the cycle path. You are arm in arm, Johnnie's cone in his left hand, yours in your right. He's chosen chocolate, and you have strawberry. You walk along the promenade between the pale-green beach huts and the sea.

'I don't blame them,' says Johnnie. 'Nice and safe.'

'What?'

'The pier. For the starlings. Nothing's going to get them on the pier, is it? No one can get out there.'

'They're rebuilding it, look, joining it back to the beach. I read it in the paper. They've got Lottery money.'

'They ought to leave it alone,' says Johnnie.

'It'll fall into the sea if they do.'

You walk on. You watch the starlings, millions of them it seems, rising and falling above the end of the pier.

'Wouldn't you think they'd bang into one another?'

'No. Animals've got more sense.'

'They're not animals, they're birds.'

Birds, millions of them, darken the sky with the rush of their wings. You think about it, strolling on, your arm hooked inside Johnnie's. It's nice to know that the way you feel has nothing to do with drink. You had a glass of wine at lunchtime – a bottle between you, that was all – then all you've had since is a couple of beers in a pub off the Kingsway. You don't like beer, so it was a safe choice.

'Look at that,' you say, pointing up at the sky, '*Damiano's Dreamworld*. Fancy it still going on. I'd have thought it'd have closed down years ago.'

The aeroplane drags its banner across the sky. *Come to Damiano's Dreamworld*. But it's late, people won't set off now.

'Where are we going?' asks Johnnie.

'I thought we could go down to the Palace Pier. I haven't been there for years. Why don't you take off that baseball cap? It's getting dark.'

'OK.'

Johnnie drops your arm, takes off the cap and crushes it into a litter bin. You dart forward to rescue it, but he holds your arm.

'Leave it, Lou. You're right, it'll be dark soon.'

You change arms so that he's on the outside, next to the railings. There are a lot of people about, kids on little trikes, couples with dogs, groups of foreign kids walking six abreast, shabby-faced men on their own. It's like London by the sea, everything concrete and man-made until suddenly you hit the water and then things could go any way.

'There's a boat out there.'

But you realize he can't see it. Johnnie's eyes aren't as good as yours, and he won't wear glasses. You've raised the question of contact lenses before, but the idea of fiddling round with his eyes makes him feel sick. He can see perfectly well, he says. The boat lags in the water, as if it doesn't want to go inland.

'Can't you see the red sails?' you ask Johnnie, and he says yes. You don't tell him that the sails are white.

In front of you a man and a woman walk, joined by their daughter. She's about six, her long skinny legs ending in rollerblades and she's talking all the time, never letting up, about how she's getting better, isn't she, she can nearly skate, can't she, tomorrow she'll be able to do it all on her own, won't she? And then there are the dark, soft tones of her father agreeing, over and over, and the mother encouraging: *Look, you push your foot like this, this way, that's it, you're nearly doing it.* They are talking in a language you don't know – not French or Italian, something more foreign than that – but all the same you can pick up every word. You glance covertly at Johnnie to see if he's listening, and yes, he is. You want to drop his arm. There ought to be a space between you. A heavy, blank space which you've made yourself, which can't keep its balance any more. *Mummy*, says the little girl in her foreign language, *Daddy*, and they both lean in towards her, to catch every word. Johnnie is listening, too. And although the little girl can't really skate yet she's actually going quite fast, with her mother on one side and her father on the other, holding her up if not actually supporting her, and bearing her along. The three of them are going slightly but perceptibly faster than you and Johnnie, and already the cheeping of the child is getting covered up by the noise of footsteps and the hiss of bicycle tyres rushing where they're not supposed to, and you hope that the bikers will be careful near the children, so you look round to check, and then when you look back the little family has gone out of sight. You look again, but they are nowhere to be seen.

'Anna,' you say, in a voice you never meant to use, and Johnnie looks at you, a sudden, naked, terrified look. And he waits in fear of what you'll say next.

'We shouldn't –' you say, and you stop. Shouldn't speak of her, shouldn't frighten Johnnie, shouldn't pick out of the blur of foreign tongues the words that say *Mummy* and *Daddy*. But you do. You have both stopped. You're a two-person island. People make way without thinking of you, parting as if by instinct when they come up behind you, joining again once they are ahead of you. You stop and Johnnie stops, and you'll never forget how afraid you are, how afraid he is, how naked in its terror is the once-beautiful face he turns to you.

'I lost her,' you say. 'We lost her,' and Johnnie keeps on staring at you as if this is the first moment of it, as if the anguish of it has only just dawned. You must have spoken louder than you meant to, because people slow down and look at you, curious, hearing the word 'lost', seeing your faces, wondering if the police have been called yet, when the search will start, whether they should offer to join in. But nothing happens, and so they walk on.

Twenty-four

You're on the pier. The Palace Pier, jazzed with light and games that suck you into electronic smog and won't let you see your way out till your wallet's empty. Kids with pinched faces lean into the machines, narrow hips touching hips of metal, fingers on the push-buttons of pleasure. You walk on, not arm in arm now, but close. The air is thick with burger grease, candy-floss and pancakes. You stop to buy waffles because you love it when the heavy metal waffle-iron closes on the pale batter, squeezing it into toast-brown squares. The girl squiggles maple syrup, looking at Johnnie. 'Is that enough for you? Is that all right?' but when it comes to you she pushes the plastic bottle of syrup towards you and says, 'Help yourself.' You walk on, eating the waffles. Lights flare on you, red, yellow, green, gold, lighting you up like presents to yourselves, and the music thuds deep inside you, too loud to be heard. You don't talk. Sometimes you stretch your mouths at each other in a smile. You eat your waffles, corner by sticky corner.

You go on into another arcade. There are cases of candy-yellow teddies with Disney eyes, waiting for the claw that fidgets above them, but never comes down. You ache with them, wanting it to happen.

'I'll win you one, shall I?' asks Johnnie, and you say, 'All right, go on,' but his coin does no more than anyone else's. The claw pinches at the air above the fur, and slowly shuts on nothing. But the machine's made up its mind you're mugs enough for a consolation prize, and it releases a dry slither of sweets into a metal chute. You find yourself scrabbling for them as if they're money. Orange, purple, lime green, tongue-pink. 'I don't like bubble-gum,' you say, and you leave them there. Johnnie shrugs and goes from your side.

'You want to try the horse racing?' he calls. You go over. Beneath a clear plastic screen, small plastic horses judder along parallel lines. The doll jockeys wear colours like the bubblegum. There's a slot to put your money in, buttons to press to bet on the colours. Johnnie puts in his coin and the light comes on, flashing: *Place Your Bets Now*. You tell him to go for the red, but he presses the green button and you both watch as the horses glide forward, first the red, then the green, the purple, the orange, the yellow, the brown. The red slides to the front, too early, he'll never keep up the pace. He jerks as the electric impulse lessens, and the brown moves past him, the plastic jockey shuddering on his plastic mount. And there, on the outside, pushed by a sudden, calculated surge of voltage, the yellow goes smoothly forward to the winning post. The race is over. Each horse glides back to the starting-line. Already you're feeding in more coins. The purple this time. There's bound to be a system. Watch what happens for the next few races, and you'll work it out.

'That jockey up on the brown, he's bent,' says Johnnie. 'He keeps pulling him up.'

'I told you there's a system.'

'You got any more ten-pence pieces?'

You empty your purse for him, but too violently, and coins spill on the floor. You kneel down scrabbling them together, and there it is, waiting for you beneath the cracks in the boards.

'Johnnie.'

'What's the matter?'

'Look. The sea's down there.'

He kneels down too because he hasn't heard what you said. He thinks something's wrong.

'What?'

'Look. The sea.'

It was there all the time, stirring thickly and blackly beneath the pier. It doesn't matter what they put up above, to distract you. Lights, music, money. It's all the same.

'Course it's the sea,' he says, catching on, kneeling beside you, but he doesn't care. He doesn't see what you see. 'You're on the pier, what else is going to be down there?'

You watch it down there, black, slithering, full. Its one toad eye winks at you.

'If I fell in there, I'd die. I couldn't bear it,' you say.

'You'd be all right. You can swim, can't you?'

'Not in that.'

'Let's go and have a drink.'

You get up from your knees slowly. You seem to be doing something you've done before, only you can't remember where. It itches in your mind, like the claw hanging over the toys.

'A nightcap,' says Johnnie.

'Are we going back? I'm not tired.' You don't want the flat yet. You don't want Johnnie asleep and all the hours open in front of you, and the little girl on her roller-blades skating away, not fast, but faster than you can walk.

'Did you know Paul was on speed when he did the Almeida flats?' you ask Johnnie, not caring if he follows the train of thought.

'Course I knew. I was living with you, wasn't I?'

'It was having two jobs on at the same time. He said it was the only way he could keep up.'

'Well, maybe he was right.'

'I don't know. I should have thought about it more. A man shouldn't come in at three o'clock in the morning and get up to do a day's work at seven.'

'But he did, didn't he?'

'I know.'

And you think of Paul, on the sites and on the phone, on the motorway at three or four in the morning, when he said he liked it because there was space to move. Sometimes he drove east and saw the sun rise, and knew he was chasing it back to where it came from, gaining a minute or more. You called it working all the hours God sent, and you accepted it. You behaved as if he could keep on doing it because he said he could keep on doing it. And you never had the guts to contradict him, even when a part of you must have known it wasn't human. There's a word you're looking for, and it's not one you'd use in ordinary speech. It stays at the edge of your mind, but you know it'll come back when you least expect it.

The water's wide beneath you. You know it. You taste maple syrup in the crevices of your teeth, and the taste of Johnnie too, as if it were yesterday and everything still to play for.

'Lou.' You hear his voice, thin at your side.

'What?'

'Don't look now. Wait. When I say, look by the hot-dog stall.'

You count your dropped coins into your purse, smile up at Johnnie, then glance round. What'll we do next? Ice-cream, roller-coaster, drink in the bar? You make your eyes as vague as clouds, travelling over the two men by the hot-dog stall. They're looking at nothing in a way that makes you know there's a something. You wait, yawn, let your gaze travel again. And there it is, like a small, definite contraction: their look on Johnnie, and on no one else. They burn into him.

'I'm a bit tired, now I come to think of it,' you say. 'I wouldn't mind an early night.' The word that's been whirring uselessly on the edge of your mind suddenly clicks to rest like a row of three oranges. *Mercy.*

Twenty-five

'Who were they?'

'Nobody. Just a couple of guys.'

'Not the ones –'

'No.'

'Well then, it's all right.'

But you say it knowing it's not, almost asking for the angry spurt of breath as he says, 'It's not fucking all right. I don't want anyone knowing I'm down here.'

'They saw you, that's all that happened. They don't know where you are. They don't even know you're staying. You could have been down for the day. Loads of people go down to Brighton for the day.'

'Yeah.'

You stand side by side on the balcony, in the dark. The night is still. It's like Italy, you think, the warm sudden dusk. You loved it there, though Paul didn't. Maybe it was the Romanian in you. Your mother used to talk about the heat in Bucharest in August, and how she would long to go away to the mountains with her friends. *It was hot there too, but different heat. A dry, clear heat. It smelled of pine, and as soon as you got out of the train, with your eyes closed, you knew where you were.* She spoke of those things sometimes, though rarely when you asked questions. Now it seems that her memories are yours. You too stand on the low platform beside the train that belches brown coal smoke. The steps are drawn up, the train leaves, you stand in the yellow heat with your suitcase in your hand, and the smell of pine steals over the empty station.

You stand side by side on the balcony, with Johnnie. You're right on the edge of the land. London's behind you, and the fields and woods you slept through on the way down. The country always sends you to sleep. This is where they rule off England with a firm line, and everything stops. One minute there are cars and shops and Pelican crossings and off-licences and public libraries. The next, nothing. Stones and water. And when you look into the water there are things to make you wish you hadn't. You remember an angler fish you saw in a museum once, with a label on its glass case. No one could have invented a creature that ugly: it had to be God.

You watch the cars sweep by. You don't need a jersey. It's fine to stand with your arms bare, folded, feeling the warm solidity of your own arms, your own flesh. Johnnie picks up the bottle of whiskey from the wrought-iron table and pours some into his glass, some into yours.

'We made a mistake,' he says. 'We shouldn't have come here. I should have taken that boat from Harwich.'

'What's so great about Denmark?'

'There's a man in Copenhagen, he owes me fifty grand.'

But you know Johnnie. There's always someone he knows who can take you there quicker, get stuff cheaper, cut the prices, get the tickets. All he's got to do is give them a bell.

'And he's waiting there, is he, for you to turn up and ask him for it? Got it all ready in a box under the bed?'

Johnnie's face shutters. You've broken the rules. You don't hold Johnnie's promises up to the light. You let them lie on the table or you change them for real money. 'It's sorted,' he says, and you know that it is. It's all there in his mind, clearer than the balcony or the black, whispering sea, or you with the glass in your hand from which you've hardly drunk, because you know you need to keep your mind clear.

'What's his name?' you ask.

'Hans,' says Johnnie, straight away, without needing to think about it.

'That's a German name.'

'Maybe he had a German mother, I don't know.'

'So Hans owes you fifty thousand.'

'He was in on the deal with me. We were going to come out with fifty thousand each.'

'But it didn't work out.'

'It would've, if Hans hadn't screwed it.'

'So he owes you what didn't happen.'

You turn away, walk to the edge of the balcony, look down. Once the daylight's taken away, there's nothing friendly about the big blocks of buildings, the wide lawns, the sharp silhouettes of beach huts and the sea beyond. You are glad you're up here on the second floor, not down there where there could be anything. You think of what Paul said about Johnnie, when his boatload of dreams evaporated somewhere between Zennor and Land's End.

'I don't understand how he can be so fucking careless. If you're going to go into that kind of business, setting everything else aside, there's money in it. There's got to be. But he still screws it up. All he's getting is the risk without the outcome.'

'Maybe that's what he wants,' you said, and Paul looked at you as if you were mad. But you knew you were right. And you know it now. No one could be as careless as Johnnie, all the time, without putting some thought into it. He's got a system. With one hand he takes it, with the other he throws it away. There's no man in Copenhagen, though that isn't to say Johnnie's lying. There'll be a Hans of some sort. He's probably got a flat and benefit and a job sometimes, and a dream which took on flesh when he met Johnnie. Johnnie can always be the flesh of other people's dreams. He shines back at them, a bright reflection of what they most want. That's his talent. But Paul doesn't recognize it, even when the talent is working on Paul just like it works on everyone else. The trouble is, it works on Johnnie too. The dreams flash off him, and he believes them.

'Why don't you stay here?' suggests Johnnie. 'Have a bit of a holiday. We've got the flat for the month. I'll get the train up to London tomorrow. There's a boat from Harwich in the evening.'

'You shouldn't go to London. You should stay here.'

You say it dryly, not as you want to. That's the best way with Johnnie. If you can sound professional, like a doctor, as if there's nothing personal to you in what he does or doesn't do, then he sometimes listens. He's terrified of illness.

'You tell me why.' He sounds as if he really wants to know, so you get started.

'Because all that'll happen if you stay here is that you'll get bored.'

'I can't stay here for ever. I've got a life, haven't I?'

'We're not talking about for ever. We're only talking about now. You stay here for a few weeks and everything'll blow over.'

'Blow over,' he jeers, but longingly too, as if there's just a thread of a chance that you might know the symptoms of his disease better than he does himself. That's when you know he really is in trouble.

'I can get money,' you say. 'I can go up to London. I can even go and see Paul.'

'They want to mark me,' says Johnnie.

'What do you mean?'

'You know.'

And you believe it. They want to put a stop to the dazzle of Johnnie. Almost nobody has what he has. Mark him, spoil his looks, make him something you feel pity for, not desire.

'You don't know what it's like,' says Johnnie. You nod. It's true, you don't know what it's like. You can only guess and go slowly and hope the ground holds. Beauty's even stranger in a man. It's something apart, like the shape of a baby's head, designed to move you. You know it and you try to resist it, but it moves you all the same, each time, helplessly, somewhere so deep it's as if it was born in you. You can't wipe it away, any more than you can destroy your own fingerprints.

Twenty-six

You lie down, side by side, and the breeze from the window ripples over your skin. You can't sleep in a shut room, whatever Johnnie says. He's made you lock the French windows at the front, and draw the bathroom blinds even though the bathroom window faces a blank brick wall. When the phone rang he wouldn't let you answer it.

'It can't be for us,' you said. 'No one knows we're here.'

The phone takes incoming calls only. You let it ring, ten, fifteen, seventeen times. It seemed against nature not to answer it. On eighteen, it stopped. You were just thinking of taking it off the hook when it started to ring again, with anonymous, piercing urgency.

'Can't you pull the plug on that fucking thing?' said Johnnie.

'It'll only be someone selling double-glazing. Let it ring. It's not doing us any harm.'

'It's doing my head in,' grumbled Johnnie, but then he wandered off to the bathroom, and a little later you heard the shower on 'boost' and knew that he couldn't have heard the third set of rings, or the fourth. And then the phone gave up.

Johnnie lies on his back, naked in the staring eye of the central light. He wouldn't turn it off. You wear your cream satin nightdress, very plain apart from a bit of distraction at the neckline, and wish to God he didn't have to have the light on. It's not like when you're twenty and you can't wait to get your clothes off and show what you've got. Now it's a question of which way to lie to make it look as if you've got two stomachs, not three. And here you are, stranded in the wreck of yourself just when you most need the looks you wasted for years. Not that you were ever one of those women who always look good. Sonia, for example. See Sonia once and you've seen her, you don't need to look again. You were beautiful sometimes. You would feel the power switching itself on and off in you, like that light. Off for good now, you tell yourself grimly, so don't start getting your hopes up. You doubt if anything else will be getting up tonight, either.

You lie back, propped on your own pillows, and Johnnie's. He prefers to lie flat, and he does so now, looking up at the ceiling. You watch him as if you have never seen him before. You take him in: the black hair you ran your hand over when he was a kid, the hair running in a dark line between his nipples, down to the base of his stomach, his penis lying curled sideways, as if you weren't there.

You half-smile. You think how strange it is to find yourselves here, and how strange that your tenderness for Johnnie rolls up in you like waves, rising, breaking, sinking back, rising again as if it will never end. It makes no difference to him at all. He's so used to people looking at him like this that he doesn't even notice it. He's had it from Paul all his life, and where Paul left off there were plenty of others ready to begin.

You watch him grope for the whiskey bottle at the side of the bed. He's trying to pour it without looking, the silly bugger, and it doesn't work. Whiskey slops on the floor. The carpet will stink of it. You'll have to remember to buy one of those carpet-cleaning aerosols that smell like the air-freshener in department-store toilets. You can't bear them. And what's worse are those poor sods they keep in there all day, dashing into the cubicles to wipe the seat every time a bum comes off it.

Johnnie fumbles with bottle and glass. 'You want a drink, Lou?'

'No, I'm all right.'

'Are you feeling OK?' he asks, propping himself up on one elbow, mocking you. 'You don't seem like yourself tonight.'

'I told you. You drink it if you want it, I've had enough.'

You can't believe it's you saying those words: *I've had enough.* And meaning them too. Feeling nothing for the whiskey except a sort of surprise that there isn't more of it. He's going to feel rough in the morning. That's three-quarters of the bottle gone. You've never seen him let it get to him like this before. His eyes are thick with whiskey, and his face looks knocked out of shape. Yours must look like that, most of the time, but it's not something you can notice about yourself, even in a good mirror.

Johnnie flops back on the bed, making both of you bounce up and down. It's a very good bed. You looked under the mattress protector, just to be sure. He's closed his eyes now. Anybody who didn't know him might think he was starting to relax. The white light overhead picks out every detail, but you couldn't say it was harsh. Just clear.

He turns into your arms. They're already open, like they were always open for Anna when she'd fallen, even before she opened her mouth to yell. It's all here in the room with you: the pier with its lights and black water underneath, the horses trying to gallop but fixed to fail, the smell of candy-floss, scorched rubber, chips. You see the faces turned on Johnnie, casual. You see them sharpen. You remember that cat, in the garden. She shot her steel claw through the water and got one of the fish. She couldn't get the big carp with their thick white flesh, but she pulled out the little orange one. It looked as if it was burning as she snatched it out of the water, and bit its head off. But you can't let yourself think about how it feels to be a fish. Instead you think: pond, fish, cat, and that blunts it. It turns into a story which has already been told a hundred times. The fish swims, the cat waits, the pond is deep, or else not deep enough. Her head closed round the orange carp and stripped off its flesh. She let you see her eat it, and when she'd finished she licked off her paws, dipped her head and rasped the velvet pads until she was perfect outside as well as in.

Like a cat going to communion.

The sun was blinding. That was when Johnnie came through the door and you saw the darkness of shadow at his feet like a pool of ink or blood. He said, 'How's it going?'

There was something between you then. The tight ball of flesh that was Anna, stretching your flesh to bursting-point. You on one side and Johnnie on the other. You didn't touch. You lied and kept on lying, and you made Anna no one's, and pretended not to understand what you were doing. But now you know it was a sin.

Here he is now, on the other side of your flesh, held back from you by the bulk of your breasts and stomach and thighs. Nothing's going to happen. He's had too much whiskey, and besides . . .

You stroke his hair. His eyes are closed now. You feel the length of him, his heat, his whiskey sourness. He'll be asleep soon, and then you'll slide him off you if you can, and turn the light off.

He'll go to Harwich, and you won't be able to stop him. But you'll go with him.

Twenty-seven

Anna's warming milk for the kitten. No one else is up yet, because it's not even six o'clock. She's used the last of the milk, but she's going to walk up to the village and buy some before they notice.

A car's coming down the track. It stops, there's a long silence, then the clunk of a car door. A minute later tyres slew on gravel in the turning circle, and the car's away off up the track again. It must have been someone who was lost and came down here by mistake. Anna turns back to the stove and lifts the pan off the burner. The milk's too hot now, she'll have to cool it. She turns with the pan in her hands, heading for the sink under the window, and freezes. There's Sonia, hurrying past the window towards the front door. Anna ducks, but it's OK, Sonia hasn't seen her. She ducks and the milk rises to the edge of the pan in a wave and slops out over the tiles.

She's down on the floor, swabbing it with the wrong cloth, as Sonia opens the kitchen door. There Sonia stands, not quite indoors yet, still shining with the beautiful earliness of the day, body tingling, mind blank with bliss. Anna sees none of it. She smears milk on to the tiles and doesn't dare look up. Slowly Sonia rouses herself, takes in the child, the mess.

'What are you doing?'

'I was making some warm milk.'

'Give that to me.'

Sonia seizes the cloth, rinses and wrings it in the sink, squirts bleach into the water and dunks the cloth vigorously up and down, as if she would like to drown it.

'Can't you tell the difference between a floor cloth and a dishcloth? she demands. But Anna is making herself small, rubbing a bare milk-slimed foot against her calf. She doesn't answer. Sonia's already into the sink cupboard, fetching out a floor cloth, brandishing it at Anna.

'Here. This is what you do it with.'

Anna takes the cloth, but she does nothing. The kitchen reeks of chlorine and spilt milk, and she feels sick.

Suddenly Sonia's face changes. 'Oh leave it, Anna. I'll do it. What were you up at this time for, anyway?' She takes the cloth from Anna, bends down and wipes the floor briskly, getting into all the corners. In a minute the tiles are clean and the cloth disposed of. Sonia, triumphant once more over dirt and disorder, fills the kettle.

'Cup of tea, Anna?'

Anna nods, hypnotized. Sonia's turned the water full on, smacking the jet of it into the kettle. Her strict fair hair has come loose, curling damply around her face. Her skin glows with fresh colour.

'Is it raining?' asks Anna.

'Raining! It's a beautiful day. I don't know why you want to spend all your time in the barn. You ought to learn to ride.' She smiles a flushed and secret smile. 'There's nothing like it. I'm off all day tomorrow. We're going up on the hills, and we won't be back before dark.'

Anna's astonished. Sonia has never talked to her like this. In fact they rarely talk at all: as if by instinct they avoid each other, one coming into a room as the other one goes out, one moving aside to let the other pass so their bodies never touch. But now look at Sonia, swooping up to take mugs off their hooks, diving like a dancer into the fridge for milk. She is packed, electric with happiness. Anna can feel it coming off her.

'Did you use the last of the milk?'

192

'I'm sorry, Sonia, I didn't know there wasn't any more till I'd poured it, I was going to get some more –'

'We'll have it with lemon. You like tea with lemon?'

Anna nods.

'OK. Listen, I'm going to have bacon and eggs. You want some, or are you going back to bed?'

'Can I have a bacon sandwich?'

'Yeah, all right.'

Anna leans against the cupboard, watching Sonia. She is so quick and perfect in everything she does. Her hands tap the eggs and the shells fall neatly in half, as if she has cut them. She tosses the bacon easily into the frying-pan and it humps up, frizzling. Sonia turns it with a flick of her wrist, then drops in the eggs one by one, each egg swirled round in a glass before it hits the hot pan.

'Do it like that and you'll keep the yolk in the middle,' she tells Anna. The bacon spits, the eggs chuckle in the fat. Anna realizes: *Sonia is young*.

'How do you want it, soft or frizzled?'

'Frizzled.'

Anna gets out the tomato sauce and cuts thick slices of white bread. It feels strange to be moving around the kitchen like this, with Sonia, not minding the touch of her as she brushes past. Here in the kitchen, with the lights still on even though there's a new day getting stronger outside the window, and the bacon curling and going crisp while the eggs lie bubbling in a veil of white, Sonia's like someone else. She's pulled off her riding jacket and tossed it on to the door knob. There are stains of grass and sweat on her white T-shirt, which is rucked around her stomach so Anna can see the flat elastic stretch of Sonia's skin, and her navel, a deep dint in the brown flesh. Normally Sonia changes her clothes as soon as there's a spot of dirt on anything she wears, but today she doesn't seem to care. She's forgotten about herself. And now she's dipping her finger straight into the yolk of an egg as it fries. She lifts her finger golden and dripping to her mouth, and sucks it. Anna fetches two plates, two mugs.

Sonia tips bacon on to Anna's plate, and the rest of the panful on to her own. Anna makes her sandwich as she likes it: a coating of tomato sauce on the white bread, a layer of lettuce, the hot bacon, the sandwich clapped together again. She lifts the sandwich to her mouth. Chewy, sweetish bread, lettuce just wilted by hot fat, bacon crackling between her teeth, the acid sweetness of tomato sauce to cut the taste of fat. Sonia folds her bacon over with her finger and pushes it into her mouth. Neither of them moves to go into the long, polished dining-room. They eat standing up, greedily. Sonia's swaggering, she doesn't care. Her mouth is wide and her lips shine with bacon grease. Her teeth tear at the flesh of the bacon and she cuts the yolks out of her eggs and swallows them whole.

'I should have fried that bread,' she says. Anna watches her over the thick bacon sandwich, but says nothing. Sonia's look is sharp now, and direct, lighting hard on Anna. 'Makes you wonder what we're doing here,' she observes.

'What do you mean, Sonia?'

'You and me. There must be people like us up and down the country, sitting in kitchens. We weren't born to each other, we didn't choose each other. But here we are living together.'

No, thinks Anna, *we didn't choose. My dad chose, if anyone did. But I don't think anyone did. And here we are.*

'I suppose you could call us a family,' Sonia goes on. 'The more you think about it, though, the stranger it is, a family that isn't blood or choice. Don't you think it's strange, Anna?'

'I don't know,' says Anna. Her hand has crept to her left pocket, and she is fingering a piece of folded paper.

'People say all sorts of things about stepmothers,' says Sonia. 'They'll even say them to your face. Do you think of me as your stepmother, Anna?'

Caught, Anna just stares. But Sonia's face isn't hostile. She wants to know.

'I've got a mother,' says Anna.

'I know,' says Sonia, and then she says no more. She will never know how grateful Anna is that she says no more. She thinks of Grace Darling. *Boldly, bravely, resolutely.* She thinks of the waves thrashing over Grace Darling's oars as she bent her back and rowed to the rescue of the drowning men. She didn't ask anyone, she just went. If she hadn't gone they would have died, on the rocks and in the dark. She touches the piece of paper she tore from Fanny Fairway's Comprehension book.

Sonia yawns. Her arms go up, her golden forearms, her silky underarms. Her breasts lift as she draws her arms up and behind her head, yawning luxuriously until her eyes water. There is a smell of her in the kitchen: not her perfume, but her flesh. Anna sees that she is beautiful now that she has kicked her cool neatness aside like clothes at bedtime. She is beautiful and her arms are strong from riding. What she wants, she'll have. She moves boldly, challenging the room even though there is only Anna in it. Anna is almost shy to be with her. She watches, and thinks of what Sonia has said. *Not by blood, and not by choice.* Why *are* they together then, her father and Sonia and Anna? What happened to bring them here? Who chose it, and is it Sonia who is unchoosing it now, opening her arms to new things and taking off the old ones like dirty clothes?

'I galloped on the mare yesterday,' says Sonia. 'I didn't think I would. But you've got to go for it.'

'What was it like?'

But Sonia doesn't answer. Her mind is inward, turning over what Anna cannot reach. She turns over what she won't speak of: the spread and stretch of the mare under her, the fleeting wildness beneath its taught paces, the smell, the heat, the harsh slippery sides, the gripping that makes her thighs ache, the smell that comes off on her clothes and her skin. The way the mare shudders all over and spreads her forelegs and puts her head down at the end of the gallop, and when Sonia gets off her legs are trembling too. She walks round to the mare's head and her hands go up to the mare's muzzle and the mare tosses her head up sharp as if to shake Sonia off. But she doesn't really want to shake Sonia off. Her neck arches, her head comes down, nudging Sonia's jacket sleeve. Her bright, flaring curious eyes are on Sonia's face. She noses down, feeling her soft wet lips into Sonia's hand and then she whickers and Sonia feels the spurt of mare's breath against her fingers.

Sonia picks up a piece of bread which Anna has cut but not eaten. Slowly she begins to wipe it around the inside of the pan, soaking up the savoury fat of the bacon and the golden runnels of broken egg. She sweeps the fat-rich bread right around the pan, brings it to her mouth, bites.

'All the same,' she says, 'who are we kidding? It's not really like a family. It's not real, like —'

She stops. With her bread in her hand she frowns as if she's going to struggle to say what it's not like. But the cool harness of daily life is settling on her. She won't say any more.

'What are you digging up the money for?'

Anna sits back on her heels. 'You're not to tell anyone.'

'Don't be stupid. You know I wouldn't.'

'I'm going to my mother's.'

A pang of loss shoots through him. He's always known it could happen. He's even practised Anna saying those words in his head. *I'm going away. I'm going back to London.* But he hasn't guessed what it would feel like to see her head stooped over the grave of her money, digging it out. She can go anywhere she wants with a thousand pounds. She'll never need to come back.

'You can't stop me,' she says coldly, as if he's someone else, not David but a boy she doesn't know.

'What happened?' he asks.

'Nothing happened.'

'Yes it did. You wouldn't be going off.'

And he knows. He watches her so close he can see the thoughts twisting in her eyes.

'It was Sonia,' she says after a while.

'What's she done to you?'

'Nothing. Only she's right, what am I doing here? What's my dad doing here? We're not a family. There's no reason for us to be together.'

'What's she been saying that to you for?'

'It's true.'

'She's got no call to talk like that to you,' he says out of a depth he hadn't known was in him. He burns with anger at the thought that he's only ten years old, not even eleven yet. Someone can hurt Anna and there's nothing he can do about it. Even if he told his mum she wouldn't want to get drawn in. She'd say Sonia might have gone a bit far but there was bound to be more to it than David knew. He could just hear his dad saying that Anna was probably exaggerating. His dad likes that word. He'd tell David to keep out of it. *They won't be here long. They'll soon be going back to where they came from.*

'You could phone Childline,' he tells Anna, because he's seen the stickers in the phone box.

'Courtney Arkinstall phones Childline all the time. She's got her own counsellor.'

'Those Arkinstalls, they've got to have everything that's going.'

'She says it's always engaged. She has to try loads of times.'

'Will you really go back to London?'

'Yes,' says Anna. 'It's not Sonia's fault.' Her hand is back in her pocket, her fingers stroking the sharp fold of the paper. 'I won't live with my mother though. I'll just stay with her. She's got a pull-out sofa in the sitting-room.'

'She'll want you to live with her.'

'No. She knows I can't. She's got an illness, she can't look after me.'

'What do you mean?'

'She told me, it's an illness. People think it's something you choose to do but it isn't, it's like having a leg off so you can't walk.'

'What do you mean?'

'It's why she can't look after me. She's an alcoholic.'

'She's not.'

'OK then, she's not.'

'I didn't mean I didn't believe you.'

'I know.'

They are silent for a while. Anna brushes soil off her palms, then suddenly she smiles at him, a big, sparkly smile that comes from nowhere he knows, and covers more than he can imagine.

'So I've got to sort myself out,' she says. 'It's not my mum's fault. When I'm grown-up I'll get a job and pay for her to go to a clinic. My dad thinks she's got no will-power, but she has.'

Anna has found the edge of the crisp packet with the money in it. She pulls it out and shakes it, showering earth. Inside the packet, the money is as fresh as when they left it.

'It's not taken root then,' says David. 'Let's count it again.' He'd forgotten how new the notes were. He wants to have his hands on the wad of them, one more time. After it's been buried like that, it doesn't seem to belong to Anna as much as it did before, when she opened the letter. It could be anybody's. Anna wants to watch out. Everything'll get taken off her, unless she holds on tighter than she's doing. He thinks of Sonia in the Land Rover, with her pale hair scraped back and her sunglasses and her face not looking at anybody or caring about anybody as she drives up to the stables. She looks so perfect. She makes him want to hurt her, driving through the village like that with her head up and looking at no one, as if none of them are real.

Suddenly, without wanting to, he sees Anna's head bobbing on the other side of the wall, as she walked down the lane that day they threw the grit at her. Her hair hid her face. They peered through chinks between the stones and knew she couldn't see them. She didn't know they were waiting for her. They were crouched down, the four of them, Jack Barraclough's knees digging into him, Billy's stinky peanut-butter breath in his face. They were hot and excited, shoved in as close as they could to the wall. They could hear her feet coming down the track. And then JohnJo swung his arm back with the handful of gravel in it and let it fly over the wall. They heard her feet stop. Billy laughed out loud, not a real laugh but a laugh for Anna to hear and know they were there. His red mouth opened and there were his teeth with the paste of peanut butter stuck to them, inches from David's face. Billy flung his handful of stones and then Jack threw his but most of his hit the wall and spattered back at them. Only David still had his handful. They'd got it from the grit heap up at the high road.

'Go on,' said Billy, and David threw his, aiming to do what Jack did and hit the wall, but he was a better shot and the stones went over. He didn't know if it touched her or not. The next minute they were thudding away over the field, Billy and Jack and JohnJo laughing the same loud, loose laughs, as if they were brothers. He nearly wished he could laugh like that too and fall down in a heap by the high road with Billy and JohnJo and Jack. They were telling themselves how they'd made her run for it, how they'd hit her on the bum as she went off running. But he said he had to go home. They looked at him, and Billy said, 'Go home then.' He went slowly, to show he wasn't running. But that was all he did.

'There's more than I need here,' says Anna. 'We can share it.'
'No,' he fires up. 'I don't want it. It's yours.'
She's silent, fingering the notes. He thinks of his dad, and

what his dad would say if he saw David here with Anna and a thousand pounds between them. They are a family. His dad has never hit his mum, or him. Only a smack in the right place when it's wanted, that's what his mum always says. Or else his dad says he'll knock him into the middle of next week, but he never does. They're not like the Arkinstalls. He's seen Billy reel out of the door from a crack on the head, and squat down in the space between the coal bunker and the wall, staring at nothing. You'd best not go and talk to Billy then. If he thinks you've seen anything he'll beat you up for it in the playground next day. Sometimes Courtney'll come out and find her cousin. She doesn't talk, she just gives him a piece of her chewing-gum, and takes one herself, and they cram in side by side in the gap, chewing their gum for so long it probably doesn't taste of anything.

'Don't be angry, David,' says Anna.

'I'll come with you,' he says.

'What?'

'I'll come with you, to your mum's. You shouldn't go on your own. It's not safe in London.'

Still she doesn't say anything. He feels an itchy red in his cheeks. Maybe she thinks he's after a free holiday in London, stopping with her.

'It's all right, I won't stop. I'll go with you, then I'll come back.'

'Will you?'

'I've said so, haven't I? But we'll have to use your money for the tickets, because I've only got £6.40.'

'And we won't be here when school starts on Thursday.'

'What'll Fanny Fairway say?' he asks derisively.

'Don't keep me waiting when I call your name in the register, Anna O'Driscoll. Are you deaf, or daft, or both?'

'Stupid cow.'

'Yeah.'

'She ought to retire. She's way past it, my dad says. She was there when he was at school.'

'I'll never see her again,' says Anna, grasping it. She looks round at a world gone temporary. 'I've got to take the kitten,' she says.

'Have you not given it a name yet?'

'There's only him left. He knows I'm talking to him. He doesn't need a name. Will you really come with me?'

'I've said so, haven't I?'

Twenty-eight

You can't remember a morning like this since you were a child. On a summer holiday once, in Norfolk. Coming out of the guest-house door in your shorts and cardigan, clutching a big metal bucket and spade. The air was cold on your legs, but everyone said it would be hot later. The smell of the sea. Dad with his hand on the gatepost, looking down the gravel lane to the rise of the sea-wall, breathing in the air. And suddenly you ran, pelting down the lane, bucket clanging against spade, sandals slapping, plaits flying. How fast you used to run. And Johnnie's still asleep, flat out at the bottom of the world and likely to stay like that until ten o'clock at least. Missing a beautiful morning like this.

They were a funny lot in that guest-house. You smile, remembering how Mrs Lamb always gave Dad two sausages with his bacon, while everyone else only got one. And she'd put the rack of toast bang in front of Dad, then linger behind his chair, breathing heavily, while he ate. Once Mum reached across and helped herself to one of his sausages, just to tease.

A man with a dog slows, catching your smile, taking it to himself. His dog sniffs your legs, and you bend down, recognizing the breed.

'What's his name?'

'He's Marcus.'

'He's a Staffordshire bull, isn't he? We used to have one when I was a kid.'

'That's right. Lovely dog. I've had him since he was eight weeks old and I've never had a cross word out of him. Course they don't like strangers, as a breed.'

'I know. My mum never had a moment's worry about me, as long as I had Claude with me. I used to go all over. Dad said he was better than a bodyguard. Not that you worried so much, then –'

'You won't get a more loyal dog than your Staffordshire bull.'

'That's true. I used to take Claude all round, down Loxford Lane, across the park –'

'Barking Park?'

'Do you know it?'

'I only grew up there. Levett Gardens, off Goodmayes Lane.'

'I know. We were up by South Park.'

'It's changed a bit since then.'

'I haven't been back, not since my dad died.'

'There's nothing to take you back, is there, once they've gone? I'm the same.'

He's a big man, early fifties, maybe more. A tan always takes a few years off. Balding, but he's got his hair cut close so it looks all right. He's got more idea than some of them. Nice jacket, nice shoes.

'I take Marcus the same walk every morning. Down as far as the pier, then back up the Hove end, past the King Alfred. He likes it up there. They still bring in a bit of fish, and there's a few boats. He likes the smell of fish.'

'You're out early.'

'Always am. We do this one before breakfast, then I'll take him out again in the evening for an hour or so, over to Shoreham Harbour or up on the Downs. Somewhere he can have a run.'

'It's a full-time job, isn't it, giving them enough exercise.'

'You've got to do it, otherwise it's not fair to the dog. Half the problems these owners have, saying the dog's vicious, it's all down to lack of exercise. If you can't be bothered, don't get the dog, that's what I say.'

'Oh, I agree with you.'

You stand, satisfied, in agreement. It's going to be another perfect day, though at seven-thirty it's still cool.

'You're retired, then, are you?'

'Semi-retired. I was in business in London. You'll find there's plenty of London people down here.'

He thinks you're living here, new to the place, wanting a few tips. You won't tell him you'll be gone in a few hours, when Johnnie wakes. Talking like this makes staying seem real. You could have a life down here, like him. A proper life. A dog maybe. You'd soon get to know people, with a dog. Little waves curl and flop on the bank of shingle. There's a faint breeze, wrinkling the surface of the sea.

'You could be anywhere,' he says. The dog's claws scutter on the tarmac. They're at the railings now, overlooking the beach. He points away to the right. 'See that chimney? That was the power station, before they blew it up.'

'What did they go and leave the chimney for?'

'I don't know. Probably got a preservation order slapped on it. That's the way things are down here, but you get used to it. I don't mind a chimney doing nothing, not now I'm a man of leisure.'

You could learn things like that. It's not beyond you to get to know a new place. You could live here, you feel suddenly. You've been a fool, always thinking you were stuck with what you'd got. People do move on.

But the dog tugs at his lead. 'He's telling me to get a move on.'

'He's been very good.'

'Nice to meet you.'

'And you.'

'Not a lot like Barking, is it?' he says, looking out at the water.

'Not a lot.'

'I tell myself every day, I'm a lucky man.' *And you're lucky too,* that's what he's saying. *You made your luck, like I made mine. Here we are on the promenade, miles of sunlight every way we look. We're the ones that got away.*

Twenty-nine

'These chips are good.' You're surprised, because nothing else about the pub is. It's empty but for you and Johnnie. The back end of nowhere, the last stop, more or less, before Harwich. The notice swinging outside said 'All Day Food'. Inside you saw the peeling veneer, the coasters that look as if someone gave up waiting for their sandwiches and took a bite of the cardboard instead, and a sad, skewed dartboard. You wished you'd driven on, but then a girl came and took your order as smartly as if she was in a French restaurant.

The Ladies has no towel and no toilet paper, but it's not too bad. You looked at yourself in the mirror and wondered about all the mirrors in which you were going to see your reflection before you got old, and how strange it is that no one knows where they'll end up. Just as well, you told yourself briskly, looking at the crumple under your eyes that doesn't go away any more, even after a good night's sleep.

And it's nice sitting here, eating chips and drinking ginger-beer shandy, a proper ladies' drink if ever there was one. You can hardly believe it's you. The back door is wedged open and the bright spring air gusts through, riffling the sheets of last year's calendar. The girl asks if you mind the door and you say no, you like it.

'I can smell the sea again,' you say to Johnnie. 'Seems funny, doesn't it, that we left the sea this morning and now we're back to it. Shows you how small England is.'

Johnnie stretches out his legs and picks up his pint of Guinness. For the first time, he looks relaxed. He's got the same feeling as you've got. Now you've left, you can't believe you ever thought you could stay in Brighton. You've got to keep moving, because it's the only way to keep this bubble round you both, that might be happiness. Because you're passing through, you don't have to answer all the questions that might rise up if you stayed in one place. You can sit most of the day side by side with Johnnie in the rented Citroën, flicking through the radio stations to get the best music, lighting a cigarette and watching him take his left hand off the wheel so you can put it between his fingers. Or you can put it straight into his mouth. He draws in the smoke and lets it spill out of his nostrils and you breathe in the smoke that's been inside Johnnie. You watch the houses flash by and sometimes you say something to Johnnie, but most of the time you're silent.

You've got the suitcases in the back, and your passports. Johnnie thought it was a risk going back to your house, but you had to go. It smelled shut up and stale, and your tulips were dead in the vase. You touched them and all the petals fell off the stems. You took all the clean underwear you could find, and your passport, and a few other things you thought you might need. But you couldn't think straight. Coming back was nothing like coming home. You checked your other handbag, and there was about two hundred in notes, so you took that. You thought of the thousand you'd sent Anna, and wondered if you could ask Johnnie about it again, about how Anna was and what she'd said and how she looked, but you decided it was better not. He was all on edge anyway, from being in the house. He didn't like being back in London, he said it gave him a bad feeling. There were too many people who knew him. You said, 'They can't all be looking out for you,' making light of it because he was making it so heavy. But he just looked at you and said, 'You think I'm paranoid, don't you? I told you, I'm getting a bad feeling. I mean it.' He kept looking out of the windows, as if he was in a film. He wouldn't go back to his flat, even though he was running out of clean clothes. All he'd say was that he could buy more stuff once he got to Denmark. *With what?* you wanted to say, because you'd already discounted Hans and the fifty thousand. Then he went off to sort out the hire car.

As a last thought you slipped the diamond-and-ruby ring Paul had given you when Anna was born into your bag. You'd never liked wearing it. You took a few other bits of jewellery that didn't take up much room, but you made sure Johnnie didn't see you. He'd be wanting to start up some new rubbish with what you could get for them. You wanted to phone Paul, just to let him know that Johnnie was all right, but with Johnnie in the flat there was no chance. And what would you say to Paul anyway? *Johnnie's OK. Don't worry, he's with me.*

You've done enough to Paul already. Leave it.

Johnnie came back with a rented Citroën, old but fast. You sat back in the passenger seat and stretched.

'Nice car. Have they got somewhere you can leave it in Harwich?'

'Yeah,' he said, with the extra-clear look he always got on his face when he was lying. You left it. What did it matter? It was only a car.

'Yeah, they're good chips.' You've got a bowlful each, rough-cut, thick, glistening. They've used real potatoes to make these. Johnnie shakes on more vinegar, cuts up his sausage, tastes it, pushes the rest aside.

'Stick to the chips, Lou.'

And you do. You're hungrier than you've been for a long time, because you haven't got the drink to fill you. Johnnie keeps telling you how many calories there are in alcohol. You're surprised, because you'd got into the habit of thinking of drink as nothing. You asked him how he knew, and he told you about a girl he went with, who took out her pocket calculator every time they went to a restaurant, before she'd pick from the menu. She kept a booklet in her bag which gave the calories of everything from gin to avocados. You wouldn't go that far yourself, but maybe cutting back on the drink will have a good effect, apart from that of not being drunk.

'What about the car? Where're we going to leave it?'

'I told Charlie we'd leave it in the car-park. He's got a friend coming up this way next week. I said I'd pay the charges for him,' he adds, with an air of virtue which makes you want to up-end his chips in his lap.

'Since when were you so bloody straight? And what's all this about *Charlie*? I thought you were going to Hertz.'

'For fuck's sake, Lou, you've been in the car. Does it look like I went to Hertz and hired it? I went to Charlie Sullivan's garage. They know me there.'

'What were you playing at, going anywhere near Charlie Sullivan at a time like this?'

'He's never there. He owns it, that's all. The thing about Charlie's is, there's nothing on paper.'

'*Charlie*. Is he your best friend or something? I thought he was dead by now. I haven't seen him for years.'

'People like Charlie don't die. Hey, you'll like this, he told me he was thinking of going to live in Brighton. We had quite a chat about it.'

'I thought you said he was never there?'

'What's it matter if he was? Charlie's all right.'

'Well, he must have changed a bit, then. He used to be into everything, worse than fluoride in the water.'

'He's an old man now. He's mellow.'

'And you liked the car.'

'I liked the car.' Johnnie smiles, and finishes his chips. He sits back satisfied, and you don't tell him he's got a bit of grease round his mouth. It can be a relief when something takes the edge off the way Johnnie looks.

'Why are you smiling?'

'Nothing. Just feeling fond of you.'

'You sound like my granny.'

'You never knew your granny.'

'You know too much about me.'

'I know I do. I wish I didn't. I wish we could just start over and not know anything.'

'Yeah.' He exhales sharply, through his teeth. 'It's a new start, though, isn't it, going to Denmark? You and me.'

'Do you really think so?'

'Don't you?'

You can't say it. If there's a time to tell Johnnie that he's doing the same thing over and over, and so are you, then this isn't it. All you do is change the shape a little bit, each time, so it feels different. Instead you say, 'I love you, Johnnie,' because it's true, and he might as well hear it. You don't think it'll frighten him now. There's no one else in the pub and the pub is nowhere, and you're going nowhere, both of you. It makes you feel freer than you've ever been with Johnnie.

'That's nice,' he says.

'Yes, it is. Listen, when we get to Denmark, I'm going to send a postcard.'

'Who to?'

'Our daughter.'

His pupils move, but nothing else. 'Our daughter?'

'Anna.'

'You shouldn't say that.'

'Why not? It's true.'

'But you can't just say it like that.'

'Yes you can. You can say anything. It feels better if you do. Like I can say I'm fat and I drink too much and I'm forty and I love you. You don't have to do anything about it, but if you don't ever say it then nothing's ever going to happen. Is that what you want?'

Thirty

It's getting rough. You feel you're treading water, not boards. The ship leans until you think it'll never get its balance again and then it starts the slow tilt back and you straddle your legs, brace your feet and just about keep upright. It's the slowness you hate. For a long time you couldn't decide if the movement came from the ship or from inside your head where the schnapps rocks back and forth in bright sloppy waves. There's a group of Danish women at the bar, ordering drinks, grabbing at the bar-rail as the boat goes into its first heavy roll. Their faces shrink out of focus then slam back again in sharp detail. They're having a good time. You hear their shrieks of laughter as the boat rolls back, but you're really watching the barman, who's jamming glasses into place with plastic holders. He looks bored, angry even, as if the sea's not really part of the deal. Last time you went to the bar, he banged down your drinks without looking at you, with your change beside them.

You get up and struggle round the banks of seats with your glass and Johnnie's. Suddenly you're at the bar and the barman puts both his hands flat on a Black Label towel and shouts at you, 'Yes? What you want?'

You imagine a thick green wave climbing up the ship, not knowing where to stop. Water pours through the tacky orange bar, dragging the barman from his place behind the bar, stripping off his jacket and hosing him away down the deck. He begs and pleads but the water takes no notice.

You smile at the drowned barman.

'Two schnapps. Doubles,' you say.

After a while you aren't in the bar any more.

'I don't think I can go down those stairs,' you say.

'It's not as bad as it looks,' says Johnnie, but how would he know?

The boats shakes like something having a bad dream. If only it would go up and down like a see-saw, the way you thought boats went in storms, but the storm has long since stopped sounding like sea and water. There's an express train howling round the funnels, circling closer and closer. You think of the shipping forecast, which has always been your favourite lullaby. *Wind backing north-easterly, gale force ten, locally storm eleven, precipitation in sight...* You'd like to hear that voice now, but it's gone, shrunk back into the guts of a million radios. Like Brighton, packed up into a white box of gulls and waves. You can't believe it was only this morning you were walking there. You can't believe you were ever fool enough to give up the solid ground under your feet.

You try to pull open a door on to the deck, but it's barred. One of the crew sees you trying to force the bar up and shouts, 'You don't go out there now,' as if he's the barman refusing to serve you. You rest your face on the glass but you can't see anything. Black, streaming water. You cling to the bars and imagine a key of rock gouging the tin can of the hull. You don't know where you are.

'We've hit something,' you say.

'We're only hitting the waves,' Johnnie shouts in your ear, and you hear him and turn to look at his face, and for once it's Johnnie giving and you taking, grasping it gratefully.

'I wish I hadn't given up smoking,' you scream, as the ship throws you apart again. You think of rocks and wrecks and the long empty shore where no one will come. You're miles out of Harwich, and you can't get back to where you came from.

You're hitting the waves, that's all. No one else is frightened. You've been keeping a sharp eye on the crew's faces, the way you watch air hostesses when there's turbulence. As long as they keep on fiddling with mini-bottles of whisky and telling you about the duty-free, you know you're all right. You're not too keen on these announcements in Danish which might be anything until they give the English version afterwards. What does the Danish for *Abandon Ship* sound like? You'd be last into the lifeboats, that's for sure.

You're hitting the waves, that's all. You think of the waves laid out in front of the ship like endless rows of sleeping policemen, solid, tarry lumps of water.

'Let's go down to the cabin,' says Johnnie, speaking directly into your ear. His breath tickles and you shiver all over. 'One of us is going to break a leg if it goes on like this.'

He's drunk, like you. He's got to be, after all those schnapps. The whites of his eyes are reddened and scored with blood vessels. You look at each other, so close you don't need to have any expression, then you look away. The ship plunges, and you watch your fingers like somebody else's fingers, clutching the scarred metal of the bars that one of the crew has slotted into place over the deck-doors. Your fingers look as if death wouldn't rip them off. You'd never have thought you could hold on to anything so hard. You thought you were busy giving everything away. *North Utsira, South Utsira, Channel Light Vessel, Finisterre.* You're missing some of them out. It's terrible how you can forget things you've heard a thousand times.

What if a ship can stop being a ship? What if it doesn't want to be one any more? Like you stopped being Anna's mother. It's changed sides. You can smell a hot, electrical stink that frightens you. You want to ask Johnnie if he can smell it too, but you're afraid in case he says yes, and then it'll be true. A metallic smell, like burning wires. You can't even tell if the ship's moving forward any more. Maybe it's trapped in a box too, a box of storm.

You're too soft for this. You don't want to be in this fight between ship and corrugated-iron sea and wind racing like an express train. You feel how soft you are, you and Johnnie, and how easy it is to hurt you. You stepped on to the gangplank and believed the sea was there to take you where you wanted to go. Now you know it can do anything it wants with you.

Your head hurts. At first it was a laugh, a bit of weather to spice up the crush in the bar and the drink and speeded-up closeness of everybody. People grabbed at chairs or bar railings. They whooped and clapped each other for keeping on their feet and getting to the table with half the drinks still in the glasses. It was all right until a lurch of the ship caught one of the Danish women with a glass in each hand. She fell with her weight on the breaking glass, and suddenly there was bright red blood between her fingers, falling on the orange carpet. She was too shocked to open her hand. The barman uncurled her fingers for her and his blank bored face looked alive for the first time that night as he drew out a long splinter of glass. He was binding up her hand tightly with a white cloth and people were talking about finding a doctor. The woman sat on the floor with her legs splayed out in front of her, while someone else held her bandaged hand up in the air as if she was a boxer who'd won the fight. The barman was telling everybody what to do.

'Let's go,' said Johnnie. He looked bad, and you remembered that he'd never liked the sight of blood. Who does, you thought.

All you'd been able to get was a cabin with twin bunks. It's tiny, but it's clean, and it has a shower-room as well as a porthole. You wanted to wake up and look out at the sea.

You sit down heavily on the bottom bunk. The pitching of the ship doesn't feel so bad when you're sitting. Apart from a tight feeling behind your eyes, you're perfectly all right. It's just a bad night at sea, like thousands of bad nights this boat has battled through safely. Shaking up the passengers a bit doesn't matter. Johnnie's holding the ladder to the top bunk, wondering if he can get up it. He decides he can't, and he clambers in past you to lie on the bottom bunk, tucked in against the wall.

The bunk isn't too bad. They've boiled and starched the sheets until the edges rip apart like sticking plaster, but there are two pillows, and a cover with roses on it. The roses look as if they could be scraped off like paint, but all the same, it's a gesture. A touch of the high life in a ferry on the grey North Sea.

'Think of all the water underneath us,' you say. You look at Johnnie, but his eyes are closed and perhaps he's already asleep. You hope that he is. This should be the best part of the journey, the middle part where you can't do anything but let the boat carry you. You eat, drink, sleep. The boat makes the decisions, not you. You've got to let it lurch on and take you both with it. There's the name of the port on your tickets, but it's only a paper name and it doesn't have to mean anything yet.

You think of the water underneath the Palace Pier. There could be anything down there, and the North Sea is the same. Not clear, but murky and packed with life.

Dad loved the water. He said the dirty old Thames was the greatest river in the world. He showed you how strong it was, and how you had to have respect for it. He used to take you down to Tilbury to watch the boats go out, and he'd point out the currents, and tell you about the tide. It went out past Sheerness and Shoeburyness, he said, past Sheppey and Canvey and the Isle of Grain. People had been going that way for thousands of years, even before there was London built on the marshes.

'Look at that orange box, Lou. That's going to go right out to sea, and if it's lucky it'll miss being smashed in the shipping lanes, and it'll end up in France or Holland. Think of that. There's been more traffic on this piece of water than anywhere else in the world. Once you're out of the estuary you can go where you want. The tide's been going in and out of here longer than there've been people to watch it. It's only because of the river that London's here at all.'

He made you see what it was like before the Romans came. He said history wasn't everything, it was only what got remembered.

'People standing where we're standing here, Lou, waiting for the tide. They went everywhere. They didn't have bridges over the Thames then, every time they went over the river they went by water. They set off around the world in boats no one'd use on a pond in the park these days.'

You knew by the way he said it that it meant something to him. *They set off.* Your dad would have hated all the safety legislation they have these days. Life's not safe, he used to say, why kid yourself? He let you stand on the edge of the dock, but his hand was always there. He thought you should go out and have a good time, as long as you didn't hurt anyone. He'd been in the Merchant Navy in the war. You asked him about it once, where he'd been and what it had been like, but he said there was no point dragging all that up again, it was over and done with. Mum said he'd been to Russia. Russia, you said. Yeah, said Dad, I don't recommend it, though I was all for Uncle Joe at the time. Most of us were. We thought a sight more of him than we did of Winston, whatever they tell you in your history book.

You stood and held Dad's hand while the gulls screamed and a hooter sounded, once and again. His hand was big and warm and you swung out, clinging to it, until you were leaning over the water, then he brought you back again. The boats for Sweden sail from Tilbury, he told you, always have done. You watched the brown water and the cranes prickling the sky, and you wanted to go, too.

'Can we go on one of those boats, Dad?'

'Yeah, all right, when you're a big girl I'll take you.'

The orange of the sun hid in the fog. It was getting dark but you didn't want to go, and you knew Dad didn't either. He told you about the pilots the ships took on to get them out of the river. They knew every mudbank and current.

'They'll drop the pilot farther down, once they're out in the open water. He's got a skill, see, even the captain of the ship won't know what the pilot knows. He's got the knowledge, like a cabbie, only the sea's harder than roads, because it doesn't stay the same. It only takes a storm to shift a sandbank. They've got to trust him.'

'If he gets it wrong, will the boat sink?'

Your dad shook his head. 'He doesn't get it wrong.'

Then the lights were coming on and Dad took you to a caff for sausages and chips, and you drew a picture of the river while Dad smoked and chatted to Dot, who kept the caff. You never mucked about when you were out with Dad.

'We had a good day, didn't we, Lou?'

You didn't need to answer, you just squeezed his hand tighter.

'I'm going to say to Paul, we've got to tell Anna. Not for us, but for her. Everyone has the right to know who they are.'

You say it aloud, because Johnnie's sleeping. You know it isn't the schnapps talking, and that you'll feel just the same the next morning. The sea's calming down now, and you don't feel tired any more. You could sit here for ever, uncomfortably perched on the edge of the bunk while Johnnie sleeps with his face against the wall. There's a laundry smell, and the smell of those oranges you put into a carrier bag at the last minute. They were beauties, big navels with the tight skins that split open to show the packed fruit. You'll have one each for breakfast tomorrow, if Johnnie keeps on with this rubbish about not wanting to go to the restaurant in case someone sees him. It didn't stop him going in the bar, though, did it?

You reach out to the bunkside switches and turn off the lights. You'll rest for a while, then you'll investigate the shower.

It's about the size of an upright coffin, but you've already tested the water and it runs hot. Fresh water, not salt.

You lie down carefully alongside Johnnie, though there isn't really room for you both, and you're hanging over the edge of the bunk. You'd better curl in to him so you're like a couple of spoons. The dark is lovely, like soft thumbprints on your eyelids. Not pressing or hurting, just saying, *It's all right, you don't need to move. You don't need to do anything at all.* Warm and dark. Even the rocking of the ship isn't frightening any more. It's like being held in someone's arms, being hushed every time you try to move or think. Like rocking Anna when the top of her head was so soft you only touched it with your lips. You don't know if you're rocking, or being rocked. You curl in closer to Johnnie and you'll do anything, you know it now, anything to keep him like this, resting, safe, at ease because you're here.

Thirty-one

And there's the train, ripping its way down the right-hand side of England. Leeds to London in less than two hours. On it, among the businessmen travelling at resentful full-price, and crowds of kids who go for two pounds each on family railcards, there are two children who have paid for their own tickets with good money. Returns from Leeds to London, child fares. David did the thinking behind that one. He knew enough not to buy tickets to London from the local station, and not to buy his own return along with a single for Anna. If they're brother and sister, why would one be staying, and the other coming back?

They are brother and sister. They've got the story ready in case anyone asks: they're going to London to stay with their aunt, because their mother's having another baby. Their dad saw them off at Leeds, and their aunt's meeting them in London. Yes, they've done the journey on their own before.

But no one's asked. The conductor clipped their tickets, said, 'Mum and Dad not with you then?' and gave them back. He didn't sound as if he wanted an answer, not with the whole packed, swaying train to deal with.

Brother and sister. David's looking after half the money, in case they get mugged at King's Cross. Anna's told him about the men who wait for kids coming in off the northern trains. They ask if you're looking for somewhere to stay, then they take you off with them and make videos of you which they put on the Internet. Suddenly he sees that she knows a lot of things he doesn't know. If he'd come to London on his own, he thinks, he might have listened to those men. He might have thought it was the right thing to do. At home Mum always says, 'David's got his head screwed on. I don't have to worry about David,' but he feels like a book that's been turned to a new page his mum has never read. At home Anna was the one who asked the wrong questions, and everyone knew she didn't belong in the village as soon as she opened her mouth. Now he's going where it's Anna's voice that fits, not his.

He asked her, 'What should we do when we get to London, Anna?' and straight away she said, 'We'll get out of King's Cross.' He'd thought they'd take taxis, with all that money, but Anna says it's better not. The taxi-driver might remember them. He's bound to check if they've got the money for the fare before he takes them, and that means he'll get a good look at their faces. And it'll stick in his mind, because most kids on their own don't have money for taxis. It'll come back to him, when he hears something on the News about two kids who have gone missing.

'We can go on the Circle line, and change,' she says.

'We won't be on the News, will we?'

She eats another Minstrel. 'I don't know. They put things about missing children on the News, don't they?'

'Only when they've been murdered. They wouldn't bother with us, because I left a note.'

He's been to the buffet twice already and bought them a stack of drinks and burgers and microchips in cardboard boxes. 'Here's your chips.' David plonks the cardboard box on the table in front of Anna, and squeezes in next to her. The train's packed.

Anna picks at the edge of the box. 'Is this really chips?'

'Yeah, I had a look inside mine. And here's your burger.' He gives her the yellow polystyrene burger box, sachets of tomato sauce, mustard, salt. 'I couldn't remember what you wanted on it. You've got relish.'

'Another conductor came around,' says Anna. 'I told him you had our tickets.'

'I know. He asked me for them.'

'Was it all right?'

He nods, mouth packed with food. He'd been frightened, in case somehow, by looking at him, the man could tell they'd no right on the train.

It'd all been so easy. Anna had her backpack ready, and left it in the woods down by the bridge. They'd go to town that way, along the track, not through the village. When Anna came down to meet him, she had the kitten with her, in a shoe-box with holes in it. She swung up her backpack, but she held the box in both hands as if it was jewels.

'We'll get a proper cat-basket in Leeds market,' David said. The market was right by the station, he knew that. He was still on home ground then, knowing more than Anna. He looks sideways at Anna, skinny and pale, shovelling in her chips as they rush south, towards where she's at home.

'You've got your mum's address, haven't you?'

'You think I don't know where she lives, don't you, just because I don't live with her?'

'No, I don't –'

'You do. You're just like all of them. You think my mum didn't want me, that's why I live with my dad. You think she'd move house without telling me where she was. You think I've only got Sonia for a mother. It's what Fanny Fairway thinks, that's why she keeps asking me what my mother does.'

Her face is paler than ever, her eyes spitting out anger.

'No, I don't,' he soothes her in desperate whispers. 'I don't think any of it. It's your mum's money paid for the tickets, isn't it?'

She frowns as if she's trying to read something off a blackboard where it's written too small. Then she shoves her box of chips over to him. 'You have the rest if you want. I'm going to feed the kitten.'

He shoots a look at the woman opposite and says, 'You'd best do it in the toilet.'

'Why? Would you like to have your dinner in the toilet?'

'What if she fetches the conductor?'

'She's too busy stuffing herself.' It's true. Two rounds of ham and pickle sandwiches, an Eccles cake that sprayed crumbs all over Anna's comic so she couldn't stop laughing, a big packet of teddy-bear crisps. Anna couldn't believe the crisps. 'I thought you only had those at little kids' birthday parties.' Now the woman opposite is working her way down a box of Roses chocolates which have gone soft in the heat of the train. Every time she pops a chocolate into her mouth, she wipes her fingers on a blue flannel she keeps in a plastic bag. Her face is shiny with food, but her eyes are small and restless and unkind.

'Go on, take him in the toilet, Anna.'

The woman doesn't like them whispering. She thinks they're talking about her. She shifts in her seat, charged, ready to speak.

'What's wrong with feeding a kitten? See that man down by the doors, he's changing his baby on the table.'

'Anna, *go on*.'

And she goes suddenly, giving in, with the new cat-basket and the pint of milk they bought in Leeds market, and the medicine dropper which is too small for the kitten's hunger.

The train rushes on. All these fields are flat, no hills at all. He wonders if that's what all of southern England is like, or if they've just chosen the flat bits to put the railway line through. He doesn't like it. If you can't climb to the top of a hill, how will you know where you are? He thinks of Mum, finding the note he'd left taped to a packet of frozen puff pastry in the freezer. He knew she'd find it there, because she'd already told him she was going to make sausage rolls for tea. It was hard to write it, when Mum was in the next room, sorting the washing, calling out to him they'd have to go into Halifax for his new school shoes on Saturday. He could have called back to her. If she'd come in just then, she'd have seen what he was writing.

Dear Mum, Anna's running away from her stepmother so I've gone to look after her. I'll be back tomorrow.

He put that bit in about Sonia because he wanted everyone to know what she was really like. The next time she went swishing through the village in her Land Rover, everyone would stare. They wouldn't want her up at the stables any more.

P.S. I've got money for food, so don't worry.

Mum would know he was all right. She'd know he could look after himself. *David's got his head screwed on.* She didn't know he knew about King's Cross and the men who said that if you hadn't got anywhere to go you could always come back with them, but she'd understand that he had to look after Anna.

Thirty-two

Johnnie wakes in the dark. He's sweating and the thud of the engines is part of the nightmare as he struggles to find out where he is and who is crushing him against the wall. The dream swirls in his head, sickening him.

'Lou. Louie!'

'All right, I'm here.'

It's pitch dark. He clutches at her while his free hand slaps the wall, trying to find a way out.

'You're OK, Johnnie, we're on the boat.'

'What's the matter? Is it sinking?'

'Don't be so bloody stupid. You woke me up, that's what's the matter, yelling and shouting.'

'Can't you put the light on?'

She snaps on the light. 'You're here.' He sees her propped on her elbow, smiling. She sees him sweat-sodden, eyes stunned with coming out of his dream too quickly.

'You haven't been asleep,' he accuses her.

'No. You know me. I never sleep when I'm on a plane either. I've got to keep it up in the air, haven't I? It's hard work.'

'What time is it?'

'Half-past three. You want a drink of water?' She holds out a blue plastic bottle towards him, and he drinks greedily.

'It's being on the boat. It gives me a headache.'

'That's not what's given you a headache. Anyway, it's not so rough now.'

'Turn that light off, Lou, it's too bright.'

The dark folds round them again.

'What was the dream?' Her voice comes so calmly out of

the dark, like part of it. And then he can't see her. It makes it easy to speak.

'I was in Africa somewhere, reporting for TV because there was a famine. I was in this room with a nun, staring at her bed.'

'I bet she was pleased.'

'She didn't even see me. The sheets were all over the place because she'd just woken up and jumped out of bed. Then there were five little baskets on the floor, with five babies in them. She was kneeling down on the floor, looking into one of the baskets. Suddenly she grabbed this baby and then we were rushing through big doors, like church doors. I knew the baby wasn't breathing right, and a priest was running along behind us, a great big fat bloke speaking German, running along trying to help with the baby.'

'What was all that about then?'

She feels him shrug. 'I don't know.'

'It was your dream. You could know if you wanted to.'

'Yeah. But I wasn't the right person to be dreaming it, was I?'

'What do you mean?'

'I've never done anything like that for anyone, have I? What would I have a dream like that for?'

'You had too many talks from those mission priests when you were a kid.'

'I was in the way,' says Johnnie. 'I got in their way. They couldn't get past because I was stood there blocking the doorway. And this nun was small, like a bird, and she wouldn't even let the priest push past me. They weren't angry. They were just – too busy with important stuff for that. *They didn't even see me.* Not really. It was like I was invisible. There wasn't enough of me to make up something they could look at. I tell you how I felt. I felt *threadbare.*'

'It was a dream.'

'Yeah, I know. But it seemed real.'

'Was the baby OK?'

'I don't know, do I?'

'You know, Johnnie, you'd make a good TV reporter.'

He laughs, unwillingly. 'It makes you not want to go to sleep, when you have dreams like that.'

'It doesn't sound so terrible to me.'

'It's not what happened. It's what it made me feel.'

'What?'

'Like crap. Like I really am.'

'You mustn't say that.'

'Don't you ever feel that?'

'I feel all sorts of things when I'm in the mood, but I don't take it for the Gospel truth.'

'You think I'm crap really, don't you? Paul does. He can't hide it. He wants to put barbed wire round my life to stop me screwing it up.'

'He loves you.'

'Yeah, I know that,' he says, his voice brushing it away.

'He loves you more than anyone.'

A sigh, a gasp of breath in her ear that hits her harder than a fist.

'I know that,' he says again, and this time it's all there, the lostness of things that can't be changed, the knowledge that what he's made of himself is what he is.

'All I've done is fuck people up,' he says.

'He's your *brother*, Johnnie. He loves you. Where you are, that's where he wants to be. That's not so bad. All he wanted was to help you, when he knew you were in trouble.'

'It was more than that. I can't move without him knowing. I can't even breathe. Everything I've done, he knows. *Everything*. It's been the same all my life and I've never been able to stop knowing how much he wants me and using it to screw him up.'

'Here, I'm going to put the light on. I'll peel us one of those oranges. I don't know what your mouth's like, but I need something to get the taste out of mine. You turn over and hide your eyes if you don't want the light in them.'

'I don't mind the light.'

She gets up and rummages in her carrier bag. A spray of orange hits his hand as she digs into the fruit and starts to peel it.

'Do you want more water? I've got another bottle in here.'

She's got oranges, biscuits, a block of chocolate, a bottle of whisky. She peels the orange, shucks out the baby inside its navel, divides the fruit and offers half to Johnnie. It's sweet, cool, ripe. He eats his half eagerly, then asks if she's got any more.

'I'll do you another. They're wonderful oranges, have a whole one this time; it'll do you good. And I bought some nuts and raisins.'

The nuts are salted almonds, the raisins plump muscatels. She's bought them separately, to mix. That's like Lou. She never buys pre-packed rubbish. Or she didn't use to, until she started drinking. He eats the whole orange, thirstily, then swigs from the bottle of water.

'It dries you out, that schnapps,' she observes.

'What time is it?'

'Nearly four.'

'It'll be morning soon.'

'We don't get in till seven in the evening. We might as well go up for breakfast, then come back to bed.'

'I don't like walking round the ship.'

'You walked to that bar fast enough.'

'It was stupid. It was taking a risk for nothing, like us going down the pier.'

'There's no one on this boat, Johnnie.'

'How do you know?'

'Even if someone did see us in Brighton, they'd never have been able to follow us here.'

'What about the car?'

'What do you mean?'

'The car. I went to Charlie Sullivan's garage. They know me there.'

'You told me that already.' The words make her so tired she can hardly get them out of her mouth. Because he's done it again. He's set himself up, the way he always sets himself up, and then he lies there and looks at you, knowing himself, daring you to know him. *You watch a fish rise to the surface. Johnnie's finger tickles its velvety sides.*

'I could lift it out, just like that. It wants to be caught.'

It's when they come off the Tube that David first feels frightened. Anna stands there looking lost while people part round her as if she's no more than a metal pole. It's rush hour and the smell of all the people jammed together makes him feel sick. He doesn't like the tiled white walls. Then Anna seems to wake up. She glances round, taking her bearings, and moves towards the yellow WAY OUT sign. He goes after her, but she is quickly swallowed up in the crowd, and he can't see her any more. He tries to push through, but the wall of backs and legs won't give way. Suddenly he's panicking, knowing she's moving away from him while he's forced to shuffle at the same nothing speed as everyone else. She'll be on the escalator already, thinking he's right behind her. He'll never see her again.

'Anna!' he shouts. 'Anna! Wait for me!'

And there she is, astonishingly, right beside him, as small and pale and cool as ever. She's walked on the spot back to him, letting the bodies flow past her. She's doesn't mind the crowd any more than trout mind a current.

'What's the matter?'

'I thought I'd lost you.'

'It's OK. It's always like this at rush hour. I'd have waited for you by the exit.'

But he knows already that there is more than one exit. He could see himself running from one to the next, sweating, out of place, desperate.

'I'd have found you,' she says. Then, even more surprisingly, he feels her hand take his. She looks so cool, but her hand is warm. 'Let's hold hands,' she says, 'then we can't lose each other.' They go up the escalator side by side, squeezed in on the right-hand side, the kitten's basket held in front of Anna so it won't get knocked. The kitten mewed a lot in the train, but now it's silent. It's been quiet for ages.

He wants to look back to see how far they've come, but Anna stares quietly ahead. She doesn't seem excited, even now they're nearly there. He wonders what it would be like if it was his mum, waiting there, and he'd been the one who'd said, 'I'll stay for a while,' and known that was all it could be. Anna says her mother can't help herself, because it's an illness. There are clinics, Anna talked about them on the train. She knows about them. They work, but they cost a lot and her dad says it's not worth it, not unless someone has the will-power. He says her mum would be all right for a couple of months, then it would all start again. But Anna doesn't think it would. When Anna has the money, when she has her own life, she'll get her mother to go in for treatment. But no one takes any notice of you until you're grown up. They'll have to wait.

Anna's had to go far ahead of him in her thoughts. He still can't imagine leaving his parents, even though he's done it.

They come out into grey, warm daylight. There are papers blowing about, and it looks dirty. Maybe Anna lives in a poor part, he thinks. He looks up the street, at the red buses and black taxis. There's a stall of postcards and he catches himself thinking of buying one for his mum and dad.

'Is is far to where your mum lives?'

'No, you go down here, then you turn right and go on a bit.'

He wants to ask if she's sure, because although she's walking like she knows where she's going, her face is empty. He feels a bit stupid holding her hand now they're out in the daylight, but there's no one here who knows him. No one for hundreds of miles who knows him, or any of the Ollerenshaws. The faces flip past, hundreds and hundreds of them. More people are talking into mobile phones than to each other. Suddenly there's a flower stall. He stops, pulling on Anna's hand.

'I ought to get something for your mum. Which flowers does she like?'

'You don't need to get her a present.'

'Well, it's not a present, is it, seeing as it's her money.'

Anna cracks a smile. 'She likes freesias. Those ones. Do you know, my mum told me most men can't smell freesias, even though they've got such a strong scent.'

He bends to the bucket of freesias and snuffs the white and cream waxy flowers. The scent is strong and deep, and he can smell it. They've put a bit of fern with the bunches, to make them look nice, and a curl of ribbon round the wrap. Funny to think the first time he ever buys flowers, they're for someone he doesn't know.

'I'll have these ones.'

He pays with a ten-pound note. He's only got two twenties left in the new wallet he bought on Leeds station. The rest of the money is spread out, in his backpack, in his jeans pockets, in the inside pocket of his jacket.

The next shop they pass, he looks in the window. He scans the prices quickly and realizes there's not one thing in the window he couldn't buy if he wanted to. Not that it's his money, he knows that. But it makes you feel different, when you know you could have anything you want. You're just choosing not to.

When they come to the house it's narrow and creamy-white, a bit like the colour of the freesias. Anna's mum lives in an end terrace with a high wall around the garden at the side. It's right on the street, no garden in front, no garage, no car-port. Just a flight of stone steps leading up to the front door, with black railings on either side. He can't even see a bell. But he knows already that he was wrong about this being a poor part, so far wrong that he's glad he didn't open his mouth.

Anna lets go of his hand, and mounts the steps. She turns what looks like a screw beside the front door, and deep inside the house he hears a bell ring. The noise of the bell dies away but nothing happens. After half a minute, Anna rings again, but he knows from the set of her back that she doesn't think anyone's going to answer.

'She's maybe gone to the shops. Does she leave the key anywhere when she goes out?'

'No.'

Anna rings again, but before the sound's finished she's already turned away. She picks up the basket with the kitten, and comes back down the steps. 'She's not there.'

'No.'

'What're we going to do?'

'Can you not get in another way?'

'No. She's got locks on all the windows.'

'What about the garden? Can we get over the wall?'

She frowns. 'There's a gate at the back, from the alley, but it's always locked. Mum never opens it. There's stuff growing over it.'

'We could try.'

'*It won't be open.*' She sounds angry, agitated. As if she doesn't want it to be open. As if now they're so near, she wants to get away again. But they've nowhere to go. Hotels don't take children on their own.

'We might as well have a look,' he says carefully. 'I'm good at climbing.'

Silently, she leads him round the back, down the alley where the bins go. The door's half-covered with creeper. Black dust comes off on his hands when he pushes it aside, and suddenly Anna says, 'People sleep here sometimes, only they get moved on.'

It doesn't look like a door that's ever opened, but there's a handle, there under the creeper. The handle turns, and though the door's stiff, he has a sudden, sure feeling that it's only the stiffness of swollen wood. There is no lock. It's going to open.

'Give us a hand. Quick, before someone comes.'

He knows it'll open, like his dad knows sometimes when he's watching a race. Dad'll spot a horse ten lengths back from the leaders, coming up on the outside. 'Keep your eye on Polygon Lad,' he'll tell you. He never says that unless he knows the horse is going to do it, and he can watch you watch it fly to the finish like a kite going straight up, as if all the jockey had to do was let it go. On TV you can't see the sweat and you can't hear the thunder, but he's been with Dad to the races and he knows what it's really like. The lather flies off the horses and hits you like spit. The horse that's been in the lead all the way is struggling now and the jockey's up on his heels, arse high, whip coming down in choppy swipes because he knows how he's made the running and he's cursing himself now because the horse is running his heart out but he might as well be standing still. He glances round and sees Polygon Lad still gaining and he knows he's got as much as he can from the horse but maybe there's an ounce more to be pounded out as they come round the last bend and go into the straight. And as he flails and flounders Polygon Lad floats past them. He wins as if that's what God fixed from the moment the race began.

Thirty-three

They are in the garden. Light strikes back from the white walls and David blinks. It's warm in here, and still, and secret. Anna's smiling as she goes to crouch by a little pool. She scoops her hand through the water, and brings it up dripping.

'There used to be fish in here, when I was little. And there's a fountain that lights up at night.'

'Can you turn it on?'

'No. The switch is inside the house.'

They turn to look at the house. It stares back blankly through its closed windows. The blinds are half-drawn, too. David goes to the French windows, and tries one of the catches.

'Don't do that! You'll set off the alarm. Someone'll come.'

'Where do you think she is?'

'I don't know. She doesn't usually go out.'

'You don't think she's gone on holiday, do you?'

Anna is at his side, peering into the house. They can see plates and glasses on the little table, and a heap of newspaper has collapsed off the other arm of the sofa. She's not very tidy, thinks David. His mum wouldn't go away leaving the house like that. There's even a wine bottle lying on the floor. It looks like the Queen's Head on a morning after, with fag-ends everywhere, and sticky rings of drink.

'We've got to get some more milk for the kitten.'

Yes, he thinks, and something for us and all. 'Is there a shop round here where they don't know you?'

'They won't remember me after all this time. I don't look the same.'

'Isn't there a supermarket we could go to?' Supermarkets

are safer. People don't look at you when you buy things there. They don't notice a kid with a twenty-pound note, the way a corner shop would.

She thinks. 'I can't remember. Mum never took me. I don't think she goes to supermarkets.'

'We've to find somewhere to stay, Anna, if we can't get in the house.'

'We can stay here.'

'Where?'

'In the garden. It's not cold. We can sleep under the bushes. I used to make houses there, when I was little, and the rain never came in.'

And they'd be hidden. No one can see over those walls. They can make a little house and pull creepers over the bushes until they're quite hidden. As long as they don't give themselves away, no one will ever know they're here. They look at each other, the idea glinting from one to the other. A camp. A secret place. They can live here, and no one'll ever know.

'We can buy food,' says Anna.

'Yeah, but it gets cold at night. What're we going to sleep on?'

And then it hits him again that they've got money and they can do what they like with it. They can buy sleeping-bags. They can even buy a tent, and one of those gas stoves you cook on. It doesn't matter how long Anna's mum is away, because they can make their own camp out here, in the garden.

It's dark. The kitten sleeps in its basket, wedged at the back of the tent. They've left the tent-flaps tied back and the orange flush of streetlight picks out the pallor of Anna's face, the black stain of her hair. She sleeps on her back, with her mouth open. David sleeps too, curled on his side. His face is wrinkled with dreams; hers is calm. Overhead there's the steady thud of a police helicopter, but they hear nothing. Once or twice the helicopter's searchlight crosses the garden, though it's not looking for them. It touches the bamboo, the buddleias with their unfolding leaves, and a zinc bucket. It sweeps across the little pond. Then the light swings off elsewhere as the helicopter rises and beats its way north-east, towards Finsbury Park. Anna stirs. She throws out an arm over David's body, frowns, leaves it there.

David wakes, hours later. He knows straight away where he is. He's not frightened, he's not confused. He thinks of Mum and Dad in their bedroom, fast asleep, waiting for their Teasmade to wake them up. No, he's not even homesick. He doesn't want to be there. He doesn't want to be waking up to go to school with Billy and Jack and JohnJo. He'd like to see his parents, of course; at least, he thinks he would. But they're far away and that's where he wants them. They would soon put a stop to the way his life's stretching, making new shapes. If they were here they'd have him out of the tent and down the road and on to that Leeds train in five minutes flat. And back to where he came from. All they've ever thought about Anna is that she'll soon be off, back where she came from. She doesn't count. They don't even need to say that they think it'll be a good thing when she's off and gone. It goes without saying, at home. People must have something wrong with them if they can't be satisfied but they have to go traipsing about here and there, picking up whatever they can get like a fiddler at a wedding. He hates it when his dad says things like that. He's never seen any fiddlers at weddings, though he's been to plenty. He gets dragged along, for fear of causing offence. *You're coming with us, David, like it or not. I'm not falling out with the Arkinstalls.* He's never seen *anything*, he thinks, huffing the down sleeping-bag round his shoulders. And there are things they've never seen, either.

It's getting colder. It's not light yet, but the darkness has a greyish feel. The kitten's mewing: maybe he can feed it without waking Anna.

There she is, lying on her back. Every time her breath comes out it whistles, like a sigh. It's a lonely sound, and he wonders if he makes a sound like that when he's sleeping. He leans over her, close, trying to see her face. Suddenly she moans, as if she's got a pain. But she's still asleep. He doesn't want to wake her. Very gently, he pats her cheek.

'It's all right, Anna, I'm here,' he says. 'I'll look after you.' He's never said anything like that to anybody. He'd never dare say it, at home. There, it's his mum who does the looking after, and she doesn't want anyone interfering with it, any more than she wants him and his dad messing about in her kitchen.

He'd better stay awake and keep a look-out, in case Anna moans like that again. It'll be morning soon, and they can try the little stove. He chose a dark-blue one, with a little brass burner, and he's stored the gas cylinder well away from it, like the man told him. They bought a cool-box, and bread and butter, and milk and chocolate powder. He was going to buy bacon, but then he thought better of it. The neighbours would be on to them, at the smell of frying bacon. The stove's perfect: it hasn't a scratch or a splash of fat on it. He hugs the thought of the little stove, and waits for morning.

Thirty-four

There's a rap at the door.

'Room service.'

You turn to Johnnie. 'Who's that?'

He's out of the bunk, fast and silent, stepping soundlessly to the door. He motions to you to keep back.

'It can't be room service in the middle of the night.' You mouth the words more than say them.

Then the rapping comes again.

'Room service. Room service.' The voice is flat, loud, bored. You can hear the chink of china – or is it glasses?

For a second you still don't know why the words stroke your skin with ice, and then you do.

'Johnnie,' you whisper. 'I didn't order anything, did you?'

The rapping again, even louder. Don't they know they're disturbing people? Johnnie stumbles as the boat swings, and catches at the door handle.

'Room service. Pot of tea ordered for Cabin 30.'

Johnnie still has his hand on the handle. To open it you have to press the middle of the handle in, then twist.

You hold his hand still. 'They'll go away if you don't answer. They don't know you're here.'

You look behind you at the bright box of your cabin, the round black porthole, the heap of bedclothes. The bunks are bolted to the floor. There's nothing you can wedge against the handle to stop them coming in.

'Don't, Johnnie. Don't open it.'

But his hand is on the door handle, and you're fighting to unpeel his fingers.

'Keep out of it, Lou. It's got nothing to do with you. I'll sort it out.'

You grab at him but he throws you off against the bathroom wall. And you're splayed there, staring, as he twists the knob and pulls the door open.

There is no one there. You see Johnnie step forward, peering right and left, and you come into the doorway. The corridor is bright and empty. To the right are Cabins 31–40, to the left Cabins 20–29. There are arrows pointing to the emergency exits, with the figure of a running man. On the floor outside your cabin there is a tray with a teapot on it, two cups and saucers, and several foil-topped packages of milk. The china clinks with the movement of the ship. It's the sound of tea-time, safety, home. There's a little note folded on the tray. Johnnie stoops and unfolds it, and you both read: *Complimentary Service, With the Goodwill of the Management.*

'And there was I thinking all sorts,' you say. 'Is the tea hot?' Johnnie bends to feel the pot, nods.

'They must have just left it and gone away,' you say. But you can't help looking up and down the corridor again. 'You going to bring that tea inside, Johnnie? We might as well drink it, seeing as it's here.'

'You have it if you want,' says Johnnie. 'I've had enough of being stuck down here. I want some fresh air.'

'You can't go up on deck. They had the doors barred, remember?'

'They'll be open now. You have a sleep if you want. I'll bring you something down.'

But you don't feel right. You don't want to be down here in the cabin on your own, with people banging on the door bringing you stuff you haven't ordered. You'll be glad to get off this ship. 'I'll come up with you. Just give me a minute, and I'll wash my face.'

Johnnie waits while you peer into the mirror, wiping your

face with Baby Wipes. Your skin's greasy, even though you haven't slept. Thank God you've still got the kind of thick, wavy hair that only needs a comb through it. It's about all that's left on the plus side. Your face squints back at you in the metal mirror and you spit on a tissue to get a fleck of mascara out of your eye. There. That'll do for now. Just a coat of fresh mascara and some powder and you'll be respectable.

'Pour me a cup of that tea, Johnnie,' you call through the bathroom door. You hear the cups clinking. Johnnie hasn't bothered to bring in the tray. He must be crouched down in the doorway pouring it. Then a cup smashes.

'You OK, Johnnie?' you call, but he doesn't answer. You won't rush out to help, he hates it when you fuss. Probably trying to open one of those stupid milk things, then he knocked the cup over.

'Johnnie?'

You frown into the mirror. You hope he hasn't spilled the whole caboodle, because you were looking forward to that cup of tea. Or that's what you tell yourself, to quieten the chatter of panic in your ears.

'Johnnie?'

He still doesn't answer. Slowly, watching your own hands, you put down your make-up bag. You turn away from the mirror. The cabin is so tiny you could reach out and touch him if the shower-room door didn't get in the way. You take a breath, and push open the door.

But the cabin is quite empty. The outer door is still open, and there's the tea-tray on the floor. A cup lies in pieces in a swill of pale-brown tea that is slowly spreading across the corridor lino. That was the noise you heard, but now everything is perfectly still, perfectly quiet, apart from the groaning of the ship. There is no one there. For a moment the thought possesses you that Johnnie's gone to get a cloth to wipe up the mess. But something in your body is thinking quicker than you, and in less than ten seconds it has turned you back, made you pick up the cabin key and step out into the corridor on silent feet. You click the door shut behind you. You tread noiselessly along the white corridor where the lights buzz, captured in their wire cages. You have your balance now. Nothing that this sea can throw at you is going to frighten you. You know these narrow, pitching gangways now, and the steep flights of stairs. You can find your way. You carry on, keeping close to the wall. At the turn of the corridor, you inch forward, smoothing yourself against the wall. Again there's nothing. Another blank, shining tunnel of lino and cream paint. Someone's left a pair of trainers with ripped soles outside a cabin door. Halfway down the corridor there's a stairway, but it doesn't take you anywhere: as you open the door, a thick, oily wave of smell and noise rolls out towards you. The stairway goes down to the car-deck. Could he be down there? It's a good, quiet place. But they have video cameras on car decks, don't they, in case of fire? He'll be somewhere dark, where a camera can't reach. You let go of the door and its rubber seal wheezes as it shuts.

At the end of the corridor there are more arrows, pointing upwards. You'll follow them. There'll be people up there. If you go through the barriers that say CREW ONLY you're sure to find someone. There's got to be a captain to steer the ship. You go on up. At the top a noise makes you jump, but it's only a video game beeping to itself in an alcove. Ahead there's a darkened room, marked RESTAURANT. More stairs lead upwards on to the boat deck, and a draught moves against your legs.

You climb into colder air which smells of metal. No one's about. There are two deck doors here, one on your right and one on your left. You can feel a thin, fresh slice of wind piping through the gaps. You go over and push down hard on the bar, and it gives way. The bars must have been unlocked in the night.

Wind seizes the doors, bellying into your mouth and hair and dress. You snatch at your skirt but it flies up, and then you've slammed the door shut and you're on the outside, slithering on the wet deck in your bare feet, crushed by the industrial noise of the sea. You're by the engine vents. There's enough light seeping out for you to see the shiny deck tipping away from you. You hardly dare look at the sea. But the sky isn't black now. The rain has stopped and there's a dirty wash of grey on your right. The ship ploughs and shudders but your heart rises. It's the dawn. Daylight's coming and the ship's on its way to land. You know it's going to be all right now that the night is over, if you can just find Johnnie.

Behind you are the black outlines of the lifeboats. You'll go that way first. You hold on to the railings, and go hand over hand, your feet catching in the puddles. Far below you the sea churns, but you don't look at it or think about it. The lifeboat hangs over your head, monstrous. You are past the middle of the ship and you can look down the deck, but still you don't see anyone, and you don't hear anything but the ship and the sea. You don't dare to call out.

You almost miss them. You almost fall on them. On your right, in the shadow of a tarpaulined stack of life-rafts, there are three men. You don't connect them with Johnnie. You think you've stumbled on sex. One man with another lying in his lap, a third kneeling between the legs of both, applying something to the face of the man with his face upturned, who looks as if he is sprouting black roses on his cheeks. Then you hear the noise the man is making, deep in his throat. You've heard it before, you know you have. A panting noise, a noise you've made yourself as you fought not to push.

'Shut the fuck up,' says the kneeling man. He is working hard, concentrating, and you watch mindlessly for half a second before the picture falls into shape and you know what they are doing.

They haven't seen you or heard you. You could dip down now, melt behind the pile of rafts and wait for it to stop. It will stop.

You dive. You come on the kneeling man from behind, your hands spread. You bring them in and go for his eyes. Your fingers rake for the soft balls of his eyes, your nails rip and tear. He screams out and rears up backward to knock you off, and your feet slip. He knocks you back and you fall with his weight on you, and strike the back of your head on the deck.

When you can see again there's a man facing you, astride you. There's enough light for you to see the tears of blood down his face, but you don't connect them to yourself. The man astride you lifts your head and slams it back against the deck again. You feel the salt spray in your mouth as you bite your own tongue. You kick and try to bring your knees up but you can't do anything. Again, he cups your head and drags it up. Your faces stare into each other, then he bangs you down. He grabs your wrists and grinds them against the deck, grunting with effort so that a thread of his spit drops on your face. You writhe sideways and suddenly there is Johnnie's face within six inches of your own. His eyes are open, staring, his cheeks black with blood. He sees you and recognizes you but he says nothing. His arms don't come out to touch you and you see that they are behind him, tied. Another man is standing over you now and his shoe stamps on your hand. You jerk up and then you can't see Johnnie any more.

Because the men stay silent you know what kind they are. But you're no longer able to know much, because of the breaking up inside your head. For a moment you see some writing but before you have time to read it, it disappears. Hands grasp your elbows, hands grasp your ankles. The wind rushes as you are lifted up into it. Gently, you start to swing. They let you dandle there, to give you time to guess what's going to happen next, or maybe they're just working out how to do it.

They breathe hard, because you are a heavy woman. You try to scream but cough instead because of the blood in your mouth. They swing you harder. Up you go, and down, and up again, and down, hitting your foot against the life-rafts, and then you are flying.

You strike the sea at the best possible angle. There is no chance of swimming, though you are a good swimmer. The waves are on top of you at once, and they take care of you in the way the sea's always done. All those times you've stepped near it and got away: it won't happen now. When you leaned out over the dirty Thames and your dad's hands swung you back.

You are aware of him coming towards you in a small boat with an outboard engine, negotiating the treacherous currents as skilfully as any paid pilot. He is sitting in the back of the boat, steering, but his eyes never leave your face. He knows exactly where you are. All you have to do is to keep swimming until he catches up with you. He is coming in fast, judging the angle at which he will turn and sweep alongside you, then kill the engine and lift you over the side of the boat.

You think you are swimming strongly, with the slow and steady stroke he taught you Saturday morning after Saturday morning. You were always first in the water when the Baths opened. *You can go on for ever like that*, your Dad told you. *Just relax. The water's there to hold you up.* But you are not swimming at all.

Thirty-five

It's another of those rare, hot April mornings. The birds sing with a brilliance they'll have forgotten in another month. Louise's garden is packed with still, blue air, but the stone of the terrace is cold. It's April, not August, and the sun hasn't yet come round the side of the house.

The French windows are shut, and locked from the inside. In the tent both children sleep, and will sleep on until ten o'clock in the morning, in spite of the noise of a London day outside the walls. They are exhausted. David stayed awake until the sun came up, and fed the kitten while Anna slept. The kitten sucked up the milk instantly, spat out the teat of the medicine dropper, shook his head, and sneezed. *He wants more than that*, thought David, and he poured milk into a plastic bowl from their new camping set. He set the wobbly kitten down on the floor of the tent, and showed him the milk. The kitten dipped his head, and his muzzle sank deep into the milk, shocking him into another sneeze. He quivered all over, backing off from the bowl. David tipped the bowl and a small stream of milk ran out and puddled at the kitten's feet. The kitten bent to it, sniffed it, and suddenly he found his tongue and was lapping as if he'd done it all his life. The milk shrank away and was gone: he'd drunk it, all on his own. *Wait till I tell Anna*, David thought, and poured another puddle of milk. Soon he'd have him trained to the bowl.

The kitten is back in his basket, the boy in his sleeping-bag. There's a shiver in the undergrowth and a cat steps out, her back high, her nose twitching. She can smell the kitten. She halts by the rolled-up tent-flap, and paws it delicately. She is feral, orange, thin as a whip except for the taut bundle of kittens that stretches the skin under her ribs. She knows this garden better than anyone. She was born here. The smell of the kitten goads her, strange and yet not strange, spreading out on to her territory. She wants to get close enough to it to turn it over and over with her paw. She might take to it, on some whim as steely as her thin backbone.

She takes one step into the tent, puts a paw on to Anna's sleeping-bag and kneads the fabric enquiringly. Something flies past the tent, at the edge of her field of vision. She springs round and upwards, her paw flashing as she leaps to knock the butterfly out of the air. But the kittens in her belly make her heavy, and she misses. The white butterfly spirals higher, like blown paper, out of her reach. Instantly the cat walks away from her failure, to the patch of sunlight which has just struck the corner of the terrace. She settles into the stone, moving her body from side to side as if she is nesting. The patch of sun spreads as she settles, covering her, lighting up sparks in her orangeness. She kneads her belly against the stone so that even while she lies down she seems to prowl, searching, assessing, defying the weight of her pregnancy to be a hunter still. Suddenly she arches, opening out her body to its full length, revealing the swollen underside of her body and her nipples. She squirms on the stone, and lashes her tail from side to side in an ecstasy of sunlight. A few seconds later, she is asleep.

The boat from Harwich heads north-east on a quietening sea. The drum of the engines is steady, although occasionally the contents of the boat shudder, like a crateful of bottles. Things slip and slide, and are put back in place. There is a flash of sun from time to time, and a few people have finished their breakfast and are going up on deck. A member of the crew is busy unlashing a heap of deckchairs which have been stowed under canvas, as if the sun might really come out and people might come on deck to lie with their faces turned upward, their heads nodding to a private dribble of music. Someone might even consider it worth taking a photograph.

The restaurant is open now. You pay a fixed sum, and then you can eat as much as you want. There is silver on the tables, and white tablecloths, and white napkins. Slices of ham and cheese lap over one another. There is black bread and white bread with poppyseeds, there are rolls and pumpernickel and primrose-coloured Danish butter. Pitchers of orange juice are fixed into metal stands. The coffee is smoking hot. There is a bright pile of apples which nobody touches because it looks too perfect, or too expensive.

Two men sit facing one another at a little table by the broad windows that look over the sea. From time to time they glance sideways, between mouthfuls, and drink in the grey sheen of the water, the bright, pale sky, the following gulls. They break open their boiled eggs, then shove them aside on discovering they are lukewarm. They swallow a mound of white bread and ham, then push their chairs back and ruminate over cup after cup of coffee.

One nods towards the horizon. 'Clearing up,' he remarks, but the other doesn't answer. His face is raked and bruised from a bad fall out of his bunk in the early hours. He's not alone. One of the crew has a broken shoulder, where a door broke loose and swung back on him, and many passengers are still down in their cabins, sleeping off drink and seasickness. Some you won't see anything of all day.

Rain came on again, heavily, soon after daybreak. Sheets of it squalled along the decks, hosing them down. They shine, now, in the strengthening light. The ship has passed an oil rig, a container beating its way down towards Rotterdam, a German ferry. The two men watch everything, while their hands lie idle on the table, or pick up a coffee cup, or a cigarette. Only a few hours to go before they'll be back on land and then they'll be on their way south through Germany, and on to some ferry terminal in Belgium or France, where they'll buy more tickets. They'll be home by tomorrow night, and the job's done. They wouldn't have killed Johnnie, if they hadn't been interrupted. They'd have marked him, that's all, like they were told, and broken his legs. That's what Charlie Sullivan paid them for, and that's what they were doing. They were going by the book, right down to putting the note on the tray, which was a bit stupid when you came to think of it, leaving their calling card like that. He owed Charlie. It was an old debt, Charlie said, a bad debt, and he was buggered if he was going to leave it any longer. Johnnie was in the shit all round, everyone knew that. There were enough people looking for Johnnie, so this was a good time for Charlie. Johnnie owed him. *No business sense*, said Mr Sullivan, *not like his brother*. And he smiled hugely. He was quite chatty for once, though they knew that wasn't necessarily a good sign. They know Mr Sullivan has a thing about people paying their debts.

'All this is between ourselves,' he'd said, flicking that look on them like he was stubbing a fag out on the remains of his dinner. And they nodded, *Yeah, sure, Mr Sullivan*, and squeezed their faces into the shape he wanted, because they knew he never forgot a face. Or anything else.

All the same they would never have killed Johnnie. It was just that one thing led to another, once they got interrupted. If he'd been travelling on his own, the way he was meant to, the way he told Charlie he was, it would have all gone right. They'd have got him back into his cabin, and someone would have come along and found him, once the ship docked. It's not as if he'd have got stuck somewhere like Morocco, which it could well have been.

And by that time they'd have been on their way south. No one ever died of a pair of broken legs and a bit of plastic surgery. It's the truth, if it wasn't for her, Johnnie'd be alive. They know Johnnie; known him for a long time. He's all right. They've got nothing against Johnnie, personally.

'I can't stand ships,' says the man with the unmarked face. 'Makes me feel shut in, sitting here. Put me on a plane any day.'

The other moves his hands on the table. He watches them take a cigarette and flick a lighter. Then he looks surprised, as if he expected them to do something quite different.

It's not true that there are no stars in London. You have to look for them. You can't just turn your face up, like you can in the country where the sky's so big and bare. He's been thinking about that on and off most of the night, driving down to London. *I could still set up an observatory*, he tells himself.

He knew he'd be coming back to London. He hadn't needed that note of Anna's to know where she'd gone. Sonia'd offered to come too, but he hadn't wanted that.

'You'll miss your riding lesson,' he'd said to her, and had the satisfaction of seeing a flush as dark as a plum on her fair face. She'd thought she could make a fool of him: well, she'd find out different. In a way though, he didn't blame her. He'd lost interest, and she knew he had. It had been a mistake ever going up there with her. Sonia worked better part-time than full-time.

He'd known straight away Anna would be with Louise. He isn't worried, he just wants to get there as soon as he can. He keeps thinking about something stupid: how thin Anna's wrists are, how easy it would be to grab her by them. How light she is. How easy to pick her up and carry her away. But she's not alone, and she's got money. She'll be tucked up in bed at Louise's. If Louise had the sense to answer her phone herself, instead of leaving the answer-phone on night and day, he'd already know for sure that Anna was there. But Louise didn't phone him. She won't let Anna back to him without a battle now, he knows that. She's got what she's always wanted: proof. If she's a bad mother, he's no better. What's Anna telling her now? Are they sharing Louise's bed, with Anna whispering close that she doesn't want to go back to Yorkshire, she wants to stay here, at home? He switches his thoughts away, and pushes the car forward to get through the next set of lights.

He pushes forward, because he doesn't know what he's hurrying to greet. It's coming. It would meet him soon enough anyway, no matter how many minutes he idled on amber. It's rushing to get where he'll be. If he could stop and listen he'd hear the hiss of time speeding into fate, but he doesn't stop. He's got enough inside his own head to listen to, apart from the throb of Dylan on *Not Dark Yet*.

'You're notifying him as a missing person?'

Paul will nod.

'That's right. Your brother was known to us, as you're probably aware.'

The lightbulb will hiss. The tiles will glare as they throw off white light. There will be too much light on the policeman's face, and Paul will want to turn away from it, but he will keep on looking. The policeman's skin will gleam as if he has smeared it with oil.

'I'll tell you something else. Since we're alone, and this is just between ourselves. Off the record.' He will pause, dandling his promise of information before Paul. Paul will tense, and lean forward slightly as if to catch what's coming. 'A fucking little toe-rag like your brother won't be missed. And I only wish I could say that loud enough for him to hear me.'

Paul will remain leaning forward. Whatever message he's been waiting for, it hasn't come. He will make no reply.

He will wait any length of time he has to. He will ask anywhere. He will leave a message with a service which acts as go-between for missing persons and their families. And little by little, whatever it takes, he will find out.

He will carry his brother inside him for ever. They're brothers, aren't they? Closer than man to wife, mother to daughter, father to son. How can you climb out of the coils of your own DNA? All their genes are the same. They came from the same place and they've got their origins bedded in them. It's like the light of a star, bedded in an explosion that happened millions of cold years before either of them was born. There can't ever be any question of guilt or forgiveness between the two of them. It would be like trying to forgive your own right hand. When Johnnie comes back, Paul will be there. He'll see him coming, no matter how much Johnnie's changed, no matter which way the tide of wrong or right has flowed between them. He'll recognize him, no matter how many years of change have piled on to Johnnie. He'll see him coming far off, and shade his eyes and squint into the sun while his heart squeezes small then springs inside his breast. Johnnie'll doubt the welcome. He'll lag back once he gets in sight of the house, fearing to come closer. But it won't make any difference, because Paul will be running faster than he's ever run in his life, crying out loud his brother's name, racing to meet him.

There they lie, boy and girl, side by side, sleeping-bag to sleeping-bag. The backs of their hands touch: David's right, Anna's left. They shouldn't possess any power, these two: the story of another packed London morning is unfolding without them. They are children, and they are sleeping in the garden, inside the little tent they've bought with money they dug up from a hole in the ground. They have no power over their own lives, so how is it that the sight of them can stop a grown man? But it does. Paul crouches on his hands and knees at the entrance to the tent, staring at the slight dew of sweat on the forehead of his sleeping daughter. She is not his daughter, he knows that, but still she looks like him. She looks like Johnnie. The cables of their relationship are twisted into her sleeping face, and so are the roots that the past puts down into the present. Anna's face is still so soft that the knots don't show.

He doesn't move. He doesn't enter the tent and disturb the children. Perhaps he cannot. There is sweat on his face, too.

It's hot, and he'd like to wipe his forehead, but he doesn't want to move.

He doesn't move, but they have already left him. When a ship sails, the ribbon of water that widens between the travellers and those left on the quayside seems no broader, at first, than the ribbons they hold out to one another, to show they are still linked. But then the red ribbons fall, and trail from hands which have forgotten to wave. The water is a widening channel, then a gulf, and after a while it becomes the sea itself.

The children are turned to each other. Motionless, they are going somewhere he cannot go. Their hands meet, like a promise which will wait for years if it must, knowing that at long last it will be kept.